GARNET FLATS

GARNET FLATS

USA TODAY BESTSELLING AUTHOR
DEVNEY PERRY

Entangled Publishing, LLC
644 Shrewsbury Commons Ave., STE 181
Shrewsbury, PA 17361
rights@entangledpublishing.com

Amara is an imprint of Entangled Publishing, LLC.

Visit our website at www.entangledpublishing.com.

Edited by Elizabeth Nover
Cover art and design by Sarah Hansen at OkayCreations
Stock art by ShotPrime Studio and Andrew Mayovskyy/Shutterstock
Interior design by Britt Marczak

ISBN 978-1-64937-697-8

Manufactured in the United States of America

First Edition May 2024

10 9 8 7 6 5 4 3 2 1

ALSO BY DEVNEY PERRY

THE EDENS SERIES

Indigo Ridge
Juniper Hill
Garnet Flats
Jasper Vale
Crimson River
Sable Peak
Christmas in Quincy - Prequel
The Edens: A Legacy Short Story

TREASURE STATE WILDCATS SERIES

Coach
Blitz

CLIFTON FORGE SERIES

Steel King
Riven Knight
Stone Princess
Noble Prince
Fallen Jester
Tin Queen

CALAMITY MONTANA SERIES

The Bribe
The Bluff
The Brazen
The Bully
The Brawl
The Brood

JAMISON VALLEY SERIES

The Coppersmith Farmhouse
The Clover Chapel
The Lucky Heart

The Outpost
The Bitterroot Inn
The Candle Palace

MAYSEN JAR SERIES

The Birthday List
Letters to Molly
The Dandelion Diary

LARK COVE SERIES

Tattered
Timid
Tragic
Tinsel
Timeless

RUNAWAY SERIES

Runaway Road
Wild Highway
Quarter Miles
Forsaken Trail
Dotted Lines

HOLIDAY BROTHERS SERIES

The Naughty, The Nice and The Nanny
Three Bells, Two Bows and One
Brother's Best Friend
A Partridge and a Pregnancy

STANDALONES
Ivy
Rifts and Refrains
A Little Too Wild

ROUND 1

CHAPTER 1

TALIA

"Thirteen." The dry erase marker squeaked as I added a tally mark to the inside of my locker's metal door. *Thirteen.* "A new record."

Thirteen days without a patient yelling at me. Thirteen days without anyone requesting Dr. Anderson, Dr. Herrera or Dr. Murphy in my place. Thirteen days without Rachel, the charge nurse at Quincy Memorial, lecturing me for, well…anything.

Thirteen good days.

What were the chances this streak would last through Christmas next week? If I made it to twenty-two days in a row, that would mean I'd gone an entire work month without my intelligence, my education or my skills being called into question.

The door to the staff locker room opened, and Rachel stood in the threshold. *Oh, God. Don't ruin my streak.*

"Hi, Rachel." I forced a smile. "How was your day?"

"Fine." Her voice was flat. She was in her late forties and might have been pretty if she'd relaxed. Or if she'd let her hair down. But in the three years I'd worked with Rachel, I'd only ever seen her blond hair, streaked with gray at the temples, pulled into a severe bun.

Was it short? Long? No clue. Even the few times I'd bumped into her outside of work, Rachel's hair had looked the same. Was that why she was so sour? Was that bun giving her a headache? Her frown was as ever present as her hairstyle. Did she ever smile?

"I've got a problem with a chart, Talia."

"Okay," I drawled.

There was no problem with a chart. I'd spent three years getting lectured by this woman on exactly what boxes to check, how she wanted the doctors to input notes and where *her* nurses looked for patient details.

Dr. Anderson, Dr. Murphy and Dr. Herrera each had their own charting preferences. They put their notes wherever they pleased. Had Rachel ever lectured them on their charting? No. She also didn't call them by their first names. I was the lesser doctor on staff and Rachel always found a way to remind me that I was just a resident.

I was just Talia.

I was just the girl who'd grown up in this small Montana town and who'd loved it enough to move home after medical school. I'd come home to give back to my community and, maybe someday, earn the respect that Dr. Anderson had garnered in his decades as Quincy's favorite doctor.

Not only was he my boss, he was also the man who'd delivered my five siblings and me into this world. He was a staple in our town. Did Rachel razz him about meticulous charting? Doubtful.

"Should we take a look?" I returned my marker to the locker's shelf, then closed it up, following Rachel to the nearest nurses' station.

She took a seat, clicking with fury through the hospital's records as I hovered over her shoulder. When she had the chart pulled up, she shifted so I could read the screen.

It was Memphis's chart. My sister-in-law had come in for a routine pregnancy checkup this afternoon. I scanned the information for anything out of place. Medications prescribed? None. Labs ordered? Just the standard urine analysis. Baby's heart rate? Normal. The nurse had entered in Memphis's vitals.

"What's the problem?" I asked Rachel.

"Your notes."

"What about the notes?" I'd added a few quick sentences stating that Memphis was feeling fine and that her weight and blood pressure were in the normal range.

"I can't read those notes and know what concerns were discussed with the patient."

"You can read those notes and see that the patient had no concerns to discuss." I kept my smile firmly in place, but damn, this woman loved to poke at me. She'd been poking for three years and it was growing old.

This entire encounter was a waste of my time. And she'd just broken my thirteen-day streak.

Why was it always her? Was it horrible that I wished she'd retire early? Her nursing staff was wonderful. They were a joy to work with, and I would bet my annual salary that not a single one of them would have felt misinformed by the brief summary notes in Memphis's chart.

But nothing I did seemed to be enough for Rachel. She viewed this hospital as hers and I was the too-young, too-inexperienced doctor roaming her hallways, intruding on her turf.

"Anything else?" I asked. "I've got dinner plans."

Memphis had been my last patient for the day and Knox had tagged along. My brother never missed a thing when it came to his wife and kids. After the checkup, they'd invited me to dinner, and I rarely turned down Knox's cooking. He owned the best restaurant in town, and though meals at Knuckles were always outstanding, the real magic came alive when he was cooking at home for those he loved most.

Lunch today had been a stale granola bar and a protein shake. My stomach had been growling for an hour. As if on cue, it rumbled.

Rachel's eyes dropped to my waist as her lip curled.

This was a test, right? Maybe Rachel was simply putting me through some sort of resident physician hazing. Maybe she wanted to make sure I had the backbone to be one of Quincy's doctors. Why else would she be so nasty? What the hell had I done to make her dislike me so much?

Nothing. The answer was nothing. So this had to be a test.

Well, hazing ritual or not, Rachel would need to come at me with more than nitpicking and frowns. My dream was to work at Quincy Memorial. This was just as much my hospital as it was hers. My family had founded Quincy, and generations ago, the Edens had donated money to help build this hospital in the first place.

"Have a great night, Rachel." My tone held more sugar than a kid's Halloween bag. With a quick finger wave, I walked away from the desk and retreated to the locker room.

It was empty, so I let out a groan as I spun the combination on my lock and ripped the door open. Then I grabbed the microfiber cloth I kept on the shelf and erased my tally marks.

Zero. "Gah."

Hopefully Rachel would back off after my residency was

over. Was that what I needed before she'd treat me like the other doctors? A full-fledged medical license?

I was close. I was so close. I'd been lucky after medical school. Many small-town hospitals weren't accredited to take on residents, but Dr. Anderson had jumped through the hoops years ago so that he could have a resident on occasion. Dr. Murphy had been the first. Then I'd applied and Dr. Anderson had taken me under his wing.

We hadn't talked about the timing of me taking my licensure exam, but I assumed it would happen this spring. And after another few years, I hoped to earn my board certification in family medicine too, just like Dr. Anderson.

If I earned a certification, would that stop patients from giving me the side-eye when I walked into an exam room? It didn't happen all the time. It happened less than it had a year ago. But it still happened. I still overheard the whispered questions.

Is she old enough to be a doctor? Are you sure she knows what she's doing? Isn't one of the other doctors available today?

Most of the pushback I got was from men, especially older men. Even at twenty-nine years old, I was still viewed by some of Quincy's good ol' boys as Harrison Eden's *girl*.

I was a good doctor, right? Dr. Anderson would have told me if I'd been doing a bad job. He wouldn't let me treat people if he thought I'd do them harm.

My insecurities always flared up after a confrontation with Rachel.

I pinched the bridge of my nose and silently counted. *One. Two. Three. Four. Five.* Pity party over. With my black puffer coat over my baby-blue scrub top, I slung my purse over a shoulder and headed for the door.

What I needed was a nice family dinner. Knox and Memphis were waiting for me in the lobby, and a warm meal at their place plus an hour of quality time with my nephew Drake would surely lift my mood.

Instead of taking the hallway that led to the employee exit, I pushed open the door into the lobby. The reception desk was empty. Jenny, the nurse who worked weekdays, had probably left right at five. This entrance was for scheduled appointments and the occasional walk-in. The doors here would be locked soon, and if a patient came in after hours, they'd have to go to the emergency room for help.

Knox and Memphis were standing together in the center of the lobby, talking to a man whose back was to me.

The man was the same tall height as Knox. He had broad shoulders and a narrow waist. Even a hoodie couldn't hide his muscled frame. And damn, his ass was worth a second look. There weren't many guys in Quincy with that sort of physique, at least none who weren't related to me. Who was that guy?

"I'm looking for a doctor who works here," the man said. "Talia Eden."

I froze. *No.* No, this wasn't happening. It couldn't be him. Except I'd recognize that voice anywhere. Even if I hadn't heard it in seven years.

A jolt of panic raced through my body and I flew toward the reception desk, practically leaping behind the counter. My knees cracked against the hard, glossy floor, and I winced, gritting my teeth so I wouldn't make a sound.

Damn it. What was he doing here? Why was he looking for me?

"You might try the ER," Memphis said. I'd hug her for it later because I was sure she'd seen me from her periphery when

I'd walked into the lobby. "Maybe they can track her down for you. Just head out the doors and down the sidewalk to the other side of the building. You can't miss it."

I inched closer to the counter, careful not to brush the chair and make a noise.

"Appreciate it." Footsteps, then the swish of the double doors as they opened and closed.

Phew. I blew out the breath I'd been holding, but my heart stayed stuck in my throat.

"Coast's clear," Knox called.

I inched up, my eyes barely over the counter's ledge. "Is he gone?"

"Yeah." Knox nodded. "Want to tell me why you're hiding from Foster Madden?"

"Nope." Definitely not. I didn't talk about Foster Madden for a reason.

I stood and tiptoed around the desk, my eyes glued to the windows in case Foster made a return appearance. But the only thing I saw on the sidewalks was snow. "I should go."

"What about dinner?" Memphis asked.

"Rain check."

Before they could stop me, I bolted. Sprinting had never been my forte, slow and steady distance races were more my speed, but there was no way I'd risk bumping into Foster. So I tore out of the lobby, and after one quick check down the sidewalk to make sure he was gone, I hoofed it to my car.

My hands gripped the steering wheel with so much force that my knuckles were white before I'd even pulled out of the darkened parking lot. I checked my rearview mirror no less than two hundred times as I drove through town, searching for headlights that might be following me home. It wasn't until I was inside the house, sagging against the kitchen counter with a glass of wine, that I let myself breathe.

What was he doing here? His life was in Las Vegas, exactly where I'd left him. Exactly where he'd stayed after breaking my heart. Why was he looking for me now? Why, after all this time, had he come to Montana?

My stomach plummeted. I didn't want to see him. I didn't want to hear that voice or look into his stormy blue eyes. Seven years and I still wasn't ready to face him again. If I managed to avoid him long enough, would he leave?

"No," I muttered. Unless Foster had undergone an entire personality change, he would eventually track me down. His nickname was the Iron Fist for a reason. He was tenacious and persistent. Unshakeable.

But at least I'd avoided him tonight. He hadn't been able to take me by surprise. I gulped from my wineglass, then took it with me upstairs to my bedroom, where I stripped out of my scrubs and took a shower to rinse off the day.

My dark hair was wet and twisted into a knot when I returned to the kitchen. My scrubs had been traded for leggings and a ratty University of Washington sweatshirt when I opened the fridge and pulled out a carton of eggs. It wasn't a Knox Eden meal, but for tonight, an omelet would have to suffice. If I'd gone to dinner, Memphis and Knox would have peppered me with questions.

Questions I wasn't prepared to answer.

Dad knew about Foster, but only because he'd been there in the aftermath. He'd flown to Las Vegas to help me move and seen me at my lowest. Mom knew because Dad didn't keep secrets from her, but the one and only time she'd brought up his name, I'd begged her never to speak it again.

That had been during the raw days. My wounds had healed, mostly, but that didn't mean I was ready to relive the pain. It was too hard. Too humiliating.

Why was he here? After all this time, hadn't he forgotten about me?

The eggs didn't sit well in my knotted stomach but I forced myself to eat. It would be the same meal I'd have for breakfast, sans the wine. I was just rinsing my plate when the doorbell rang.

The dish brush slipped from my hand, clattering into the sink.

It was him. I couldn't see the door, but somehow, I knew it was Foster. The doorbell rang again, followed by a knock.

Why hadn't I dried my hair? Why hadn't I dressed in anything else? Scrubs would have been better than facing him with a bare face and bare feet. There was a hole in the knee of these leggings and this shirt would have fit my brothers loosely.

If I didn't answer the door, would he leave? Or would he stay here all night, knowing I was hiding inside? If I ignored him tonight, would he come to the hospital again? The last place I wanted to talk with Foster was at my work.

So I lifted my glass, draining the rest of my wine for liquid courage. The moment I swallowed the last drop, I squared my shoulders and walked through the house.

The sooner this was dealt with, the better. I'd find out why he was here, then send him on his way. With any luck, Foster would be gone from Quincy by morning.

My heart beat so hard it hurt. Every pulse resounded through my limbs. I sucked in a breath and held it as I inched through the entryway, my footsteps silent. When I reached the door, I stood on my toes and pressed an eye to the peephole.

Foster stood in profile, his gaze cast across the covered porch. He'd grown a beard. It was a nice beard. Short trimmed, so you could still make out the sharp corners of his jaw. But my Foster hadn't had a beard, just stubble on the days when he hadn't shaved.

A stab of pain pierced my heart. This wasn't *my* Foster. There was no version of Foster that belonged to me. Not anymore.

He raised a finger and pushed the doorbell again. Then he ran a hand through his chocolate-brown hair, something he'd obviously been doing a lot tonight because the ends were sticking up at odd angles.

I dropped to my heels and waited through another three agonizing heartbeats, then I flipped the dead bolt and opened the door to Foster Madden.

The man I'd dated for one year, two months and eleven days.

The man I'd loved with my whole heart.

The man I'd vowed to forget.

The view from the peephole hadn't done him justice. He was every bit as handsome as I remembered. Maybe even more now that he'd grown that damn beard.

Age had only enhanced his rugged features. He was bigger than he'd been, years spent honing his body into the perfect fighting machine. His black hoodie stretched across his broad chest, molding to his shoulders. His jeans hung on his narrow hips and pooled at the hem above a pair of motorcycle boots.

How many times had I traced the bump in the middle of his nose with my fingertip? How many nights had I drowned in those deep, ocean-blue eyes? How many kisses had I given the soft pout of his lips?

"Talia."

God, that voice. Raspy and deep. My name had never sounded as good as it did out of Foster's mouth.

"What are you doing here?"

He studied my face. "You're not surprised to see me."

"No." I crossed my arms over my chest as the chill from outside seeped through my clothes. "I saw you at the hospital."

His jaw clenched. "You saw me."

"What are you doing here?" I repeated. "And how did you know where I lived?"

Not that it would be hard to figure out. Quincy hadn't entirely transitioned into the modern age, and the local newspaper still printed an annual phone book along with putting the information online.

"It's been a long time," he said. "How are you?"

It's been a long time. How are you? "Small talk? Really? Does your wife know you're here?"

He lifted his left hand, wiggling his naked ring finger. "I'm not married."

When had he gotten divorced? This was the problem when you vowed to forget someone. It meant that in the past seven years, I hadn't once let myself search for Foster.

I hadn't peeked at his social media accounts or typed his name into Google. I hadn't watched any of his pay-per-view fights, and if his name came up on ESPN, I'd either shut off the television or walk out of the room. My brothers liked to rent UFC fights. I'd lied more than once about being on call to avoid one of their parties.

"Why are you here?" The growl in my voice surprised us both.

Pain clouded his beautiful eyes. His throat bobbed as he

swallowed, then dropped his chin.

What had he expected? Me to open my arms and welcome him back into my life?

The hurt in his eyes vanished just as quickly as it had appeared. And all that remained was sheer determination. The focused stare. The steeled spine. The flexed jaw. It was the look Foster wore in the boxing ring, usually before he won.

He shoved a hand into the pocket of his jeans, pulling out a single silver key. "Here."

I took it from him as he held it out, careful not to let our fingers brush. He wasn't mine to touch. Not anymore. "What's this?"

"My building."

"Your building." I narrowed my eyes. He'd better be talking about a building in Nevada.

Foster's hand dove into his jeans again, this time coming out with a small slip of paper. He took my other hand and pried it open.

Electricity zinged up my arm. The calloused tips of his fingers sent tingles across my skin.

His eyes flared, like he'd felt that charge too, as he placed the paper in my palm, then let me go. "That's the address."

At the street name, my heart sank. "This is in Quincy."

"Yep."

"Why do you have a building in Quincy?"

"Come tomorrow and you'll find out."

"No."

He dug into his other pocket this time, pulling out a small velvet pouch in a familiar shade of teal. "I'm guessing this will make it a yes."

"What is this?" I asked as he handed it over.

Foster didn't answer and he didn't wait for me to open the pouch. He spun on a heel and marched across my porch, jogging the few steps to the sidewalk. Then he rounded the hood of a gleaming black truck, started the engine and drove down the block.

I inched away from the threshold as his taillights disappeared, kicking the door closed. With every passing second, the pouch got heavier.

Don't open it.

Foster was counting on my curiosity. He hadn't answered a single question of mine tonight, instead leaving me with even more than I'd started with.

Don't open it.

"Gah." I stretched the top of the pouch and turned it over, the item inside dropping into my palm beside the key.

A ring. A two-carat, emerald-cut diamond inlaid on a gold band.

I gasped as the diamond glinted from the overhead light. How did he have this ring? Why?

In my other hand, I crumpled the paper into a tight ball, squeezing as hard as possible.

Then I pried it apart.

Damn him. I should ignore him. I should pretend he didn't exist. But considering I hadn't managed that in seven years, I doubted I'd forget Foster Madden by morning.

CHAPTER 2

FOSTER

The phone's ring bounced off the block walls in my new building. I pulled it from my pocket. Jasper.

"Hey," I answered.

"Hey. Just checking in. How was yesterday?"

"Could have been worse." She could have had a man answer her door last night. I knew she wasn't married, but a boyfriend would have made this more of a challenge. Not impossible, just another challenge. "She didn't slam the door in my face."

"Well, you would have deserved it if she had."

I chuckled. "This is true."

Jasper wasn't just my trainer. He was my closest friend and one of the only people in the world who knew the truth about my situation. About Talia. About why I'd come to Montana.

This was the fight of my life.

There were five rounds in a fight. And after last night at Talia's, I had a feeling I'd need them all to win.

"How's the gym?" he asked.

"Empty. Dirty. I don't know if you could even call this place a gym." My voice echoed around the dank space. "Guess that's what I get for buying a building sight unseen."

From the outside, the building was nothing more than a square box painted a dull gray. *GYM* was written on the front wall in an obnoxious shade of safety orange. The letters hadn't looked nearly as ugly in the photos my realtor had sent.

There was a bit of resemblance to the pictures. But the photos had shown a bright, clean space with outdated equipment. Either they'd been from a decade ago or he had a Photoshop magician on staff.

Regardless, I should have known something was wrong when I'd met him an hour ago to pick up the gym's keys and he'd hesitated outside the front door.

I'd hoped the interior would be better, but with every loop around the room, it only got worse.

The cement floors were covered in a coat of dust. Every single ceiling tile was spotted with water marks. Most of the paint was the same gray as the exterior, but the orange had snuck its way inside too and covered an entire wall. Not one of the floor-to-ceiling mirrors at the back of the gym lacked cracks. And there was a draft coming from one of the windows—or maybe all of the windows. The furnace was running on full blast, the fan nearly as loud as helicopter blades, and it wasn't doing a thing to cut the December chill.

"How bad is it?" Jasper asked.

"Bad. The realtor handed me the keys and bolted. He said he had another appointment, but I have a feeling he was leaving before I could pummel him. Those pictures he sent were bullshit."

"What are you going to do?"

I sighed and dragged a hand through my hair. "Get to work. I've got to get this usable."

At this point, I didn't have a lot of other options. This

building was just going to have to work temporarily.

With Christmas in five days, I doubted I'd be able to find another place to live until after New Year's. The hotel was booked—ten minutes after I'd walked through the gym's door, I'd called The Eloise Inn and asked to extend my reservation. But the hotel was booked through the holidays. I had two nights left before my room would go to the next guest. And every motel, VRBO and Airbnb within fifty miles was taken.

After the holidays, I could search for a nicer home. But I needed a gym. My training had been delayed enough these past few weeks dealing with everything in Vegas.

Eventually, I could get this place remodeled. Or I could tear it down and build from scratch. But that would take months. I didn't have months. So I'd settle for this place. I'd make the gym's small, one-bedroom apartment livable. And meanwhile, I'd convince Talia to listen to what I had to say.

If there was one thing going for me, it was the element of surprise. Part of the reason I'd bought this shithole was because it was vacant. I'd been able to pay cash with a quick close. That had been only a week ago. Talia had been surprised by the address I'd given her last night, which meant she hadn't gotten wind of me moving to Quincy.

I was banking on Talia's natural curiosity to bring her here today. I needed to see her again. I needed to see her a hundred times. Maybe then I'd realize this wasn't a dream.

Seven years I'd waited for this chance. Seven goddamn years and I couldn't risk fucking it up.

"Have you talked to Kadence?" Jasper asked.

"Last night." I walked toward the door open to the apartment.

It was in just as bad of shape as the gym. The bedroom was

empty. I counted myself lucky that an animal hadn't decided to take shelter from the winter weather in the closet. But the carpet was stained and the scent of cat piss clung to the air.

I surveyed the cramped living space and attached kitchen. I hadn't had the guts to open the fridge yet and see what was growing inside. The bathroom would need a few gallons of bleach before my skin came in contact with the shower or toilet.

On the list of renovations, this apartment was at the top.

"It's temporary," I told Jasper. And myself.

"You sure about this?"

"I'm finally free." I'd been trapped for so long I wasn't even sure how to act of my own free will. But it was time to build the life I'd missed. The life I'd held in my grasp before I'd fucked it all up.

"I hear you," Jasper said. "What can I do?"

"Nothing. I'll figure it out."

"Do me a favor? Fit in a workout today."

"Does cleaning count?" To get this place ready, I'd be busting my ass.

"That works," he said. "How's your head?"

"Not great," I admitted.

This was the first time in my life I had no motivation to train. To fight. Now that Arlo was dead and no longer pushing me to win, win, win, I just…didn't care.

I needed to find that motivation because I had a fight the first weekend in March. Maybe Talia could help. If I could get her to listen.

"Don't worry," I told Jasper. "I'll be ready."

"When should I come?"

I sighed and walked back to the gym, following my own footprints in the dust. "Give me some time."

"You don't have time."

"I know," I muttered. I didn't have time to waste cleaning up an old gym and making a crappy apartment livable. Yet here I was.

For Talia.

"Call me soon," Jasper said.

"If I don't talk to you, Merry Christmas."

"Same to you."

I ended the call and tucked my phone into my jeans pocket. Then I walked toward the ugly-as-fuck orange wall. The color was giving me a migraine but it would have to wait. The first order of business was cleaning the apartment.

I'd made arrangements to have furniture delivered on Friday. There were carpets to rip out and rooms to scour. Then I'd tackle the gym.

My stomach was in a knot as I paced to the opposite end of the space, peering out one of the grimy windows. Would she come today? Had that ring piqued her interest enough?

My palms sweated as I paced the length of the building again. I hadn't been this nervous in years. My phone rang in my pocket. Vivienne's ringtone. Jasper had probably called and told her to check in.

"Hey," I answered. "Everything okay?"

"Yeah," she said. "How about you?"

"I'm all right. It's…weird."

"I know. I was thinking that earlier when I was walking around the house." Vivienne was the only one in the world who'd understand. Because I wasn't the only one who'd just been set free. She had too. "But a good weird, you know?"

"Yeah, Vivi. It's a good weird."

"How's Montana?"

"Cold, but I'm glad to be here. I'll be busy getting the place set up."

"How is it?"

Awful. "Fine." I wouldn't tell her about the actual state of the gym. She'd see it eventually, and if she knew it was bad, she'd worry.

"Will you call later?"

"You bet. Have a nice day."

"You too. Good luck."

Next to Jasper, Vivienne was my best friend. She knew why I was in Montana. She knew that Talia had always been in my heart.

Over the years, she'd been the one to keep tabs on Talia. Mostly, Vivienne had done it to save me the heartbreak of seeing photos of Talia with another man. So she'd randomly check Talia's social media posts. She'd google Talia's name and see if it had ever changed from Eden.

The fact that Talia wasn't married had been a miracle. My miracle.

The day Vivienne and I had signed our divorce papers, she'd encouraged me to take this risk. She'd done everything in her power to help me get to Montana.

Here I was. Time to get to work.

"Okay." I clapped my hands, the sound filling the gym. I'd stopped at the hardware store this morning for a few cleaning supplies, knowing I'd have to do some work. I hadn't expected this much work and my stash wouldn't last long, but it would get me started.

I took one step for the door, but it opened. And there she was.

"Talia." My voice sounded hoarse. "You came."

She nodded, looking me up and down. Then she held up her hand, the velvet pouch dangling from her fingers. "You knew I would."

"Hoped." Yes, I'd baited her with that ring. And I'd do it again.

She tore her gaze away and let the door swing closed behind her. Then she stepped inside and tucked a lock of her dark, silky hair behind an ear. Last night, she'd had it up in a knot. Today, it was curled in waves that hung nearly to her waist.

Fuck, she was beautiful. I would have sworn she couldn't get more breathtaking, yet she had managed the impossible.

The air rushed from my lungs. My heart beat too fast. Seeing Talia was like being hit in the chest. It had been the same last night. How many times had I wished to see her face, to stand in the same room and breathe the same air, just one more time?

Beneath her black coat, she wore a pair of baby-blue scrubs that brought out her sapphire eyes. A man could find the secret to life in those eyes.

Talia walked to the center of the room, looking everywhere but at me.

"You're a doctor." *Fuck. Nice, Madden. Way to state the obvious.*

"Yes."

"That was always your dream." It didn't surprise me in the slightest that she'd made it come true.

Talia pushed up the sleeve of her coat, tapping her watch. "I'm on a break and need to get back to the hospital. What do you want, Foster?"

You. "I wanted to see you. Tell you I was in town. Thought maybe we could catch up. Go to dinner or something. The restaurant in the hotel is really good. I ate there last night."

"That's my brother's restaurant." She crossed her arms over her chest, still walking in circles around the gym. "Why did you buy this building?"

"Because I need a training facility. The other gym in town is public. I needed something I could tailor for myself. Put in a ring. Heavy bags. Mats. That sort of thing. Plus it's got an apartment that will work until I'm able to buy a house."

Talia's stunning blue eyes widened. She stopped walking and pointed to the floor. "You're going to live here? In Quincy?"

"Yes."

"Why?"

Wasn't it obvious? "You always talked about Quincy. About how your family founded the town. How it was a place where roots ran deep. I decided if I was going to relocate, why not Montana? It was time for a change. Time to get out of Vegas."

"A change." Her eyes narrowed. "What does Vivienne think about this change?"

"Does it matter? She's not my wife."

There was so much to say. So much to explain. But there was a fire in Talia's eyes, and if she was angry, she wouldn't hear me out. Maybe she wasn't ready for what I had to say. And I needed her to *hear* me. To hear the truth.

"How about dinner tonight?" I asked.

She raised her chin. "How long have you been planning this move?"

"Not long."

"I'm surprised no one knew." She scoffed. "Foster Madden moving to Quincy is big news."

Which was exactly why I'd made sure to keep a lid on the purchase of this building.

"When did you buy this ring?" She held up the pouch again.

"Was it hers?"

"No, that was never Vivienne's." That ring had always been for Talia.

It had stayed locked away in my safe until I'd finally been able to give it to her last night.

"There's a lot to talk about. If you've got to get back to work, then tonight. What do you say? Dinner?"

Her arms cinched tighter across her chest and she started walking again. "No. I don't think that's a good idea."

"Why not?"

"Because I don't want to see you, Foster. I don't want you in my town."

"Too late."

Her nostrils flared.

Shit. I'd always loved Talia's steady nature. When others would panic, she'd stay calm. It was part of the reason I'd known she'd make an incredible doctor. But every now and then, she'd get mad. And when someone pushed the right buttons, Talia Eden had a temper unmatched.

So before it blew and I really pissed her off, I changed the subject.

"There's a lot to be done to fix this place up. That orange wall has got to go. But I think the building itself will work. I'm going to set the ring up here." Marking an outline in the dust, I walked a square in the center of the floor, then pointed around the room as I spoke. "I'll put mats in that corner. Hang heavy bags from that beam. Bring in a treadmill and stationary bike."

"You can't be serious about this."

"I am. I've got a fight in March and am having a hard time focusing in Vegas. A change of scenery should help. Maybe some fresh faces. You were always good at keeping me focused.

Maybe I could enlist your help."

She gave a slight head shake. It was the same look people had after you rang their bell. I had her head spinning. "You're asking me to help you get ready for a fight?"

No, I was asking her to dinner. "Something like that. We could talk about it tonight."

"I—what?"

"Dinner, Tally." It was a mistake to use her nickname. I knew it the moment her expression blanked. Gone was the confusion. Gone was the anger.

She shut me out faster than I could blink.

"Get out of Quincy, Foster." She marched across the floor. "I don't want you here."

The cold air rushed inside as she ripped open the door and stormed outside.

"Fuck." I dragged a hand over my face. A pop of teal velvet caught my eye.

The ring.

She'd dropped it on the floor.

I walked over and picked it up, holding it in my hand for a long moment.

Was I pushing too hard? Too fast? That was the only way I knew how to go. But it was exactly how I'd lost Talia in the first place.

"Round one."

Round one was over. And I'd gotten my fucking ass kicked.

ROUND 2

CHAPTER 3

TALIA

*T*ally.

No one called me Tally. Not my parents, my brothers or my friends. Everyone used my full name.

Except Foster.

He'd thought it was so fitting, not just because of my name, but because I tended to count in tally marks. I'd watched all of his fights and sparring rounds with a notepad on my lap filled with tiny lines.

Strikes landed versus strikes attempted. Kicks versus punches. Takedowns and tap outs.

The tallies had been a way for me to curb my nerves. If I was busy keeping count, then I worried less about him being kicked in the ribs or punched in the face.

Just like tallying my good days at the hospital. Those marks, even when I had to erase them, gave me a positive focus. A goal.

Tally.

I hadn't been Tally in a long time. Until yesterday.

It was like being blasted back in time, to the days when Foster had been the biggest part of my life. The days when he'd been so close, he might as well have been the thump in my heartbeat.

And the ring...

Why? Why had he bought that ring? Especially if it hadn't gone to his wife. When had he bought it?

It looked exactly like the ring I remembered, but that was impossible. He wouldn't have bought a ring for me when he married Vivienne. But still, it was so familiar. Achingly familiar.

I'd never forget the day I saw that ring.

Foster's boss had asked him to run an errand, to pick up a pair of earrings that was a gift for his daughter. So I'd gone with him to Tiffany's because in those days, we'd been inseparable.

While we waited for the saleswoman to bring out the earrings, Foster and I wandered the store. He challenged me to a game. He asked me to pick out my favorite ring and he'd try to guess which one it was.

He found it on his first guess.

Because out of all the elaborate, glittering rings, he'd known I'd pick something simple and delicate.

A ring I could take on and off with ease. A ring I could wear on a chain around my neck at work without the stone digging into my skin. A ring that would look beautiful on my finger, even when my skin was chapped and dry from frequent handwashing and disposable gloves.

That had been a week before he'd told me he was marrying Vivienne.

A week before he'd shattered my heart.

He couldn't move here. He couldn't live in Montana. We'd cross paths. There was no way we wouldn't run into each other on Main or at a store. Quincy was too small to avoid a man like Foster. Somehow, I had to convince him to leave. Somehow.

But first, I needed to clear my head. I needed to sort out

my heart. So this morning after showering and eating a quick breakfast, I'd left the house and come to the place where I'd always found peace.

Home.

Driving in my black Jeep Wrangler, I eased down the lane to Mom and Dad's, passing under the Eden Ranch gated archway. Beyond the fences bordering the road, the snow-covered meadows stretched for miles. Evergreens covered the mountain foothills, their branches dusted in white.

A green tractor with a round bale in its forks rolled through the pasture beyond my window. A line of black Angus cows trotted behind it, each wearing the Eden brand on their ribs— an *E* above a curve in the shape of a rocking chair's runner.

I loved the ranch. I loved the open spaces and the family legacy and the animals. Throughout my childhood, I'd planned on becoming a veterinarian. I'd wanted to specialize in large animals so I could help out on the ranch with cattle and horses.

Until my junior year in high school and a wintery night had changed my destiny.

My English teacher, Mrs. Haskins, had been eight months pregnant at the time and only days away from taking her maternity leave. It had been March and a massive snowstorm had blown into town. The weather forecast hadn't predicted its severity. One moment, we were watching heavy flakes fall to the ground, and the next, a sheer whiteout. Most roads were closed for emergency travel only, and since my family lived in the country, it was impossible for my parents to drive in and get us.

So my twin sister, Lyla, and I rounded up our younger siblings, Mateo and Eloise, to wait it out. Mrs. Haskins volunteered her house as a place for us to stay until the storm died down.

We trudged the two blocks to her home and all hunkered inside. Her husband worked for the transportation department and was out driving a snowplow, so she was happy for our company.

Until her contractions started.

We called 9-1-1 for an ambulance, but by the time they arrived, I was holding a slimy newborn baby girl in my arms.

I'd never been so scared in my life.

Maybe I'd had the courage to help because I'd been so focused on the veterinarian path. I'd watched Dad pull plenty of calves. But from that moment on, my path had changed.

Mom always said becoming a doctor had been my calling.

What if I'd gotten it wrong? What if I should have stayed here, worked here? I wouldn't have to deal with the Rachels of the world. And I wouldn't have met Foster.

I shook off those doubts as I neared the house. The ranch was bustling with activity this morning, the hired men getting ready to head out for their day. As a truck passed with a couple of guys in the cab, I waved, then parked beside Mom's new Cadillac.

Every year, Dad bought her the latest model. This time, he'd gotten her an Escalade because she'd insisted on plenty of space to keep car seats for her grandkids.

"Talia." Griffin was crossing Mom and Dad's porch as I hopped out of my Jeep.

"Hi." I smiled, meeting him at the base of the steps.

In one hand, Griff had a travel mug. The other he held in the air, making space for a sideways hug. He smelled like wind and soap with a hint of campfire, probably from the stove at his place. With every passing day, he reminded me more and more of Dad.

"You look tired. You okay?" he asked. Griff had taken it upon himself as the oldest sibling to make sure we were all okay. Again, a lot like Dad.

"Good," I lied. The dark circles beneath my eyes were from two sleepless nights spent tossing and turning about Foster. "What are you up to?"

"Just dropped off the kids." He let me go and hooked his thumb over his shoulder. "Mom's babysitting today while I head out and get some firewood split. What about you? Not working today?"

"No. I'm on call all weekend, so I've got today off." My schedule was erratic at best. The standard shifts were reserved for Dr. Anderson, and the rest of us filled in the gaps. "I thought I'd come out and take Neptune for a ride. Dad said you had most of the horses still gathered in from after they got reshod."

"Yeah, they're all in the calving pasture. I'll have one of the guys bring her into the stables and get her saddled for you."

"I can do it."

"It'll save you the trouble. Head on in. Get some coffee and one of Mom's muffins. Neptune will be ready in thirty."

"Okay." I smiled. "That will give me time with the kids."

"See you later." Griff set off for the barn.

The Eden Ranch was one of the largest in the state, generations of our family having built it up. Griffin's heart belonged to Winslow and their two babies. But beyond his family, my brother loved this land.

I couldn't imagine him in a suit and tie, working in an office. He belonged in a faded pair of Wranglers and scuffed cowboy boots with a canvas Carhartt coat on his back and a dusty Stetson on his head.

The scent of hay and cattle drifted on the gentle breeze as I headed up the porch steps to my childhood home. My parents had both retired in recent years but this house would always feel like ranch headquarters. Past their log home was the barn my grandfather had built. Beside it were the stables and the shop, additions Dad had made when he'd been at the helm.

I pushed open the front door and inhaled sugar and blueberries and lemon. Did it smell better inside or out? They were both home. "Hello!"

"Talia, will you bring me that five-gallon bucket of flour beside the door?" Mom hollered.

"Sure." I shrugged off my coat and hung it on an iron hook in the entryway, then hefted the bucket by its handle and waddled it down the hall. "Where do you want it?"

"By the pantry, please." She pointed with a dough-covered finger.

I set it down, then moved around the island to inspect whatever it was she was making. "Pie? Smells good."

"I'm getting a jump on Christmas prep. This will go in the freezer." She kissed my cheek, then went to the sink to wash up. "What are you doing today?"

"Thought I'd come out and go for a ride."

What I loved most about my parents' house was that the lock on the front door hadn't been turned in decades. They didn't expect phone calls before we showed up. They were used to unannounced visitors and not once had they made me feel like I was interrupting.

This was our home, no matter how old we got.

I went to the cupboard where she kept the coffee cups and took out a mug.

"Guess who I bumped into at the store yesterday," Mom

said, picking up her own mug.

"Who?" I asked as I refilled her cup, then my own.

"Bonnie Haskins."

"No kidding?" I laughed. "I was just thinking about her on the drive over."

"She had Marie with her. That girl is growing like a weed."

Marie, the baby I'd delivered during that snowstorm. Named for my middle name.

The last time I'd seen Marie had been at the hospital. She'd come in for her annual sports physical. "She's so cute."

"She's going to give the boys at the high school a run for their money."

"You're not wrong." I smiled and sipped my coffee.

This was why I lived in Quincy. So that Marie Haskins would grow up in front of my eyes. So that Hudson and Emma and Drake would be doted on by their aunt Talia.

A tiny giggle sounded from the living room. "I heard you're babysitting today."

"Your dad is on duty until I get this pie in the oven. But otherwise, we're going to have a fun day. I bought finger paint."

"You spoil them."

"Hell yes, I do."

"I'm going to go say hi." I left my coffee on the counter, then headed for the living room, where Dad was on the floor with three babies. Emma, seven months old, was lying on a blanket with her toes in her hands, trying to shove a foot into her mouth.

Her one-and-a-half-year-old brother, Hudson, was smacking two blocks together. While Drake, my brother Knox's son, was toddling around Dad, giggling as Dad tried to tickle him.

"This looks like fun."

Hudson took one look at me and the blocks were forgotten. He shoved up on his feet and held up his hands. "Uh. Uh."

Up. Up.

"Hey, buddy." I swept him into my arms and kissed his cheek. Then another little boy crashed into my leg, so I bent and hefted Drake up too. My siblings always teased me for having baby fever. I wanted kids. Someday. And until that day came, these babies were my fix. "How are my guys today?"

Drake answered with a string of gibberish.

"Ah. Well, that sounds excellent." I put them both down and sat on the floor. "Hey, Dad."

"Hi, sweetheart. What are you up to today?"

"I came out to take Neptune for a ride." I toyed with Hudson's blocks, helping him make a stack.

"It's a pretty day. Sun's shining." No matter what the temperature, hot or cold, Dad considered any day with sunshine a golden one.

"I thought I'd swing by the hotel this afternoon," I said. "See if Eloise needs any help before the Christmas rush. I talked to Lyla this morning and she was oddly calm, considering how busy it's been."

Dad chuckled. "I thought the same thing when I talked to her yesterday. But you know it won't last. She'll be dead on her feet by the time Christmas gets here next week."

The entire town was decked out for the holidays with garland and lights and trimmed trees. Lyla owned the coffee shop in Quincy and she'd spent three hours the other night hand painting Eden Coffee's front window with snowflakes.

She had customers streaming through her door from the time she opened at six in the morning until closing at seven each night. Half were locals who'd placed special orders for holiday pastries. Half were tourists in town to enjoy the festivities.

Lyla would be exhausted by the time New Year's was over. So would Eloise and Knox. But they'd have help. The Edens pitched in to help each other, without hesitation.

"What's new at the hospital?" Dad asked.

"Nothing really." There wasn't much I could tell him, but on occasion, I'd gripe about Rachel.

Hudson threw a fist into my stack of blocks, then giggled, so I stacked them again.

"You okay?" Dad's eyes narrowed on my face. "Something is bothering you."

There was no point in denying it to Dad. He'd always been able to read my moods. And I'd rather him hear it from me than the Quincy grapevine. Knox hadn't mentioned bumping into Foster at the hospital earlier this week, but chances were, it would come up sooner rather than later. We didn't get a lot of famous UFC fighters in Montana.

"Foster Madden is in town."

"What?" He straightened, lowering his voice. "Why? What does he want?"

We hadn't talked about Foster in years. Knox teased me for being too private for my own good. But I was glad I hadn't had to explain the Foster situation to everyone. It was a story I didn't have the heart to share multiple times.

Lyla knew I'd been dating someone in college and that we'd broken up when I'd gone to medical school. Eloise knew the same. And my brothers, well…they avoided their sisters' love lives.

"He claims he's moving here," I said. "He bought that vacant gym on Lower Clark Fork Road."

The previous owner had gone broke when I'd been in high

school, and the gym had sat vacant for years. There just weren't enough people in Quincy to support two gyms, especially when the Firehouse had new equipment and fitness classes.

"Have you talked to him?" Dad asked.

"Yeah."

"And?"

I shrugged. "I don't want him to live here. But I guess I don't have much choice."

Dad's mouth flattened. "You know, I thought about buying that building to flip. Damn it."

"It's...strange." I had a feeling that even if there'd been no building, Foster would have come anyway. I forced a smile and ran my fingers through Drake's blond hair. "I'll be fine. It was a long time ago. Just a shock. But I'm going to take my ride. Get some air. Then I'll be good as new."

"Want some company?" he asked.

"I'd say you've got your hands full." I bent down to kiss Emma's forehead, then stood. "See you after a bit."

After a quick stop in the kitchen to say goodbye to Mom, I headed outside, grabbing a pair of gloves and a beanie from my car. Then I zipped my coat up to my throat and headed for the stables.

"Your horse is all ready, Doc." A hired hand saluted me by touching the brim of his hat as he strode out of the building.

"Thank you." I smiled, then walked inside. Neptune stood in the closest stall. "Hey, girl."

She huffed, butting up against my hand as I stroked her dappled gray cheek.

Neptune was one of eight horses Dad had purchased years ago. Eloise had insisted on naming them all, and at the time, she'd been doing a school project about the solar system. So each of us siblings, plus Mom and Dad, had a horse named after a planet.

"How's my pretty girl?" I crooned, opening the door to lead her out.

We walked for a bit, out of the stables and lapping the corral before I made a few adjustments to my saddle. Then I stepped my left foot into a stirrup and hoisted myself up, settling into the seat before we headed through a gate—the hired man had opened it for me—and into a field.

Dad was right. It was a pretty day. The sun cut the chill from the air. The rays reflected off the snow, and on the back of my horse, my mood instantly improved.

"Foster is here," I told Neptune because my horse was the best listener around. "I have no idea what he expects from me other than he wants to go out to dinner and talk."

Neptune snorted.

"Yep. That's what I think too. It's all horseshit. No offense." I loosened the reins, letting Neptune pick up speed to a trot. "What could there possibly be to say after so long?"

Neptune didn't have an answer this time.

Neither did I.

We rode in silence for hours, weaving a wandering trail in the snow until the crisp air cleared the fog from my mind.

I took the long, familiar path to my favorite place on the ranch.

Garnet Flats.

In the spring, the meadows would be a lush green dotted with wildflowers in red, yellow, white and purple. In the summer, the warm sap from the evergreens would infuse the air with the scent of pine. In autumn, the leaves would change, coloring the mountain foothills before they slept through a white winter.

One hundred acres of sheer beauty.

My dream had always been to build a home here. To experience the seasons through every sunrise and sunset. As I stared across the snow, my eyes flooded.

That dream had included Foster once.

For the first time in my life, it hurt to be here.

With a nudge of my leg and a tug on the reins, I turned away from the meadow. Neptune and I returned to the stables at a gallop, and by the time we arrived, we were both out of breath.

After I put my saddle away, took care of Neptune and led her back to the calving pasture to rejoin the other horses, I headed back to Mom and Dad's. I didn't want to go home, so I didn't. Tomorrow, work would be a welcome distraction, but for today, I'd use my family.

I finger painted with my niece and nephews. Mom made me a grilled ham and cheese sandwich for lunch before I helped her put the kids down for a nap. And every time Dad made eye contact, I smiled, doing my best to reassure him I was fine.

It wasn't until the sun was dipping toward the horizon that I finally said goodbye and climbed into the Jeep. Then I took the long way home so I could savor the pink and orange sunset behind the jagged mountains that surrounded Quincy's valley. And by the time I turned down my street, it was nearly dark.

Just not dark enough to miss the black truck with Nevada license plates parked in front of my house.

"You infuriating, obstinate man." I gritted my teeth and turned down the alley so I could park in my garage. After marching inside, I flew through the house and ripped open the front door to find Foster on my porch. "Why are you here?"

"Dinner." He held up a plastic bag from our local Mexican restaurant. In the other hand, he had a bottle of white wine.

"God, you are stubborn."

"It's a little cold for a picnic. Gonna let me in?"

"No." I crossed my arms over my chest.

"Are you seeing someone?"

"I can't see how that is any of your business."

"That's a no. Come on, Tally—Talia," he corrected. "It's just dinner."

It would never be just dinner. Not with Foster. "No."

"Fine." He tucked the wine under his arm and used his hand to dig in his pocket, pulling out that damn blue pouch. "You left this at the gym."

"Seriously? Stop with the ring." Didn't he realize how hard it was for me to see it?

"It's yours."

"When did you buy it?"

He held my gaze. "Right after you left."

"Why? You married another woman." Before he could answer, I waved both hands. "Never mind. I don't want to know. That ring has never been mine, and I don't want it."

"Tally."

"Don't!" My voice carried past him and into the night. "Don't call me Tally like you know a damn thing about me. Don't call me Tally like we're old friends. Don't call me Tally like you didn't lie to me each and every day we were together."

"Okay." He sighed. "I just… I want to explain. Please."

"Why? I can't believe a word you say."

"Yes, you can."

"No, I can't. I won't. I'm an intelligent woman, Foster. I'm trusting. I'm loyal. And you made me question *everything* about myself. You made me doubt my intuition. My heart. *Myself.* So no, I don't want dinner. I don't want to hear your explanation. I don't want you here. Go away."

How long had those words been bottled up? I waited for that sweet relief, for the good feeling that should have come after yelling at Foster. But my heart…hurt. It hurt. Shouldn't it feel good now? How many years had I held this anger inside? Why didn't it feel cathartic to set it free?

"I'm sorry." Foster swallowed hard. "I'm so sorry."

"It's not enough," I whispered. "It's not enough to be sorry."

"You're right." He nodded. "I just…you've always been my Tally. It's how I think of you. It's what I call you in my head."

He'd thought of me. He'd said my name in his head. The hurt doubled. Then it tripled with the apology written on his face and the regret brimming in his eyes.

This had to end. I had to be the one to end it this time. So I took a step away, gripping the door. "I stopped being your Tally the day you married my best friend. You want to give that ring to someone? Give it to Vivienne."

It should have felt good to slam the door in his face.

It didn't.

CHAPTER 4

FOSTER

Sweat dripped down my face as I hauled the last ceiling tile outside the gym, tossing it into the dumpster I'd rented last week. The cold air was a welcome break from the heat inside.

Every muscle in my body was on fire. Jasper wouldn't have to worry about me missing training sessions or cardio. Renovating this building was some of the hardest physical work I'd done in years.

I took a moment to cool down, my body steaming as my chest heaved. But long breaks weren't an option, so I headed back, surveying my progress. Luckily, this cleanup had only required energy. I hadn't run into any major structural issues that would require construction.

In the past week, the gym had become, well…a gym. Or the makings of one.

The cement floors hadn't been in bad shape after I'd spent hours on my hands and knees, scrubbing away the dust and grime. Whoever had owned this place before me had put mats down with some sort of tape. Idiot. Getting the adhesive off had taken hours.

The drop ceiling had made the space feel cramped, probably

part of why that dumbass previous owner hadn't been able to keep members, so I'd ripped out the tiles and the hanging grid. Now it had an industrial vibe, with the air ducts exposed. The electrical wires I'd hide with some coverings I'd bought yesterday. Then I'd start on paint. Two five-gallon buckets were in a corner next to my ladder, rollers and brushes.

Most of the tools I'd bought had been from the Quincy hardware store. If I was going to live here, I wanted to support the local businesses. But there were some specialty items that they didn't keep in stock, so in addition to busting my ass here, I'd spent a glut of hours behind the wheel of my truck, driving to Missoula to hit up Home Depot.

The four-hour round trip didn't exactly fit in my timeline, but I hadn't had much choice. So I'd hit the road by five in the morning, and when their doors had opened at seven, I'd been their first customer.

The added time in my truck hadn't been all bad. The drive had given me time to think. So had my long hours working here.

It had been a week since I'd gone to Talia's house with Mexican food and wine. A week since she'd yelled and slammed the door in my face.

A week since I'd seen just how much pain I'd caused her.

I didn't want to back off, it wasn't my style, but she needed time. So I'd given her time.

Christmas had come and gone. It had been a damn lonely day, so instead of dwelling on my current situation, I'd spent my holiday finishing the apartment. Making it a home.

I'd stripped the carpet from the bedroom and living area. Then I'd scoured the cement subfloor. I'd had to use a razor to scrape up all of the glue. My first trip to Missoula had been for stain-blocking primer and laminate flooring. After the bare space had been prepped, I'd hauled in the furniture. Alone.

My palms had blisters from the paint roller. My neck had a permanent kink from working on the ceilings. My lower back was screaming at me from too many hours on my hands and knees.

This project was part of my penance.

For Talia, I'd bear every ache and pain.

It didn't help my body that I'd been sleeping on my new couch since leaving the hotel before Christmas. The bedding was still in its packaging. The mattress was wrapped in plastic and the frame needed to be assembled. It was on the list, just closer to the bottom than the top.

The replacement washer and dryer, along with a new fridge, wouldn't be here until Friday, so until they arrived, I was living out of my suitcase and thriving on takeout. Besides, I'd have to get used to sleeping on the couch. My back would too.

Pain was just another part of my atonement. Everything was at stake. My life. My future.

Talia.

Would she ever hear me out? Would she forgive me when she learned the truth? Or was it too late?

Fear had been keeping me up at night. Pushing me to keep going. Fear that I'd lost her seven years ago and there was no winning her back.

Seven years was a long time.

What if we'd changed too much?

That familiar panic crept into my mind, making my insides churn. I clenched my fists and shoved the worry aside. I wasn't going to lose her. Not again. I wouldn't lose, period.

I was Foster Madden, the Iron Fist, middleweight champion of the world.

That title, something I'd worked for my entire life, was a motherfucking joke. I'd give it up in a heartbeat to go back in time. To make better decisions.

Except I couldn't quit. Not yet. This fight in March was the last on my contract with the UFC. My agent was in talks to get me another two-fight contract but should that even be my next move?

A lot depended on this move to Montana.

Besides, my body paid the bills. I'd throw a few more punches and kicks to make sure that when it did come time to retire, I'd be financially secure.

I strode into the apartment, heading for the sink in the kitchen to wash my hands. Once they were dry, I reached into the camping cooler I'd bought last week and fished out a sports drink, gulping until the bottle was empty.

Then, like I had in the gym, I surveyed the mostly empty space. Across from the couch was a TV on a stand. I hadn't even bothered plugging it in. The wireless wasn't set up yet—another item on my list. The coffee table was cluttered with more empty drink bottles and protein bar wrappers.

If I didn't get this kitchen set up soon so I could cook myself some decent meals, and if I kept working this hard, I'd cut too much weight before March. *Whatever.* I'd worry about the scale another day.

I took out another bottle of Gatorade and a chocolate chip granola bar from a grocery stack, then walked out to the gym, heat blasting me in a wave. The drafty window had been sealed, but the furnace seemed to be chugging as hard as ever. Maybe it was just me, my body producing this heat, but I went to the thermostat and turned it down five degrees. Again.

The damn thing was probably broken. Another item to be

fixed. Another day.

I shoved almost the entire granola bar in my mouth, chewing as I pointed at that ugly orange wall. "You and me. Today, we're gonna dance."

I ate the rest of my bar, wadding up the wrapper and shoving it in an open trash bag, then I set my drink on the floor and went for the paint.

Cloud gray wasn't exactly original for a wall color but it would brighten up the space from the current shade and be easy to keep clean. At some point, maybe I'd hang up photos and the American flag. I'd buy some racks for equipment storage. But my championship belts would be staying in a box.

When it came to a gym, there weren't a lot of options for style. Boxing rings and exercise equipment all looked the same. Heavy bags and mats only came in so many colors. But I'd do my best to differentiate this space from Angel's in Vegas. Starting with the trophy wall. That, I'd do without.

Maybe if I'd been less concerned with those trophies, with the money they represented, I wouldn't have gotten so fucking greedy.

Why hadn't I just stayed poor? At least without the money, I would have been my own man.

Guilt had been tormenting me for seven damn years and its claws were as sharp as ever.

I'd just picked up a gallon of Kilz, ready to prime the orange wall, when the door opened at my back. There was only one person who knew about me and this gym, so I spun around, my heart leaping.

Except it wasn't Talia walking through the door. It was an older man with salt-and-pepper hair.

"Can I help you?" I asked, setting the paint down and

crossing the room.

He nodded. "You can sell me this building and leave Quincy."

Huh? "Say that again?" Too few calories, too much exercise and too little sleep. I had to have heard that wrong.

"You can help me by getting the hell out of my town."

Damn. Guess I had heard him right. I took a step forward, ready to toss this guy out on his ass, but then I locked my eyes with his brilliant blue ones.

Talia's blue.

We'd never met in person but I'd seen photos of her father. It took me a moment to match old pictures to the man standing before me.

"Harrison Eden." I closed the distance between us and extended a hand. "Nice to finally meet you, sir."

He stared at my hand, eyebrows arched. Talia must have learned that look from her father.

I dropped my hand to my side. "Appreciate you stopping by today. Appreciate you standing up for Talia. But I'm not leaving Quincy."

Harrison's jaw ticked. "Even if my daughter doesn't want you here?"

"Talia and I have a lot to talk about."

"Like how you broke her heart? I was there. After. I went down to Vegas to help her move. You crushed her. She's not the type who will forget."

"No, she isn't. But I've loved her since I was twenty-three years old." There was no point in mincing words. I was moving my entire life to Montana for Talia, and her dad might as well know why.

"Love?" He scoffed. "You had a funny way of showing it.

Where I come from, what you did to her wasn't love."

"No offense, Harrison, but you don't know a damn thing about me or the past."

"Then enlighten me." He crossed his arms over his broad chest. He was older but the man was built.

"Talia hears it first. If she decides to share, that's her choice. Until then, you're going to have to deal with me in your town."

"She has a good life here. You'll ruin it."

"A good life? She's alone." Two nights in a row I'd gone to her place and found her alone. No husband. No fiancé. No boyfriend.

"She has her family."

I shook my head. "That's not the same."

Having parents, brothers, sisters was not the same as having a partner in life. A confidant. A friend. My biggest regret was that the person who'd been my partner for so long was Vivienne. It should have been Talia.

"Talia has a demanding career," Harrison said. "She'll settle down when she's ready."

Excuses. We both knew he was making excuses.

"I know I hurt her." I held up my hands, then stole Talia's words from last week. "Sorry isn't enough. But I'll say it. Over and over and over. Until she knows I mean it."

Harrison studied my face, like he was searching for a lie. But I'd lied enough for two lifetimes. All he'd find here were truths.

Without another word, he turned and walked out the door.

I waited until his car door slammed and the sound of his engine disappeared before striding into the apartment and sweeping up my keys from the counter.

The orange wall would have to wait.

Harrison's visit had been to run me out of town. But Talia must not have told him about my stubborn streak.

I'd given her a week. Time was up.

The drive into town took ten minutes. Other than Harrison's taillights in the distance, I didn't see another vehicle. Another reason the gym had probably failed. It was too far off the beaten path.

I'd spent my adult life in gyms and fitness centers. The best were those that you couldn't ignore. The ones you drove past daily on your way to buy a high-calorie latte or McDonald's meal deal.

The road followed the curve of the Clark Fork River. The sun was shining overhead, glinting off the water and the snow-covered banks on each side. My commute to Quincy was a hell of a lot more scenic than being stuck in Vegas traffic.

Harrison reached the stop sign ahead and took a right at the intersection, heading down Main Street. I turned left, falling into a short line of cars that were all going to the opposite end of town.

Toward the hospital.

I parked in the visitors' lot. Talia's Jeep sat in a section reserved for staff. She'd had a similar model Jeep in Vegas, one I hadn't been surprised to see drive up the other night when I'd been waiting at her house.

Maybe we hadn't changed that much after all.

I hurried inside, checking the time on the clock above the receptionist's counter. "Hi."

"H-hi." The young woman did a double take, her face flushing as she tucked a lock of hair behind her ear.

I was a hot mess at the moment, but I wasn't too proud to use the way this T-shirt clung to my chest and arms if that would earn me Talia's whereabouts. "I was wondering if you could help me. I'm looking for a doctor. Talia Eden? She's an old friend and I was just passing through town, so I wanted to surprise her and say hello."

"Okay. Yeah. Sure." She sat a little straighter in her chair. "I saw her come through just a few minutes ago. I think she was heading to the cafeteria for lunch."

"You're a sweetheart." I pointed toward the hallway. "This way?"

"Straight down the hallway and it will be on your left. You can't miss it."

"Thanks." I winked, then strode from the desk, brushing off the front of my shirt. Then I lifted an arm, taking a whiff of my armpit. "Ah, damn."

Should have showered first. I hadn't thought about impressing a woman in, well...years.

The sound of forks and chatter greeted me as I stepped into the cafeteria. To my left was an open kitchen with a grill and fryer. Beneath a heat lamp, there were a handful of paper boats filled with chicken tenders and steak fries. To my right loomed a soda machine and racks of chips. Behind the glass door of a cooler were a variety of premade sandwiches, yogurts and fruit cups.

"I'll take one of those," I told the cook in the kitchen, nodding to the chicken tenders.

"Ranch or ketchup?"

"Ketchup." Talia had always been partial to ranch. "Thanks."

I took my food, snagging a bottle of water from a drink fridge, then went to the clerk at the register. His head was covered in a blue hair net nearly the same shade as his scrubs. I dug out my wallet from a pocket, paid for my meal, then passed him for the tables in the small, adjacent dining area.

Talia was sitting alone at a table. She was in her blue scrubs with a white lab coat over the top. In one hand, she held a fry. In the other, a chicken tender.

I chuckled. Never in my life had I met a woman who ate like Talia. She inhaled her food. She chewed with fury and didn't spend her meals chatting. When she sat down at her plate, it was to consume. Fast.

There were two chairs at her table, so I claimed the empty seat, popping open the top to the plastic cup with my ketchup inside.

Talia's eyes widened. Her mouth stopped moving. She sat straighter, chewing a few more times before she swallowed. Then she dropped the fry and chicken strip into her own paper boat. "This has to stop."

"It will. After you listen to me." I dunked one of my own fries in ketchup, shoving it into my mouth.

"This is my place of work. I'm not talking to you here."

"Then I guess you'll have to let me inside tonight when I come over with dinner."

Her nostrils flared and she splayed her hands on the table. "No."

"Six o'clock?"

"Foster."

God, I loved hearing her say my name. Even when she was pissed. "Actually, we'd better make it six thirty. I've got some painting to do. Might take me the rest of the afternoon."

"I remember your hearing used to be a lot better."

I smirked and ate another fry. "Still like pizza?"

"Grr." She snarled and shoved to her feet so hard that the

chair behind her nearly toppled over. Talia caught it, then swept up her food. "You stubborn ass. If you show up at my door, plan to freeze because I'm not letting you inside."

"Then come to the gym."

"Why?" Her voice was too loud. She realized it and glanced around, grimacing a bit when a table of nurses gave her a strange look. "Why do you want to talk so badly? Nothing you can say will change the past."

"I can't change it. But I'd like to explain."

"Then what? Let's say I come to dinner. Then what?"

"Then…if you still want me to leave Quincy, I'll leave."

Talia studied my face for a few long moments, a lot like how her father had earlier. Assessing. Dissecting. Searching for the lie. "You'll leave if I ask you to leave."

"I will leave." If after we talked, if me living in Quincy would cause her too much pain, then I'd go.

Moving again wasn't the plan. But I'd figure it out. After tonight, if I truly felt like we were over and there was no chance, I'd walk away.

"Fine. Six thirty." She spun, her ponytail whipping through the air.

I popped another fry in my mouth.

And grinned at the beautiful woman storming out of the cafeteria.

CHAPTER 5

FOSTER

"You've got Vivi. Leave a message. Beep. Wait. Did you think that was the actual beep? Gotcha."

I chuckled. "Hey, it's me. Was hoping to catch you. I've got dinner plans tonight, so I won't call at the normal time. I'm not sure when I'll be free. So if I don't get to talk to you, have a good night. I'll call you tomorrow morning."

I hung up and set the phone on the coffee table. The scent of glass cleaner and whatever solution came with the Swiffer WetJet filled the apartment. From the moment I'd walked through the door from the hospital, I'd spent every minute cleaning.

Painting had been put on pause.

"What else?" Jesus, this place was empty. Tomorrow morning, I was ordering a dining set. Eating at the coffee table wasn't a long-term option. And I needed window shades.

Granted, the view beyond the glass was beautiful. Darkness had already fallen, the days short this time of year, but tonight's sunset had been breathtaking. The yellow and orange sky had reminded me of my favorite lemon and tangerine sherbet. I'd stopped cleaning long enough to take a picture and send it to

Kadence and Jasper.

Still, even with the sunset, maybe curtains or blinds would make it feel homier. Decorating wasn't my forte. Vivienne had taken charge of our house in Vegas, and I had no doubt that when she came to visit, she'd roll her eyes and demand my credit card so she could shop.

I walked to the gym, going to a window that gave a better view of the road. It was six forty-five and there was still no sign of Talia. I'd run into town to pick up pizza earlier. She hadn't come and gone while I'd been away, had she?

Or maybe she wasn't coming at all.

No, she'd come. She wanted me out of town badly enough to show tonight.

What the hell was I going to say? I'd spent years dreaming of this opportunity. One would think I'd have my speech prepared.

"Shit." I rubbed a hand over my beard. My body felt like it was coming apart and my heart was beating too fast.

How did I tell her the truth? How did I start? There was no gentle way to do this. Maybe I could just start with the crux of it all.

That I was a fucking fool.

What I wouldn't give for some equipment right now. Just something to punch. That's when I was the most centered. When I had a target.

I strode to the middle of the room, to the space where I'd set up the ring once it arrived. I closed my eyes and lifted my hands, balling them into fists. Then I shifted my feet, getting into a good fighting stance, before I let my jab fly.

Pop. Pop. I followed both punches with a right hook.

I bent my knees, sinking into the balls of my feet and did

it again. Jab. Jab. Hook. Then I added an uppercut and winced when a pinch came beneath my shoulder blade.

"Ah." I rolled my left arm in a wide circle, loosening the muscles.

Jasper would have my ass if I injured myself while I was renovating this place.

I bounced on my toes a couple times, not exactly agile in my boots, but there was familiarity in the movements. Then I did the same combination again. Jab. Jab. Hook. Uppercut. No pinch this time.

"Thank fuck."

I moved around in a circle, shadowboxing until some of the jitters eased. Then I took a long breath, filling my lungs until they burned.

Just lay it out there.

Whatever it takes.

My only job tonight was to share with Talia what I should have told her years ago.

The truth.

Headlights swept the wall and I hustled out the door, waiting on the landing as Talia parked beside my truck.

"Sorry I'm late," she said as she rounded the hood. "A guy cut his hand open while he was working in his shop this afternoon, and I got caught up at the ER."

"It's fine. He okay?"

She nodded. "It was a pretty deep cut. I did my best to sew it back together. He'll have a scar."

"But he still has a hand."

"Yeah."

I held the door open for her. "Then I'd say it was a win."

She stared up at me, and for the first time since I'd come to

Quincy, there wasn't any anger or resentment in her eyes. Talia just looked...exhausted.

She slipped past me, walking into the gym and taking the same path she had before, lapping the room. "You've been busy."

"It's been an undertaking." I closed the door, hanging back and giving her plenty of space.

She went to the orange wall, trailing her fingers along the surface. Her shoulders were slumped, her ponytail hanging loose.

"You're tired," I said.

"I've had a hard time sleeping this week." She moved to the paint buckets, examining the dot of color on the lids. "Didn't want to keep the orange, huh?"

"It's hideous." I grimaced. "Should we do this another night?"

"No." She stood tall and turned, her spine stiffening. "You'll really leave if I ask you to go?"

"Yes." I jerked my chin toward the apartment, leading the way. "Mind if we eat on the couch? It's that or stand at the kitchen counter."

"The couch is fine." Inside, she stripped off her coat, laying it over an armrest. "I didn't have time to go home and change."

I walked to the kitchen, flipping open the pizza box. "Your scrubs are fine."

"I don't wear much else these days." She took a seat, undoing the tie on her hair. "Good thing I look decent in blue."

Decent? She was fucking stunning.

I stood frozen, afraid to blink because I'd miss it as she fixed her ponytail.

She was here, in my home. She was real, wearing scrubs from a long day's work. Her fingernails were short because she'd never been a woman to fuss over manicures. No jewelry because she didn't need it to make her sparkle.

She glanced over, caught me staring.

I jerked my gaze away, reaching for the paper plates I'd picked up with the pizza. "I don't have anything fancy."

"I don't need fancy."

No, she didn't.

Except I'd thought she'd needed fancy. Or maybe that was just me. It had been my own hidden desire for an expensive life that had pushed me over the edge.

I plated a couple of slices, then took them over, setting them on the coffee table. "Water? Or Gatorade?"

"Water, please."

I grabbed two bottles from the cooler, then a couple of paper towels for napkins, joining her on the sofa.

"You don't use the fridge?" she asked.

"I opened it last week. Took a whole day with the windows open to clear out the stink. So instead of trying to figure out what died inside, I bought a new one. Should get here Friday."

"Ah." She nodded, taking a bite.

I did the same.

She chewed.

I chewed.

She took another bite.

So did I.

She didn't look at me.

But all I could stare at was her profile.

A memory came rushing back, of the two of us at this small hole-in-the-wall pizzeria in Vegas. It hadn't been long after we'd started dating. Before that day, I hadn't realized that a woman could have a sexy chew.

But the way her lips moved, the flex in her jaw and cheeks.

Another memory hit, this one of her taking me in her mouth. My cock twitched behind my jeans and I shifted to hide the growing bulge.

"How was Seattle?" I asked.

She glanced over, her eyebrows raised. "I'm not here for casual conversation, Foster."

"Humor me while we eat."

She sighed. "Seattle was rainy. School was time consuming, so I didn't get out much, but I struggled with the gray days in winter."

"You always liked the sunshine." It was the reason she'd moved to Vegas for undergrad. "Remember that time we went hiking, and on the way down, we found that rattlesnake in the path?"

"Oh, don't remind me." She shivered. "I hate snakes."

"You made us wait until it slithered off. By the time we made it to the car, I was burnt to a crisp."

"I told you to wear sunscreen."

"There's always a bottle in my truck. I learned my lesson."

The corner of her mouth turned up as she chewed. Not a smile, but the beginning of one.

There she is. There's my girl.

Maybe if I could talk about the good times, it would help ease the sting from the bad.

"I stayed at The Eloise last week. Nice place. Saw your sister at the coffee shop."

Her eyes widened, and when she spoke, her words were muffled with food. "Lyla?"

"She had another girl at the counter, so I didn't actually talk to her. You don't look as similar as I thought you would." Having only seen Talia's twin in photos, I'd thought they would be more identical.

"What do you mean?"

"She was actually smiling. Laughing. She didn't have a murderous scowl on her face."

"My murderous scowl is reserved for you. Other people consider me quite pleasant. And I've been told my bedside manner is unmatched."

I chuckled, some of my nerves settling. Maybe this wouldn't be so hard, not if we could tease each other.

"Want another slice?" I stood and collected the box, bringing it to the coffee table. Then I took another slice while she did the same. "Do you like the hospital here?"

"I do. But I'm still trying to prove myself."

"To who?"

"Everyone. I'm an Eden. My family founded this town generations ago. Most people have known me since I was a kid, including my boss and most of the tenured nurses. Not everyone looks at me and sees the adult I've become."

The defeat in her voice was enough to give me a murderous scowl of my own. How could anyone not look at her and see a brilliant and capable woman?

"I used to babysit Dr. Herrera's kids when I was in high school," she said. "Every once in a while, he'll call me kiddo. The patient tonight, the guy who cut his hand, asked if there was someone else to stitch him up. When I said no, he said he didn't mean any offense, but he remembers me as a cheerleader when his son was on the football team."

Asshole. Was that why she looked so tired? "Sorry."

"That's life in a small town. But it's a good town. A great place for kids to grow up."

I was counting on it.

Talia finished eating before me. She set her plate aside, balled up her napkin, and when she faced me, the casual conversation portion of our evening was over. "Why did you buy that ring?"

I set my own plate aside. "Because I couldn't stand the idea of it being on any other woman's hand. That ring is yours. Always has been. So I bought it. Promised myself if I ever saw you again, I'd give it to you."

"You spent thousands of dollars just in case we'd see each other again?"

"Yes." That ring was the most expensive purchase I'd ever made up to that point in my life. "I'd like you to have it."

"I can't." She shook her head. "I just... I can't. Sell it. Give the money to charity."

Never.

Either she kept it.

Or I would.

"So." She shifted again, straightening. I'd spent my life reading body language. Looking for the strike. Looking for my opponent's tell. Talia was stiff, like she was ready to take a blow. "Your explanation."

Just lay it out there.

Whatever it takes.

I opened my mouth, ready to delve into the past, but my phone rang on the coffee table, the chime at full volume because I hadn't wanted to miss any calls while I'd been working on this place. "Shit. Sorry."

Vivienne's face flashed on the screen. She had her tongue sticking out and her eyes were crossed. She called it her goofy face.

I declined it, then faced Talia again. But her eyes weren't

waiting for mine. They were locked on the screen. On Vivi's picture.

"Do you talk to her often?"

Shit. The honest answer wasn't one she'd like. "Yes. Every day."

"But you're divorced."

"Vivienne is my friend. We're no longer married, but she's part of my life." She'd been my ally through years of hell.

A crease formed between Talia's eyebrows.

"Hey." I scooted closer, reaching for her shoulder, but before I could touch her, she shot out of her seat and snagged her coat.

"I can't do this," she said as she flew through the apartment's doorway.

Fuck. "Talia, wait." I jumped to follow, jogging to catch her in the gym. When I tried to touch her elbow, she yanked it away. So I lengthened my strides, passing her to block the door.

"Move." She sidestepped to the right.

I shifted too. "You said you'd let me explain."

"Get out of the way." She sidestepped again, and I followed. "Gah. Just let me go, Foster."

"I haven't let you go in seven years. I'm not starting tonight."

She rocked back on her heels.

"Please, Tally. Stay. Let's talk." I took her shock as my opening, stepping closer. Then I lifted my hand, tracing my fingertips across her cheekbone. A current raced up my arm as she gasped.

Her eyes locked with mine, the blue pools swirling.

Yeah, she felt it too. Of course she'd feel it.

What we had wasn't the type of connection that went away with time. This was the spark that lasted a lifetime. This was lightning. It knocked you on your ass to make sure you realized just how rare it was.

I leaned in closer, bending until our breaths mingled. My fingers slid into her hair. She didn't push me away. She didn't step back. Her eyes stayed locked with mine as I closed the gap between us.

Another inch and that mouth would be mine. Another inch and I'd get the kiss I craved with every fiber of my being.

Just another inch and—

The chime of my phone echoed from the apartment. My reaction was habit. I lifted my gaze.

And because I lost focus, Talia found her opening. She ducked under my arm and slipped out the door.

"Hell." I let her leave. I let her get a head start while I took Vivienne's call and put the pizza away. Then I drove into Quincy.

This round wasn't over yet.

CHAPTER 6

TALIA

The snow on the Jeep was melting. It dripped onto the garage floor in plops.

I'd been sitting in the driver's seat, listening to the *plop, plop, plop* for so long that the cab's lights had shut off. The heat from my drive home was nearly gone. My fingers were cold, but I couldn't seem to unwrap them from the steering wheel to go inside.

There was too much space in the house. Too much light. Too many distractions.

But here, in the darkness with the plops, maybe I'd be able to sort through my feelings.

The Jeep, parked in the garage, had become a sanctuary of sorts. A cocoon where I could block out everything except the emotional hurricane raging inside my chest.

The last time I'd sat here like this had been six months ago.

There'd been a bad car accident on the highway outside of town. Both drivers had been rushed to the emergency room, and I'd been there with Dr. Herrera. He'd taken the most severely injured patient, a pregnant woman, and left me with the other.

It was a man who had lost a leg in the crash. I did exactly as Herrera instructed—stopped the bleeding, cleaned the limb and got it bandaged.

The man cried the entire time, so hard it shook the bed and made it difficult to work. But his tears weren't for his missing leg. His tears were for the woman in the other car.

He sobbed, saying how he'd never forgive himself for speeding. For texting. He prayed through the tears, asking God to take both his legs and his arms—his life if necessary—to save hers.

He cried until the medicine finally kicked in and he fell asleep. I woke him up the next morning to tell him that the woman and her baby would be fine. Dr. Herrera had saved them both.

I'd never forget that man's face in that moment. The relief. The gratitude. The tears, silent this time, that streaked down his face. Three hours later, he'd had a massive heart attack and died.

Dr. Herrera had assured me there was nothing I could have done. Yet I'd felt like a failure.

I hadn't lost many patients in my short time as a doctor. In a town the size of Quincy, we didn't have a lot of trauma, not like hospitals in big cities. That man had been the third patient of mine to die.

There were three tally marks at the bottom of my locker door, not written in dry erase, but with a Sharpie.

That day, after driving home, I'd sat in the garage, in this Jeep, and it had been my turn to cry.

There were no tears tonight. Maybe they'd come after the shock had passed.

Foster had almost kissed me.

I'd almost let him kiss me.

It had taken years for me to pick up the pieces of my broken heart. But I'd gathered them all, painstakingly stitching them together again. My instructors had always commended me on my suture technique.

Yes, there were times when I'd feel the pinch of those old wounds. But time had healed. So had distraction. Medical school had been my savior, followed by my residency.

Except here I was, dumbstruck, because an almost kiss had left me unraveled.

Shouldn't this attraction have faded? If anything, it felt more powerful. More urgent. More desperate. The magnetism between us was as potent as ever.

He'd almost kissed me.

And I'd almost let him.

What was wrong with me? What had happened with Vivienne? Why hadn't he forgotten me?

The curiosity was gnawing at me. It was getting harder and harder not to type his name into my phone to see the search results. But I'd held off for seven years. I wouldn't cave. Yet.

Foster had come to the hospital today and promised answers. God, I wanted those answers. Not knowing was eating me alive. And yet when I'd had the chance tonight, I'd bolted. One look at Vivienne's face, and pain had sent me scurrying out of that gym.

My phone rang and I jumped, knocking my leg into the steering wheel. I plucked it from the console's cup holder, Lyla's name on the screen. "Hey," I answered.

"Hi. What are you doing?"

"Oh, nothing."

I hadn't told her about Foster yet. Maybe I should have found the time over Christmas, but she'd been swamped at the coffee shop and I'd been avoiding the conversation. With everyone.

Lyla knew I'd dated a man named Foster. She knew we'd broken up my senior year of undergrad, but I'd led her to believe it was because of my move to Seattle.

She'd be pissed when she learned the whole story. She'd be mad that I hadn't leaned on her after he'd broken my heart.

But I wasn't like Lyla.

I wept alone in dark garages. She wasn't afraid to shed a hundred tears in her coffee shop, even if there were employees or customers around to witness her cry. Lyla shared her life daily on Instagram. The last selfie I'd taken had been months ago.

If she had a crush on a guy, most of Quincy knew about it before they'd even had their first date. The last time I'd gone on a date had been during my last year of medical school when another guy in the program had asked me out. I'd faked a stomach bug in the middle of dinner when he'd hinted at going back to his place after dessert.

I'd tell Lyla about Foster. Eventually. Just not tonight.

"What are you doing?" I asked her.

"Just got home from the shop." Lyla yawned. "I wanted to say hi."

"Hi." I smiled at my sister's voice. "Want to do something this weekend? I'm not working or on call for a change."

"Sure. As long as I can be in bed by nine."

"I'll come to the shop on Saturday afternoon. We can hang out until you close, then go to Knuckles for dinner. I'll buy the wine."

"Perfect. See you then."

"Bye." Saturday, I'd tell her about Foster. Probably.

I closed my eyes. *One. Two. Three. Four. Five.* Garage time over.

On a long sigh, I climbed out of the Jeep and trudged inside. I flipped on the lights as I moved through the house, shedding my coat and shoes before heading to my bedroom.

But I didn't strip off my scrubs and dump them in the laundry to take a shower. Instead I walked into my closet, fished the stepstool from the corner and hefted down the tote I hadn't touched since I'd moved in three years ago.

I set it on the floor in my bedroom, sitting next to it as I popped off the lid. The scent of plastic and paper and stale air filled my nose as I lifted out my high school yearbooks. Beneath them was a disorganized mess of photos and mementos.

At the top of the pile was a *Wicked* program from when I'd taken Mom to the show one weekend in Seattle. She'd flown out to visit me while the musical had been traveling through the city. Beneath the program was a seashell necklace from my senior trip to Cabo. There was a silver dollar my great-uncle had given me before he'd died.

I lifted out the unorganized clutter of photos. Most of the pictures were old, taken by Mom or Dad when I was a kid.

There was an envelope from the one-hour photo shop that had closed years ago on Main. It was a photography studio now, the owner specializing in senior portraits and newborn photo shoots. She'd come to the hospital a few months ago because she'd been having migraines, so I'd written her a prescription.

Everything in this box, the pictures or trinkets, was linked to a person in Quincy.

Except for a single photo, buried at the bottom of the tub.

A photo I should have thrown out seven years ago but hadn't been able to let go.

It was a photo of Foster and me at Lake Mead. Vivienne had taken it with the disposable waterproof camera she'd brought along—she hadn't wanted to risk dropping her phone in the water.

We'd rented paddleboards and spent an afternoon on the water. Foster was sitting on his board, his legs dangling in the water. I was standing on mine, holding my paddle with its blade in the water. My red bikini was nearly the same color as his board shorts. Vivi had teased us for coordinating outfits.

Foster and I were smiling at each other. Talking. I hadn't realized Vivi had even taken the picture until she'd gone to a CVS and come home with a stack of pictures. Most had been scenery shots. There were a few of Vivi and me that Foster had taken. Another shot had been of Foster and me kissing.

Those I'd left in a scattered pile on Vivi's floor the day I'd moved out. I'd wanted her to have to throw them away. I'd wanted her to have to clean up the mess she'd made.

But this one hadn't been with the others. It had been stuck in a notebook in my backpack, hidden for me to find the day before I started at the University of Washington.

Maybe I should have ripped it up. But I'd been so relieved that this little piece of him had survived. So I'd tucked it away, buried it beneath the tokens from my childhood and hadn't let myself look at it again.

Knowing it was here had been enough.

I pressed a hand to my sternum, rubbing at the ache.

We'd been so attached to each other. So *addicted*.

Foster had been training for a fight and his body had been ripped. We'd spent a lot of that summer hiking, soaking up the sun and each other before I moved to Seattle.

He'd planned to help me move. Foster had insisted he'd drive the U-Haul, then fly back to Vegas after I was unpacked.

We hadn't really talked about him moving permanently. I'd assumed it would happen when he was ready. After I'd settled into school. Long distance for a few months hadn't worried me in the slightest. Whenever the topic would come up, he'd always say, *Don't worry, love. We'll figure it out.*

So I hadn't worried. I'd had that much confidence in *us*.

Until he'd come to the apartment one night, stood in my bedroom with the boxes I'd already packed and dropped the bomb.

He couldn't be with me anymore, not when he had feelings for Vivienne.

Not when he was going to marry her.

Sometimes, I still couldn't believe it was real. Even after all this time. Even after he'd married her.

Was that why I'd gone to the gym tonight? Because deep down, I wanted—needed—it to have been a lie?

It was because of Vivienne that I'd even met Foster. She'd grown up in Vegas. We'd met our freshman year at UNLV because we'd lived in the same dorm and both majored in biology.

Her plan had been to teach. Mine, medical school.

My sophomore year, I'd moved into a condo with two women from the dorms, but I'd always felt like the third wheel. Vivienne had been in a similar situation, so our junior year, we'd moved in together.

Her father owned a gym in Vegas, the type where they trained boxers and mixed martial arts fighters. One day Vivienne convinced me to tag along with her for a workout.

I walked through the door and Foster was in a ring. He was sparring with another guy, both dripping sweat. I didn't notice him at first, too busy taking in the place.

Vivi and I were the only women in the building.

Then a timer dinged and the fight in the ring stopped. Foster took the mouthguard from his teeth and laughed. Then his smile drifted my direction and that was the beginning.

It took time for us to get together. There were months of flirting at the gym before he asked me out. But after that first kiss, he was mine. For over a year, he'd been mine.

Why the hell did I have this picture? I'd positioned my fingers on the top edge, ready to tear it in half, when the doorbell echoed through the house.

I dropped the photo like it was on fire.

I scrambled to my feet, backing away from that box as the doorbell rang again.

It was Foster. And at the moment, it felt safer to answer the door, to face him, than to hold that photo. To know I didn't have the strength to rip it in half.

So I hurried downstairs and to the front door.

He stood with his arms crossed and his jaw set in that adamant line. When I flipped the lock and turned the knob, he strode inside before I could object, forcing me to shuffle backward as he kicked the door closed behind him.

"Foster—"

He silenced me by inching closer. So close I had to crane my neck to keep his gaze.

"W-what are you doing?"

"Did you feel it? At the gym?"

"No."

"You're still a horrible liar." He bent lower, so close that his breath caressed my cheek.

His hand trailed down my arm, and even through the cotton of my scrub top and my long-sleeved shirt beneath, I felt tingles. It was like a spark running along a fuse, moving faster and faster, until it reached the firework and *boom*.

Foster leaned in closer, his mouth a whisper from my own.

Why couldn't I push him away?

"Feel that?" he whispered.

Feel it? It was burning me alive.

"I came here to talk." He reached for my hair, touching the same place he had at the gym.

My gaze dropped to his lips.

"Fuck it," he growled, then his mouth was on mine, soft and

supple and exactly like I remembered.

He swept me into his arms, holding me tight as his tongue stroked my bottom lip before sliding inside. The scrape of his beard pooled desire in my core.

The scent of his cologne swirled around me, rich and masculine. Like fresh-cut cedar and leather. His taste was another memory, Foster with a hint of cinnamon gum.

His lips moved over mine as our tongues tangled in perfect unison. He groaned against my mouth, the vibration sexy and deep in his chest. His hold grew tighter.

Foster kissed me like our lives depended on it.

I kissed him with every bit of frustration and longing and heartbreak and hope I'd kept locked away.

God, what were we doing? Why was I so weak when it came to this man? But I didn't stop. Not until I felt his arousal dig into my hip.

It was the turning point. Either we ended this kiss. Or clothes would hit the floor.

I tore my mouth away and squirmed to get out of his arms. We were both panting, our eyes locked. His gaze searched mine, maybe for forgiveness. Then he reached for me, but I swatted his hand away.

"Don't."

He froze.

I took a step away. "Don't kiss me again."

"Talia—"

"You need to leave. Please." My voice cracked. "You need to leave Quincy."

His jaw clenched. "No."

"You promised you'd leave if I asked."

"You promised to hear me out."

I raised my chin. "And what if I said it didn't matter? It's over, Foster. It's been over."

He dragged his thumb across his wet lower lip. "That kiss was not from two people who are over."

No, it wasn't. But it was just chemistry. Attraction. That toxic addiction that had ruined me once. "Did you cheat on me with Vivienne?"

I'd asked him that question years ago, the night he'd dumped me.

"Never."

I'd wanted so badly to believe him then. I wanted so badly to believe him now. I studied his face, searching for the lie. Except I couldn't see it. I hadn't seen it years ago either.

"You don't believe me, do you?" he asked.

"I believed everything about you once. That changed when you married my best friend."

Foster's jaw clenched as he shook his head. "You don't know what happened."

"I was there." I tossed out a hand. "I *lived* it. Nothing you say will change the past. Nothing you say will make me forgive you."

He gritted his teeth. "Nothing? And you call me stubborn. I forgot how infuriating you can be."

My jaw dropped. "Are you turning this around on me?"

"I'm asking you to just fucking listen."

"And I'm asking you to leave. I guess neither of us is going to get what we want."

"You want me gone? Fine. I'm gone." Before I could speak, he turned and yanked the door open.

My heart cracked as it slammed behind him. The silence that followed was deafening.

I'd asked him to go. I'd wanted this, right?

So why did I feel like going to the garage to cry?

ROUND 3

CHAPTER 7

FOSTER

I was in a shit mood.

"You're in a shit mood." Jasper's voice filled the cab of my truck.

"I'm a ray of goddamn sunshine compared to yesterday." Or the day before that. Or the day before that.

In the three days since I'd stormed out of Talia's house, I'd worn a permanent scowl.

"Take it things with your girl aren't going well," Jasper said.

"Something like that," I muttered.

I'd told her I was leaving, but that had been an angry declaration in the heat of the moment. No way in hell was I leaving Quincy. Not after all that I'd been through just to get here.

Not after that kiss.

"I pushed too hard." My hands relaxed on the wheel as I drove into town.

It was the realization I'd come to after fuming for the last three days. I'd bulldozed into Talia's life, and instead of giving her time to absorb the shock, I'd just applied more pressure.

I was pushing myself just as hard because of what was

coming—of *who* was coming. The calendar was advancing too fast.

"She's angry," I told Jasper.

"Can't blame her for that."

No, I couldn't blame Talia. "I've got to get her to remember what we had."

"How are you going to do that?"

"Hell if I know." I scoffed. "Any ideas?"

"You've got to be really desperate if you're asking me for advice with women."

I chuckled. "This is true."

Jasper and I had known each other for years. He'd started coming to the gym about a year after Talia had left. He was a good fighter and sparring partner, but where he excelled was in training. No person on earth pushed me the way Jasper pushed. Hiring him had been a no-brainer.

But when it came to women, Jasper was more the *love 'em and leave 'em* type. He'd been married for a short time in his early twenties, before we'd met. He didn't talk about his ex. He didn't talk about why they'd gotten divorced. But whatever had happened had made him shy away from anything that resembled a relationship.

Jasper's biggest commitment was to my career.

"How's the gym?" Jasper asked.

"It's coming along. The ring showed up this morning." The delivery crew had hauled it into the open space of the gym and set it up. I'd ordered it the day I'd bought the building and had paid a small fortune to have it expedited, considering their normal turnaround time was three months.

The open space at the gym was now filled. The mats had shown up yesterday along with the heavy bags. The treadmill was coming tomorrow. My list of shit to do was dwindling.

Soon, I'd be able to focus on prep for this fight in March.

"It's only been eleven days," Jasper said.

"Really?" Eleven? I did the math in my head. "Seems like longer."

"Probably because you haven't been sleeping. Am I right?"

"Maybe."

Sleep had been a luxury. There was simply too much work to be done. But the interior of the gym was now painted. Goodbye orange wall. I'd hauled away the rest of the garbage and the dumpster was no longer out front. The apartment was clear and would serve as home for a while.

I'd busted my ass to get it done in time.

"What's next?" he asked.

I sighed, stopping at the intersection before turning down Main Street. "Couple more days to finish up. I need to clean again. Stock the fridge."

A new washer and dryer had been installed along with the refrigerator. The lack of sleep, the backbreaking days, had been worth it.

"The exterior needs to be repainted and most of the windows will have to be replaced sooner rather than later. But it's good enough until spring." I yawned.

"Get some rest," Jasper said. "You're no good to me if you're dead on your feet."

"Will do, boss. See you soon."

"Bye."

Jasper would be here next week, ready to whip my ass into fighting shape.

I tossed my phone into the passenger seat, then pulled into a parking space outside the coffee shop.

The sky was a brilliant, cloudless blue. The afternoon sun reflected off the Christmas garlands strung above the road. Two men, each on a ladder, were unwrapping the pine-bow garlands twined around the lampposts.

Restaurants, offices and retail shops lined both sides of Main. The Eloise Inn, the tallest building in town, had a large wreath on its brick façade that would probably come down soon. And at the jewelry store next door to the coffee shop, a woman was removing the red and green ornaments from the winter wonderland scene in her window.

I'd miss the holiday decorations. Hopefully I'd be here next year to see them again.

After shutting off the truck, I pushed outside and was hit by a blast of cool, pine-laced mountain air. My mood instantly improved.

"Nice day, isn't it?" The man parked beside my truck dipped his chin as he unlocked the door to his SUV.

"Sure is." I nodded back, then stepped onto the sidewalk, filling my lungs with that fresh air as I zipped my coat up higher.

Sunny as it might be, it was still damn cold. But at least the view didn't disappoint. If I had to give up the rocky and arid mountains of the Mojave, I couldn't think of a better replacement than the towering indigo peaks with white caps that surrounded Quincy.

The snow had been cleared from the sidewalks, but every roofline was covered in white. It only made the afternoon brighter.

It was hard to be grumpy in downtown Quincy.

A kid's squeal of laughter caught my ear. I followed the sound to a familiar face.

It was the man I'd seen at the hospital when I'd come to

search for Talia. He'd been in the lobby with a pregnant woman, probably his wife.

He carried a little boy with rosy cheeks. Both were wearing matching black beanies.

The boy had on a pair of boots, snow pants and a bright green coat. He squirmed to be set down, and the moment those boots hit the pavement, he was off, running for the same destination as mine.

Eden Coffee.

I'd run out of coffee at the gym, and after yawning for the tenth time in a row, I'd decided to swing into town. But instead of the grocery store, I'd come here. Talia's sister had a hell of a display case of pastries and my stomach growled.

The man smiled at his kid, opening the door so they could both walk inside.

Who was he? There was more familiar about him than just the run-in at the hospital.

I strode toward the green building.

Eden Coffee was written in gold letters on the shop's door. There was a bit of frost and fog around the edges of the black-paned windows. A chalkboard sandwich sign was out front and someone had written the daily specials—snickerdoodle latte and a cranberry bagel—in white block letters.

Aromatic coffee and sweet vanilla greeted me when I went inside, a bell jingling over my head.

The first time I'd come here, while I'd been staying at The Eloise, I'd expected something Western. Rustic. But the walls were painted the same green as the outside of the building. It had a trendy and modern vibe, not unlike a hip cafe you'd find in a city. Wooden tables and chairs lined the walls, a few occupied this afternoon.

The man and the little boy were at the counter. The kid was pressed against the glass display case, his mittens keeping him from leaving fingerprints as the beanie was plucked off his head, revealing a static mess of blond hair.

Cute kid.

"Hey." Lyla rushed out from around the back, rounding the corner. She wore a green apron with a dusting of flour on the front. The same flour was on her nose.

Even though they were twins, any fool could tell her and Talia apart.

Or maybe I'd just been a fool over Talia for far too long.

"How's my little Drake today?" Lyla picked up the kid and kissed his cheek. "Want Auntie to make you something special?"

Wait. Auntie? So that man had to be—

Hell. How could I have missed it? That had to be Talia's brother. Griffin or Knox. I'd never met either of them before, but Talia had shown me pictures ages ago. Except he hadn't had a beard in the photos. They'd all been younger.

But he had the same dark brown hair as Talia. And as he smiled at his son, the same bright blue eyes crinkled. He resembled Harrison too.

Maybe I should have hit the grocery store. I wasn't sure I had the energy to deal with an angry older brother.

Except it would happen eventually, so I squared my shoulders and moved away from the door. Last time I'd been in, Lyla had been busy. I'd only spoken to the guy for a short minute at the hospital.

Guess I had to consider myself lucky that he hadn't interrogated me that day. Or punched me in the face. For what I'd done to Talia, I deserved two black eyes.

But this was inevitable. I wanted her, and I'd have to prove to everyone I was worthy. That this time was different. And since the past three days had sucked, I might as well add this on.

My mood couldn't get a lot worse.

My boots thudded on the floor, drawing attention from the Edens.

Lyla smiled and handed the boy—Drake—to his dad. "Hi. Welcome in. What can I get for you?"

There was nothing but an honest question in her gaze. No glare or contempt. Nothing that said she'd be spitting in my coffee.

Okay. "Americano, please. Double."

"For here or to go?"

I gave her a sideways glance. That was it? She'd just take my order? "Uh...to go."

"You got it." She nodded and rounded the counter, immediately getting to work.

"You're Foster Madden." The man shifted the kid to one side so he could hold out a hand. "I saw you at the hospital the other day."

"Yeah." I braced as I shook his hand. *Here we go.*

"Knox Eden. Nice to meet you. I'm a fan."

A fan? "Oh, um, thanks?"

"Watched your fight last summer." Knox chuckled. "Was pretty glad when you won. Couldn't stand the other guy."

The fight where I'd knocked out my opponent, a loudmouth asshole from LA, in the first round. "Yeah, he's something."

"Didn't seem to teach him much. I saw him in an interview a while back, still running his mouth about a rematch."

He wanted to talk about the fight? Seriously?

"What brings you to Quincy?" he asked. "You're at the old

gym on Lower Clark Fork Road, right?"

Wait. What was happening?

"Sorry." Knox mistook my confusion. "Small-town gossip. Someone new moves to town, everyone talks about it. You were looking for my sister. Talia."

Okay. Now we were getting into it. "Yes, I was."

"Didn't realize you knew each other."

What. The. Fuck?

He'd heard about me through gossip? Not Talia. Small-town gossip. He didn't realize I knew his sister? Yeah, I knew his sister. She was the love of my goddamn life.

My head spun like I'd been the one blindsided with a right cross. Knox, her brother, had no idea who I was other than a professional MMA fighter.

"College," I said, summoning every ounce of calm to keep from seething.

"Here's your coffee." Lyla set a paper cup with a jacket on the counter. "Anything else?"

"No, thanks." I pulled my wallet from my pocket and handed her a twenty.

How could Talia not have told her family about me? We'd been together for over a year. She'd been the most important person in my life. Everyone in my life had known about Talia. Friends. My parents. Arlo.

But she hadn't told her brother? Her twin sister?

They weren't playing dumb, were they?

Talia had pissed me off the other night. She'd made me so damn mad after that kiss. But this? This was fury. This fucking hurt.

Had I really meant so little to her that she'd kept me a secret from her siblings?

"Here you go." Lyla held out my change.

The door jingled behind me as I took the bills. I needed to get the fuck out of this shop. Get the fuck away from anyone with the last name Eden.

Not trusting myself to speak, I dropped a couple bucks into her tip jar. Then I picked up my coffee, raising it to Knox as a farewell.

"See ya around," he said.

I turned, ready to escape, when a beautiful face stopped me in my tracks.

Talia stared, those blue eyes wide, as they darted between me, her brother and her sister. No scrubs today. She was in jeans and a gray coat with a trimming of fur at the hood. Her boots hit at the ankle and she had a pair of thick cream socks bunched above them.

She was dressed for winter. Her hair tumbled in waves over her shoulders. Her cheeks were the same pink shade as her lips.

The woman who held my heart in her hands.

All this time, I'd thought the reason she hadn't gotten married was because maybe, just maybe, I'd meant enough. Enough that she'd remember me. Enough that no man could compare.

Except she hadn't cared enough to even tell her brother my name.

A happy wail erupted from Drake and he squirmed to be set down, then rushed straight for Talia's legs.

She picked him up, kissing his cheek. "Hi, buddy."

Another day, another time, the image of them together would have made me smile. That was what I'd hoped for once. A family with her.

Except today, I was in a shit mood.

And Talia was the reason.

So I didn't bother with a hello or even a tight smile. I walked around her, straight for the door.

The cold air singed my nose as I marched for my truck. I had the keys in my hand when a voice called my name.

"Foster."

I slowed, gritted my teeth and faced her. Goddamn this woman. Even though I was pissed, just the sight of her made my heart skip.

Her hands were stuffed in her coat pockets as she stopped on the sidewalk. "I thought you were leaving."

"I'm not." I lifted my coffee to my mouth and took a sip.

"Oh." Talia dropped her gaze to her boots. "What did you tell them?"

"Who? Your brother? Not much. But I guess that's about all you told him too." There was no hiding the frustration in my voice. My blood was as hot as the coffee in my hand. "He has no idea we were together, does he? Does Lyla?"

She swallowed hard. "Knox knows I was dating someone in college and that it didn't work out."

"Someone." I was just a someone. I had to force myself to relax my hand before I crushed the cup in my fist. "You didn't even tell him my fucking name."

"I told Lyla. And my parents."

"Right. Forgot about your dad. At least he knows enough to come to the gym and bust my ass for showing up in Quincy."

"What? When?"

"Does it matter? You made sure to tell him the bad. But you didn't bother to share the good."

The year we'd been together had been the best time of my life. I'd cherished every memory. I'd replayed countless moments. Just to keep her close. To make sure that she was always front of mind.

Maybe she'd spent these years only replaying the end.

My fault. It was my fault. But fuck, it hurt.

"Were you ashamed of me?" Because I'd been poor. Uneducated. Because I'd used my fists to make a living.

"What? No."

I wanted to believe her. "Then why?"

She hesitated. "It's complicated."

"Yeah," I muttered. "I guess it is."

I left Talia on the sidewalk and climbed into my truck. It took effort not to glance at her as I drove away.

"Fuck." I pounded a fist on the wheel as I turned off Main.

Damn it, I wished Jasper were here. Because today, what I needed more than anything was a fight. Anything to numb the pain and distract myself from reality.

I was losing her. I was losing her all over again.

Or maybe she hadn't been mine to begin with.

CHAPTER 8

TALIA

Foster was mad. When I stacked our sins against each other's, his outweighed mine tenfold. He didn't get to be mad. So why wouldn't this guilt go away? It had been plaguing me for three days.

"Okay, spill," Lyla said the moment she flipped the lock on the coffee shop's front door. "Who was that smoking hot guy earlier?"

"Someone from the past." I sighed, toying with the rag I'd been using to wipe down tables. "It's complicated."

The same explanation I'd given Foster on the sidewalk earlier. It sounded just as trite and pathetic as it had the first time.

"You don't want to talk about it, do you?" She walked to the table, taking one of the chairs and turning it up onto the table.

"Not really."

She frowned but didn't hound me for details as we worked in silence to close the shop.

I finished wiping down tables and turning up the chairs while she worked behind the counter, cleaning the espresso machine and hauling the unsold pastries to the refrigerators.

The light beyond the windows faded fast until darkness had settled and the glow shining through the glass was from the downtown streetlights.

Lyla cleaned the kitchen as I swept and mopped the floor, the two of us making short work of the closing routine.

Part of me envied Lyla for owning this shop. She set her own hours. Her choices were her own. There was freedom here I'd never have as a doctor. Not that I could imagine doing anything else with my life. But it made times like this special. I never complained about cleaning the coffee shop or folding linens at The Eloise or washing dishes at Knuckles or moving cows at the ranch.

My family was full of entrepreneurs and had been for generations. The ranch was the biggest enterprise, but the Eden name was splashed all around town. If we didn't currently own a given business, chances were, one of our relatives had in the past.

In recent years Mom and Dad had pushed hard to retire by selling some of their investments. Giving each of us kids the option to step in.

Only Mateo and I hadn't taken over a business. My youngest brother was flying planes at the moment, but I hoped he'd find his way back.

Montana had a way of tugging us home.

I'd made the decision to live my life here, beside my parents, siblings, grandparents, aunts, uncles and cousins.

And now Foster.

He was staying in Quincy. I refused to acknowledge the relief I'd felt when he'd told me he wasn't leaving. I also wasn't letting myself picture the hurt on his face when he'd asked me if I'd been ashamed.

Never. I'd never once felt ashamed of loving Foster. But I should have told everyone about him. I should have been honest about our breakup.

Lyla came out of the kitchen with a towel in her hand. "I'm done in the kitchen. What else needs to be finished out here?"

"Nothing." But instead of picking up my coat so we could go to dinner, I turned over one of the chairs and slumped in the seat. "That guy? That's Foster. The man I dated my senior year of undergrad."

"Really?" Lyla rounded the counter, taking down another chair to sit at my side. "I was busy and didn't catch his name when he was talking to Knox. He's gorgeous."

"I know." I groaned. Foster had only gotten sexier with age. This would be so much easier if he weren't still the handsomest man I'd ever seen.

"Why is he here? Think he wants to rekindle things?"

"He's here…" For me. To make amends. To talk. Maybe to seek forgiveness. He hadn't come out and said he wanted to try again, but that kiss the other night was impossible to ignore. "It's a mess."

"You broke up because you moved, right?" she asked. "If he's living here, maybe the timing will be right this time."

"He broke me," I whispered.

"What do you mean he broke you?" She sat up straighter. "What happened?"

The story of our relationship rushed from my mouth, like it had been waiting years to be freed. By the time I was done, there was as much hurt on Lyla's face as there had been on Foster's earlier.

"You never told me any of this," she said.

"It's not exactly easy discussing how your boyfriend married your best friend."

"College roommate," she corrected. Lyla had always referred to Vivienne as my roommate, not my best friend, because that title she'd claimed in the womb. "I get that it's not easy to talk about, but you should have told me."

"I'm sorry."

"Knox didn't know about Foster either. Does anyone?"

"Dad does. Foster was supposed to help me move, but after the breakup, plans changed. Dad came to help me with the U-Haul. I was pretty upset. He knows what happened and you know he doesn't keep secrets from Mom."

"Unlike you." Lyla scoffed. "I'm mad at you."

"You're not alone," I muttered.

"We don't keep stuff like this from each other." She flew out of her chair, swiping a can of glass cleaner and a rag from the counter. She went to work on the display case—the display case I'd already cleaned—erasing invisible fingerprints and smudges until the glass squeaked.

"I'm sorry, Lyla."

She whirled, eyes blazing. "I tell you everything. You're not just my sister, you're *my* best friend. You help me through the bad days. You didn't even give me the chance to be there during yours."

"I'm—"

"Shush. I'm on a roll." She started pacing. "You're brilliant. You're an incredible doctor and you help so many people. But you suck at letting anyone help you. Would it be so hard to not be perfect?"

Ouch. "I'm not perfect. Far from it."

"I know you're not perfect. You can't cook worth a damn. Not that you'd ever admit it. Not that you'd ever admit how you're really feeling. Here you are, after working all week at the hospital, cleaning my coffee shop."

"I don't mind."

"That's not the point and stop interrupting me." She held up a finger. "I don't need you to help me clean. But I know you want to, so I let you. Get the difference?"

I kept my mouth shut.

"That was a real question you have to answer."

"Yes." A smile tugged at my mouth. "I should have told you about Foster a long time ago. I promise to tell you the next time a man breaks my heart." Not only because I should lean on my sister, but because it was important to Lyla that she be given the chance to show up on my bad days.

"Thank you." She gave a single nod. "So what are you going to do about Foster?"

"Ignore him?"

She laughed. "A single woman does not ignore a man who looks like that."

"God." I dropped my face into my hands. "I don't know. I don't *know*. He kissed me three days ago, and I can't stop thinking about it."

"Good?"

"Remember when we were fifteen and you got your first kiss?"

Lyla walked to her chair, taking a seat with a dreamy smile. "Jason Palmer."

"I made you tell me every single detail that night." We'd snuck out to the barn so that no one would hear us talk. I'd been curious and excited and a little bit jealous. Lyla had always been more daring with boys. "You told me it was better than rainbows."

"I do love rainbows." She gave me a sad smile. "This kiss with Foster wasn't just good."

"It was better than rainbows."

"Oh boy. As your sister, I'm obligated to hate him for what he did to you. But as your best friend, I will support you in whatever you decide. What are you going to do?"

"Ask him to leave?" I shrugged. "I can't. It's too late."

Lyla reached over, placing her hand over mine. "Too late for rainbows?"

"The rainbows disappeared in the storm." The storm of Foster and Vivienne.

"Then maybe you can get some closure. He wants to explain. What's the harm in letting him try?"

The harm? That I'd fall for him. And he'd break me again.

We sat together in silence for a few moments, until I stood and put my chair on the table. Then together, we walked to Knuckles and ate a quiet dinner. When Lyla started to yawn through dessert, I signaled for the check.

"I love you," I said, giving her a hug as we stood between my Jeep and her car in the alley behind the coffee shop.

"I love you too. Good night."

"Night."

Lyla drove in one direction on Main as I turned the other. Except when I reached the street that led to my neighborhood, I kept going straight until I found myself on Lower Clark Fork Road, following the dark curve of the river out of town.

Maybe Lyla was right. Maybe I needed closure with Foster. Maybe then the pain and frustration would go away. Maybe then I could truly forget.

And damn it, I had a few things to say myself.

Foster was mad at me. But he didn't get to be mad.

With every mile, my heart raced. My own anger blossomed until my grip on the steering wheel was punishing. The lights inside the gym streamed through the windows into the night. I parked, hopped out of the Jeep and hurried inside, not giving myself a chance to second-guess this visit. To cool my emotions.

Heat blasted me in the face as I stepped inside.

The gym was nothing like it had been earlier in the week. In the center of the space was an elevated boxing ring. The mats and skirt around the base were a bright blue. Black ropes stretched from corner to corner. And in its center, wearing nothing but a pair of shorts, was Foster.

His body, those cut muscles, glistened with sweat. His chest heaved with labored breaths.

Desire pooled between my legs. My core clenched. *Fuck.* Coming here tonight was a mistake. He was too tempting.

Watching him train had always been such a turn-on. During his fights, I'd sit on the edge of my seat, hoping that he'd win. Panicked that he'd lose.

But on the nights he won—which was most of the time—we didn't make it out of the parking lot before I dragged him into the back seat of his truck and tore his clothes off.

"What do you want, Talia?" Foster's voice held a razor-sharp edge.

I wanted to look at him and feel nothing. I wanted to be able to rip that photo of us in a hundred pieces. I wanted to sleep at night and not have his face haunt my dreams.

I wanted him to stop being mad at me, because damn it, he didn't get to be mad at me.

Heading for the ring, I climbed its edge. Then I bent and slipped between the ropes, marching straight into his space.

"You don't get to be mad at me." I poked a finger into his

bare chest and was met with nothing but solid muscle.

He glanced at my boots and the flecks of snow that had made their way inside. His jaw clenched. "Take your shoes off. This is a brand-new fucking ring."

My nostrils flared, but I bent, peeling off one boot to throw over the ropes followed by the other. They each landed with a thud on the concrete floor. I was a little shorter without the boots, so I stood on my toes and poked him again. "You did this. Not me. So you don't get to be mad at me."

"You didn't bother telling your family about me." He planted his hands on his narrow hips. "We were together for a year. Admit it. You were worried about what Daddy would say when you brought home a guy like me."

"Oh, fuck you." I slammed both hands into his pecs, pushing as hard as I could. He didn't even rock on his heels. "How can you say that to me? How can you think I'd be ashamed? Fuck you for thinking I ever cared about money."

"Because you had it!" He threw out his arms. "You fucking hid me, Talia. You hid me."

"I loved you." I pushed him again, giving it my full weight. "I was twenty-one years old, living in Las Vegas, a thousand miles from home. My parents knew your name. Everyone knew I was dating a guy. But no, I didn't get into the details of my love life with my brothers."

"Excuses, Talia. What about your sister?"

"She knew enough. I didn't know what was going to happen to us. I don't know why I didn't tell her, okay? It wasn't to hurt you. Or to hide you. I was leaving and we never talked about it."

"We talked about it."

"Oh, really? When? I was moving to Seattle and all you ever said was 'We'll figure it out.' " I tossed those air quotes in his face.

"We would have figured it out."

"Was that before or after you *married* Vivienne?" This time when I pushed, I gave it all my weight. I gave it seven years' worth of anger and heartbreak. And this time, he had to take a step back to keep his balance.

"I loved you for 437 days." I didn't give him space. I crowded him, making a fist. "One year, two months and eleven days."

It had been a long damn time since I'd thrown a punch. But we were in a fighting ring. And damn it, I wanted this fight. So I threw a jab at his nose.

He blocked it with a flick of his wrist. "What the fuck?"

"I thought you said you had a fight coming up." I threw another jab, the muscles in my arm tensing. "You wanted my help, right? Well, here you go."

"Talia, knock this shit off."

"No." This time I threw a punch with my right arm, aiming for his kidney.

He knocked it away with his elbow, backing away and around the ring.

But I just kept following, throwing pointless punches that never landed against his skin.

"I hate you for choosing Vivienne." Another punch.

"I hate you for not loving me the way I loved you." Then another punch.

"I hate you for being so fucking hard to forget." A tear dripped down my cheek as I threw the next punch. My eyes flooded and Foster was blurry but I just kept on swinging. "Ashamed of you? I would have done anything for you."

"Talia, stop." He grabbed my hand but I yanked it free, and this time when I threw my punch, uncontrolled and vicious and with all my might, he let it collide with his chest.

Pain exploded through my hand, my knuckles aching. "Son of a bitch."

"Shit." Foster seized it, completely unfazed that I'd hit him as hard as possible, and peeled my fingers back, inspecting my hand.

"It's fine." I ripped it away, retreating to the other side of the ring and turning my back to him as I shook out my knuckles. Once the pain faded, I sniffled and wiped my eyes dry.

Nice, Talia. I'd just completely lost my mind.

I tugged on the ropes, ready to make an escape, but Foster's hand closed around my elbow, stopping me.

"Tally, I'm sorry." It was as sincere as his other apologies. Little by little, they were sneaking their way inside.

"I was never ashamed of you," I whispered. "Never."

Foster hadn't talked much about his childhood while we'd been together. He'd taken me to meet his parents at lunch once and they'd both seemed nice. But we hadn't gone to his parents' house. We hadn't spent much time at Foster's apartment because it had been in a rough neighborhood.

"Will you look at me?" he asked.

I dragged in a shaky breath and turned. A small block of black letters ran in a vertical line along his ribs. Earlier, I'd been too busy gawking to notice them. Then I'd been too busy punching.

But now, there was no missing them.

GARNET FLATS

"What is that?" I pointed to the words, meeting his gaze. "Why do you have that tattoo?"

It was the only ink on his body.

He closed his eyes for a long moment, his shoulders

slumping. "You told me once that your great-grandmother loved to hunt for garnets."

"Great-great-grandmother," I corrected.

She, along with my great-great-grandfather, had founded Quincy. Our family had lived here ever since. People joked that you couldn't throw a rock down Main without hitting an Eden.

It wasn't entirely inaccurate.

People called our immediate family Quincy royalty—either in jest or jealousy. I really hated that term. We were just people who loved this town enough to stay and build our lives in the community. We were a family who cherished our roots and our stories, like my great-great-grandmother's.

She'd loved hunting for garnets. By the time she'd died, she'd amassed quite the collection. Most had been turned into jewelry, handed down through generations. I had a pair of garnet stud earrings. Lyla and Eloise each had necklaces.

Garnet Flats was the area on the ranch where she'd found most of her garnets—hence the name. Dad used to take me there to hunt for my own in the summers. Mom would pack us a picnic lunch and we'd have a daddy-daughter date. I'd never found a gemstone of my own, but that spot had become my special place.

It had been one of many stories I'd told Foster about Quincy. About the ranch. He'd always seemed fascinated by my Montana home, saying how he couldn't wait to see it for himself.

He was here now.

And my special place was inked on his skin.

"I've never heard anyone describe a place the way you talked about it," he said. "I could close my eyes and be there, standing with you in the meadows. I could see the mountains and smell the trees. I could picture the house you wanted to build. The life you wanted to live."

"Why is it tattooed on your body?"

"As a reminder."

"Of what?"

He gave me a sad smile. "Of what I lost."

The tears came back.

"Your dreams were my dreams, Tally. I lost them when I lost you." He hooked a finger under my chin. "Did I lose you?"

Yes. It should have been an easy answer. He'd chosen Vivienne. So why couldn't I say it? Why couldn't I walk away?

His eyes searched mine as he towered over me, leaning closer and closer. And just like the other night, I didn't push him away.

I wanted rainbows.

Foster's lips brushed mine. A whisper of a touch that ignited a fire in my veins.

I lifted on my toes, throwing a hand around his neck to tug him forward.

He didn't hesitate. His arms wrapped around me as he hauled me off my feet, pinning me to his chest.

One sweep of his tongue and the world outside this ring vanished. The world didn't exist. The past was a haze. My legs wrapped around his waist, locking us together.

He slanted his mouth over mine, his tongue delving deep to tangle with my own, and I melted into the oblivion. It was rainbows and stars and a symphony of desire. His lips were heaven, soft but firm. His teeth nipped and he sucked with just the right amount of pressure to make me whimper.

His hands drifted to my ass, hoisting me higher until my face was above his and my hair draped around us. Then we dropped, Foster sinking to his knees. His hold didn't falter. His lips didn't break from mine until he was resting on his heels and I was sitting on his thighs.

"Fuck, Tally." He shoved at my coat, stripping it off my shoulders.

I shook out my arms, frantic to get it off. Then he pulled at the hem of my sweater, dragging it up until it was whipped off my head and sailing across the space.

The heat of his skin pressed into mine as his mouth latched on to my neck, sucking and kissing while my hands roamed his skin, tracing the honed muscle of his shoulders and chest. His hands splayed over my spine, the strength of his body enveloping mine.

He'd changed over the years. He'd gotten stronger, bulkier, transforming from a strong young man to this Adonis. Foster's body was honed for sin and sex.

"More," I gasped as his fingers pulled down the straps of my bra.

Foster leaned forward, taking me down until my back was against the mats. He hovered over me, his lips leaving a trail across my skin as he peppered kisses along my jaw and down my neck.

My fingers threaded through his hair as he moved to my breasts. The wet heat from his mouth seeped through the lace cups of my bra as he sucked a nipple into his mouth.

"Oh, God." What the hell was I doing? Who fucking cared?

Lyla could keep her rainbows. I wanted this.

Fireworks.

My entire body was ready to combust.

"Say my name," he growled against my skin as he kissed down my belly to the hem of my pants.

"Foster," I breathed.

"Good girl."

I lifted my hips as he wrenched open the button and yanked down the zipper. Then he dragged the denim down my legs, stripping my jeans and socks, leaving me in nothing but my bra and panties.

We were a frenzy, desperate to strip the remaining pieces free. I worked my bra while he pulled down his shorts and the boxer briefs below. Before I could shimmy out of my panties, he ripped them from my body, tossing the torn lace over his shoulder.

Then he claimed my mouth once more while his arousal throbbed against my drenched core. No foreplay. Neither of us needed anything more than our mouths fused, tongues twisting.

Foster reached between us, dragging the tip of his cock against my clit and sending a shudder through my body before he positioned himself at my entrance and thrust inside.

I cried into his mouth, savoring the stretch. The wince of pain from his size. The pleasure that came when he inched his huge cock in deeper.

"Fuck, Talia," he groaned against my lips.

"Move." I wrapped my legs around him, clinging to his shoulders.

He pulled out and rocked us together, finding a rhythm that stole my breath. The steady pounding of his hips against mine sent me barreling toward the edge. The sound of our pounding heartbeats and erratic breaths filled the empty space.

Foster leveraged the power from his body, not holding anything back as he moved inside me, because we'd both always liked to fuck hard. His hand caressed my ass, drifting along the curve of my thigh until he reached my knee. Then he pushed away from where I'd had it wrapped around his hip. He lifted it higher, nearly to my shoulder. The angle sent him so deep I gasped.

Foster had learned my body's secrets a long time ago and the man had a great memory.

"You feel this?" He thrust forward and stopped, the root of his cock pressing against my clit.

"Foster." I clawed at his shoulders, my back arching off the mat.

He pulled out only to slam inside again. "Do you feel this, Talia?"

My legs began to tremble. The build was coming, my breath catching.

"Answer me." He changed his pace, bringing us together in a slow thrust. Agonizingly slow. "Do you feel this?"

Not the chemistry. Not the lust. Not the fireworks.

The impossible emotion, buried beneath it all, that I refused to name.

"Do you—"

"Yes," I whispered. Yes, I felt it.

Foster's lips found mine for another kiss, his tongue plundering, his cock hitting that sweet spot inside, until stars broke across my eyes and I came apart, shattering into a thousand pieces, crying his name. My orgasm triggered his own and he came on a roar as I pulsed and clenched around his length.

It took minutes, hours, to float back to earth. Maybe because I clung to haze and pleasure, knowing reality was going to sting. Foster held me tight until the sweat from our bodies had cooled and he rolled off me, collapsing into a boneless heap at my side.

The light from the fireworks faded.

The rainbow disappeared.

I squeezed my eyes closed, not wanting to see my strewn clothes or the torn panties on the other side of the ring. They were the evidence of my weakness.

But I couldn't stay on this mat forever, so I shoved to my feet and collected my jeans, dragging them up my legs. I stuffed my socks and bra into a pocket and tugged on my sweater. Then I climbed out of the ring to put on my boots and coat.

"Talia." Foster hadn't moved from where he lay in the ring, naked. He opened his eyes, turning his head to stop me with that stormy blue gaze. "Did I lose you?"

"You lost the woman I was."

"And the woman you are now?"

I wished I had an answer. I didn't. So I left him in the ring and drove home. And rather than cry in my garage, I let the tears fall in the shower instead.

CHAPTER 9

FOSTER

January first. A new year. A fresh start.

And for the first time in a long time, I was beginning a year as my own man.

Unless Talia would have me. Then I'd be hers until the end of my days.

I'd given her yesterday to think about Saturday night. I'd taken that time to think about it too. We'd always been combustible together. And fuck, it had felt good to lose myself in her body. To feel her pulse around me. To see that desire in her eyes. To hear her say my name as she detonated.

My hopes were up. The chances of forgiveness were slim, yet still…

I hoped with abandon.

Talia had said I'd lost the woman she'd been. Well, I sure as hell wasn't going to lose her again. Not if I could help it.

So I'd begin this year with honesty. With a confession that was long overdue.

I'd spent most of my day at the gym, cleaning and busting my ass to put the finishing touches on the place. The last of the equipment was set up, and I'd managed to squeeze in a decent workout.

Then I'd come into town this afternoon for groceries, driving by the hospital on my way home to see if Talia was working. Her Jeep had been in its regular parking space, meaning I'd had more time to kill. It was the first time in my life I'd been glad for the laundry.

The sun had set hours ago. The waiting had been agony and it had finally driven me out of my house and into town. To Talia's.

My stomach was in a knot as I parked outside her house. The lights were on inside, casting a glow onto her snow-covered lawn. We'd gotten a flurry this morning and her sidewalk was dusted in white.

In the corner of her porch was a blue shovel, so I got out of my truck, zipped my coat higher and got to work. The scrape of the shovel filled the cold dark night as I delayed for a few more minutes.

As I gave myself just a bit longer to hope.

I was on the last porch stair when the door opened. Talia stood on the threshold, no makeup, her hair damp—flawless— and dressed like she had been on my first night in Quincy. Leggings. And an oversized sweatshirt.

A UNLV hoodie.

I had one to match.

"What are you doing?" She wrapped her arms around her waist.

"Clearing your sidewalk." I set the shovel aside and surveyed my work. "It probably took me twice as long as it would have taken you."

"It's great. Thanks for doing it for me."

"You're welcome. Suppose I'll get more practice living in

Montana."

I waited for her to contradict me or to argue and demand I leave Quincy. But she stayed quiet. Maybe after Saturday night, she realized now why I wouldn't leave.

My breath billowed as we stared at one another. There were a thousand unspoken words between us, so thick they were a cloud of their own.

"About the other night—"

She waved it off. "We don't have to talk about it."

"We do. I didn't wear a condom." Not that I'd had one to find. I hadn't needed condoms in a long damn time.

"I'm on birth control."

"'Kay." There was a hint of disappointment in my voice. A baby with Talia wouldn't have been an unwelcome surprise. "I, um…haven't been with anyone in a while." The fact that I'd managed to last more than five seconds had been a goddamn miracle. Being inside Talia's body was heaven on earth.

"Because of your divorce. Right."

"Something like that," I muttered. No, it hadn't been because of the divorce. But that clarification would come later. "Gonna make me stand out here all night? It's not exactly warm."

"You can come in, but only because if you get hypothermia, I'll be the one to treat you. I've spent enough time at the hospital today and I have a twelve-hour shift tomorrow."

I laughed, expecting to see a smile on her face too. But she looked like she'd just stubbed her toe. "What?"

"Don't laugh."

My grin faltered. "Why?"

"Because I like it." Talia shifted sideways and motioned for me to step inside.

As she closed the door, I toed off my boots and stripped out of my coat, hanging it on a hook in the entryway. Then I followed her deeper into the house, drawing in a long breath of her scent. Coconut and citrus.

I'd gone to sleep a happy man on Saturday night because I'd had that smell on my skin. Thank fuck she hadn't changed her soap over the years. I would have missed it.

"Great place," I said as we entered the living room.

"Thank you."

Her house was charming and cozy. The walls were painted a soft tan that complemented the leather sofa and armchair. The walnut coffee table had six marble coasters, one of which held a mason jar full of ice water. She'd always been worried about condensation rings ruining furniture, so she'd kept coasters everywhere.

The fireplace against the wall was made of the same brick that had been used outside for the porch's stairs. The hardwood floors looked original, with the occasional ding and scuff to add character. A thick area rug took up most of the room, the hints of dark green in the pattern coordinating with the potted snake plant in the corner.

The house was older, probably built before open concept had become the rage, so each room was separated by walls and arched doorways. And above the couch, instead of paintings or prints, was a gallery wall of photos. The picture in the center was of her family.

It was older, a larger version of the copy she'd had at her apartment in Vegas.

Talia walked to the couch, taking a seat against one end and folding her legs into the cushion like she was curling in on herself. Like she was bracing for what was coming.

I took the opposite end of the couch, giving her some space as I leaned my elbows on my knees. "Nice sweatshirt."

She glanced down, like she'd forgotten which one she'd pulled on.

"You bought me the same one, remember? You thought it would be cute if we matched."

"The sleeves were too short, so you never wore it."

"No, the sleeves were fine." It had been one of two white lies I'd told her. "I didn't wear it because I didn't want people to think I'd earned it. That I was going to college."

"What?" She cocked her head. "Why?"

"I barely finished high school. Got my diploma and knew that I'd never make it through another math or English class. The idea of college...that was for people like you. Not me. And when I put on that sweatshirt, it reminded me of everything I'd never have. Everything I wouldn't be able to give you. A poor kid from a poor neighborhood whose best skill was throwing his fists around. A guy who was lucky to have twenty bucks in his pocket and knew he'd never be able to give you the world."

She pulled her knees into her chest. "I never needed the world."

"But I wanted to give it to you anyway."

Back then, I'd been wrapped up in material possessions. I'd defined success as money and status. Everything my parents had been bitter about not having. The resentment they'd held toward each other because of why they didn't have it.

If I could go back in time, I'd kick my own ass.

Talia hadn't needed cars or a fancy house. All she'd needed

was to fall asleep in my arms every night and wake up to my face every morning.

"You didn't talk about your childhood much," she said.

"No." And I'd only introduced her to my family once. At a lunch, not dinner, in an effort to keep it as short as possible.

While she'd always talked about her family, I had avoided that subject at all costs. It was like our positions had been reversed. She'd told me everything but hadn't shared me in the opposite direction. And I'd told everyone about her, but shared nothing about them to her.

"We didn't have much money when I was a kid," I said. "Dad worked at a tire shop, changing tires and patching holes. Mom worked as a bartender at a sports bar off the strip. Together, they brought in decent pay, except they usually came home with half of it because they'd left the rest at a casino."

"They had a gambling problem? I had no idea."

"Not something I liked to talk about. It caused a lot of problems between my parents. They fought all the time. They'd get mad when one lost too much. The next time, it would be the other."

"I'm sorry."

I shrugged. "It's who they are."

Neither of my parents would change. I'd accepted that. And these days, instead of being angry at each other, they were often angry at me too. They resented me for my wealth because I didn't share it with them, not the way they wanted me to.

Every time I gave them money, they'd blow it in weeks. The two cars I'd bought for Dad had been hawked for cash. The same was true with the jewelry I'd given Mom.

I worked too hard for them to gamble away my money. So I'd bought them a house that was in my name so it couldn't be sold. They received nice gifts on birthdays and at Christmas, and I didn't ask what became of those gifts.

"Growing up, our house wasn't peaceful," I told Talia. "The normal volume was a shout. I think that's why I got into fighting. It was an outlet. A way to quiet the noise. I had a friend in high school who started boxing and he took me to Angel's one day."

Angel's gym, owned by Arlo Angel. He'd been my savior at that point in my life. He'd taken me under his wing and trained me personally for years. Probably because he'd seen natural talent and a fuckload of pent-up aggression.

"I didn't respect my dad," I told Talia. "I didn't listen to my mother. But Arlo...he was my hero. He took a pissed-off kid and gave him a future. He told me I could be great, so I fought to be great. I needed that. I needed someone who believed in me. I needed something to fight for." And for far too long, Arlo's approval had been the source of my motivation.

"Understandable," she said. "He's a charismatic man."

"Was," I corrected. "He died in November. Heart attack."

Talia gasped. "Oh, I had no idea. I'm so sorry."

"I'm not. A lot happened with Arlo. None of it good."

"What do you mean? You loved him."

I blew out a long breath. Telling this part of the story was never easy. Probably why I'd only shared it with Jasper. "I stopped fighting for Arlo when I met you."

"Huh?" Her eyebrows knitted together. "I don't understand. You were fighting at his gym."

"He wasn't the motivation. Not the bulk of it anymore. At first, I fought because I needed the outlet. Then I fought to make him proud. Then I met you. It wasn't about me anymore, it was about you. I had no education. No hopes of being a lawyer or banker or businessman. My talent was in the ring. So I fought to win, because winning meant the brightest smile on your face. It meant hearing you cheer my name. And it meant money."

It had all come down to money. Fool that I'd been, I'd thought money had mattered.

"You talked about your family. Their businesses. The ranch. The hotel. I knew you came from money. And I promised myself that I would never make you take a step backward. I wouldn't drag you down."

Talia sat straighter, letting go of her knees. "Are you saying you broke my heart because you were acting like some sort of martyr? You let me go to find someone 'better'?"

"No." I gritted my teeth. Just thinking about her with another man had sent me spiraling more than once in the past seven years. "I was going to fight anywhere they'd let me. I was going to fight every time, earn every dime. Until my body was broken. I was never going to let you go."

"But you did. You chose Vivienne."

I met her blue eyes brimming with pain and betrayal. A million apologies wouldn't take away the guilt. A lifetime wouldn't be long enough to make up for the hurt I'd caused her. "I'll never forgive myself for what happened, Tally. For what I did to you."

"But...why?" Her voice sounded so small. "What happened to us? We were happy. I thought we were happy. Weren't we? You should have told me you had feelings for Vivienne."

"I didn't."

Her hands balled into fists on top of her knees. "You *married* her."

"Because Arlo blackmailed me into it. Either I did exactly

what he wanted, including marrying Vivienne. Or he'd turn on me."

"For what?"

"For throwing a fight to make fifty thousand dollars."

CHAPTER 10

TALIA

"W-what?" I shook my head. "You threw a fight? When? Which fight?"

I'd gone to every one of his fights and he'd lost twice. Both times, it had been by decision and so close a call it could have gone either way. Foster had taken a beating but delivered the same. He hadn't held back. No one could have watched either fight and said he'd let the other guy win.

Foster gave everything he had when he was in the ring. Always.

"It wasn't a fight you watched. About six months before we, um..." He swallowed hard.

"Before we broke up."

"Yeah. One of the guys at the gym approached me about an underground fight." Foster cringed at the admission.

"No." *Oh my God, no.* "You didn't."

Even as someone who hadn't been rooted in the fighting world, I knew that underground fights were nothing but trouble. It hadn't happened often, but every now and then, I'd heard a whisper at Arlo's gym about an underground fighting ring. Mostly the chatter had happened after a fighter had been badly hurt.

I'd asked Vivienne about it once. She'd told me those fights were dangerous, but the guys did them for the money.

Not only was it illegal—if caught, the participants could be arrested for assault—but they risked their standing with the UFC. For Foster to have done this, he'd put his career in jeopardy. And his life. The rules in illegal fights were...flexible.

Vivienne had told me that one of the guys in the gym had gone to an underground fight and his opponent had done an eye gouge. The man had lost his eye.

"I'm not proud." His voice was hoarse, rough from the scrape of brutal honesty. "It was, without a doubt, the biggest mistake of my life. I've regretted it every day since."

Foster wore a stoic expression most of the time. He faced the world with his shoulders squared and his guard at the ready. But when he dropped his hands, when he gave you his vulnerabilities, you were in. All the way in.

"You did it for the money," I said.

"I did it for the money."

"Because you thought I needed it?" I flew off the couch, rage brewing in my chest. All that pain, all the tears and anguish, because he'd thought I'd needed money? "Stand up. I need to punch you again."

Foster obeyed immediately.

"That is insulting," I spat. But when I met his gaze, clouded with humiliation, my anger fizzled.

He would let me punch him, over and over and over again. But it wouldn't make me feel better. It wouldn't fill the hole in my heart.

"I needed you. Not money."

"Took me losing you to figure that out."

I swallowed the lump in my throat, refusing to cry. Not tonight. "How did Arlo get involved?"

"Arlo had always been involved." Foster sighed, sinking back into his seat. He waited to continue until I was seated too, my hands tucked beneath my knees to keep them from fidgeting. "The first fight I agreed to was small. Not a huge payout, a thousand bucks, but more than I'd make at the gym working all day. And a decent supplement to what I was winning with the UFC fights they were giving me at the time."

He'd been a new and upcoming talent, but he'd needed fighting experience for the UFC to give him higher-paying matches. He'd been putting in his time with the league, and to pay his bills, Foster had worked as an instructor at Angel's. Those days, Foster had been in one of two places. At the gym, or with me.

Except that wasn't really true, was it? Because he'd also been sneaking off to these illegal fights.

Cockfighting. That's what Vivienne had called it.

"The second fight was bigger," he said. "Better payout. I figured I'd do it, maybe two more, and walk away. The fight was at this warehouse and they'd set up a makeshift locker room. I was sitting on a table, waiting for my turn and taping my hands, when the door opened. And in walked Arlo. I thought he'd heard about it and was coming to bust my ass, haul me out of there. But he just smiled. Said it was about time I decided to make some cash."

"What?" I blinked. "He knew."

Arlo had always seemed so righteous. So rule abiding. He'd rail at fighters when they took cheap shots during sparring matches. And when I'd asked Vivienne about those underground fights, she'd told me her father hated them.

He'd been a kind guy, a beast of a man, with a belly laugh. How many, including me, had he deceived with his easy smile?

"Oh, Arlo knew." Foster scoffed. "He was very experienced in that world. Knew all the organizers. Knew the fighters. Knew how to place his bets and walk away with a pile of cash."

"But, the gym? If he got caught—"

"He would have been cut out from the league. So would all of his fighters. That's why he never invited any of us to the underground fights. We found our way there without him. And once we entered that world, we weren't allowed at Angel's. He didn't want to risk having a fighter get busted and leak it back to the gym. Hell, none of the guys from the gym ever knew he was involved or making money off them. Arlo would stay hidden in the wings, watching and betting. The next time that fighter showed up at Angel's, Arlo would ban them."

"But not you."

"I was the exception."

"Why?"

Foster shrugged. "I don't know. Maybe because we were close. Maybe because he believed I'd eventually make it to the top of the UFC. The underground fights made money, but nothing like my contract now."

Millions. He had to be making millions from his fights and sponsorship deals.

"And Arlo wanted a piece of it," I said.

Foster nodded. "He wanted that glory. To call himself Foster Madden's mentor."

"Not just a mentor. You married his daughter."

"Divorced his daughter."

"When?"

"When did Vivienne and I get divorced?" He waited for my

nod. "Exactly three weeks after Arlo died."

Which meant they'd had to have filed for divorce right after Arlo's death. Apparently in the past seven years, their marriage had crumbled. How much of a role had Vivienne played in this scheme?

"So Arlo was blackmailing you this whole time?" I asked.

"He never let me forget my mistake. The day that motherfucker died, I celebrated with cake and my favorite vodka."

"What about the fight? The one you threw?"

Foster dragged a hand over his beard. "It's the only fight I've intentionally lost. Seven years and not a day goes by I don't feel sick over it."

For fifty thousand dollars. It wasn't a small amount but it seemed a low price for his morals.

"If I had just waited—" He shook his head. "If I had just stayed on the path, I would have made that in spades. But damn it, I was young and Arlo pitched it at exactly the right time. You were starting to plan your move, and he planted these seeds of doubt. How hard it would be to be apart. How you'd make new friends. Meet other men. How many plane tickets a decent payout would buy to visit you in Seattle."

I'd feared most of the same, leaving Foster behind, worrying that too much distance would create a rift between us. Worrying that we'd grow apart.

"Please don't take that as me putting any of the blame on you going to school," he said. "Arlo played on my greatest weakness."

Me.

"Why didn't you tell me?" I asked.

"Like I said. I'm not proud."

He'd kept these fights a secret. For six months. Nearly half the time we'd been together.

I closed my eyes, letting it all sink in. Replaying moments in a new light. "There were nights when you'd come to my place after the gym with cuts. That one time your ribs were all bruised. You told me it was from sparring. But it wasn't, was it?"

"No."

"You lied to me."

"Yes, I did. I'm sorry."

So many apologies. They were getting heavy.

"I'd been picking up underground fights about once a month," Foster said. "Making a grand, maybe two, on each. You'd just brought boxes to the apartment to start packing. That's when Arlo approached me. He said there was a bigger payday. Fifty grand for a single fight. That was over three times as much as I could make in my tier with the UFC. Add that to what I'd already made, it would have been the last one. But for me to get that fifty, it wasn't with a win. The organizer of the fight was bringing a contender and if I won—"

"The organizer would lose more than if he paid you fifty on the side."

"Yeah. So I fought the bastard hard. I gave it all I had until the last round when I feigned fatigue and let him pummel me against the ropes. Then took a hook to the temple and woke up to a nightmare."

I gulped, a shiver rolling down my spine at the idea of him getting knocked out. "And where was I during this?"

"With Vivienne. I knew I wouldn't be able to face you afterward, so I asked her to plan a girls' night."

I remembered that girls' night. He'd been invited to a

bachelor party and knew it would be late, so he'd crash at his place afterward. Another lie. But I'd believed him. I hadn't feared he'd cheat. I hadn't thrown a fit that he'd be going to a strip club. I'd trusted him entirely, enough to believe that he'd actually been out with friends.

Instead, he'd been dealing with a concussion.

My pulse raced, my stomach twisting into a knot. It was hard to hear the truth. To know I'd been naive in my trust. To realize I'd been duped. I stood from the couch, unable to keep still when I felt like crying or screaming or crawling out of my own skin.

"Why would Arlo need to blackmail you?" I asked. "You threw his fight. Was he trying to get more money?"

"He was trying to get me to stay. After that fight, I told him I was done. With all of it. Even the UFC. I felt so dirty and cheap, I didn't want to fight again. So I told Arlo I was quitting and moving to Seattle."

"You were going to move with me?"

"Well, yeah." He spoke like he was stating the obvious. "I told you we'd figure it out. I wasn't sure of the timing, but I was always coming to Seattle. Did you really think I'd be able to stay away from you that long?"

Yes. No. Maybe. "It was a topic we both avoided too often."

"I didn't like talking about us being apart." He sighed, rubbing his beard again. Was that his nervous habit now? Or just something he did while he was thinking of what to say? "Arlo didn't want me to leave. For the obvious reason."

"Money."

"For every penny I made, he took a cut. That fight I threw? He didn't make a cent that night. Because the whole point was for him to trap me. From that point on, every time I got paid, he'd have his hand out. Sponsorships and endorsements, I'd give him a cut. Whatever he wanted, he took because he had the information to tank my career."

"You had information on him too, though."

"That he bet at the fights? Yeah. I could have fucked him over. But people don't talk about those fights for a reason. That's a good way to get beaten to death."

I flinched. "They would have killed you?"

"Worse. They might have come after you. Arlo knew you were important. When I told him I was out, he didn't argue. He just calmly told me to reconsider. He talked about how dangerous it could be in Seattle for a woman. How there was never any guarantee people were safe."

"He threatened me?" That son of a bitch.

"I don't know what he would have done but I wasn't taking that risk. Not where you were concerned. So I stayed. I played Arlo's game."

"Until he died."

"Until he died," he repeated.

"What about the other fighters? Aren't you worried someone will come forward? Take Arlo's place and blackmail you for money?"

He shook his head. "Not really. Like I said, people stay tight-lipped. Most fighters are tied up with families you don't betray. And I didn't use my real name. I was only a part of it for a short time. Just a handful of fights. That fight I threw was my last. There are no pictures. No cameras allowed. If someone was going to blackmail me besides Arlo, they would have come forward by now."

Foster sounded so sure. Maybe my doubts were because I'd just learned all of this, but it seemed like the type of skeleton that never left your closet.

"I'm sorry, Tally." He looked up at me with tears in his eyes. With a regret so deep it was like staring into a black hole. "I'm so fucking sorry. I made the wrong choice. If I could go back, do it all differently, I would. Please know that."

More brutal honesty. My heart felt like it had been turned inside out, then outside in. My head was a scrambled mess. I walked to the window, staring out into the dark night. What to feel? What to think? "You should have told me the truth."

"I didn't want you mixed up in it."

"Don't." I whirled away from the glass. "Don't you fucking dare. Did you really think so little of my ability to handle the truth? What if someone had come after me in Seattle? I would have had no idea. You made me a part of that blackmail and left me in the dark. You were a coward. *Do not* say you were protecting me."

Foster shot off the couch. "You really think I wanted you mixed up with that trash? Of course I was protecting you from it, Talia. I would protect you from anything that could cause you pain."

"Except yourself."

He recoiled, his body tensing like I'd slapped him.

"Fuck." I pinched the bridge of my nose.

"You're right. The only person who ended up hurting you was me. But I was scared. When I say it was dangerous, I'm not downplaying that. These aren't men who obey society's rules. If you cross them, they take their revenge to the extreme. You think I would have been able to live with myself if someone had come after you? Hit you? Raped—" He shook his head. "I can't even think about that."

I shuddered, not wanting to think about it either. "And

Vivienne? Was she safe because she was Arlo's daughter?"

Foster scoffed. "She didn't even realize she'd been swimming with sharks her entire life."

"Is that why you married her? Because of Arlo?"

He hung his head, giving me a barely there nod. "Yeah."

"And Vivienne went along with it?"

Had she always loved him in secret? Had she just been waiting for us to break up before making her move? Had she even been my friend? Or had it always been about Foster?

While Foster had broken my heart, having my best friend stomp on the shattered pieces had turned it into dust. Her betrayal was something I'd never forget.

And she'd won. I hated her for winning. For being able to call herself his wife.

Foster raked a hand through his hair. "She...it's complicated."

I was really starting to hate that phrase, even though I'd been the one to use it first.

"Arlo wanted us together," he said. "The marriage was his idea."

"Oh, and I'm sure she put up a fight," I deadpanned. Vivienne would have gone along with it because she'd gotten Foster. Maybe she'd been after the money too.

"She didn't want our marriage either."

"Right." I scoffed. "And I'm sure she put up a hell of a fight on the way to the altar."

"She feels awful about what happened."

Vivienne felt so awful that she'd married him anyway. She'd slept with him anyway. She'd worn his ring anyway. She'd taken his name anyway. Yeah, she must feel awful.

Why was he defending her? Why was he so loyal to her?

Didn't most people break ties with their ex?

Did they talk about me during their phone calls? Had he told her how I'd fucked him at the gym on Saturday?

My frame tensed, my hands fisting. My feelings for Foster were a jumbled mess, but when it came to Vivienne, one emotion rang clear.

Fury.

"I'm done with this conversation."

"There's more to talk—"

"Good night." With that, I walked through the living room and up the stairs to my bedroom.

And left Foster to show himself out.

CHAPTER 11

FOSTER

Weren't confessions supposed to make you feel better? I'd expected to feel lighter after confiding in Talia. But there was no relief. I was fucking miserable.

The pit in my stomach felt miles deep. My head throbbed and I couldn't focus. This morning's breakfast had come up ten minutes after it had gone down.

It reminded me a lot of the days after our breakup. The days when I'd hardly been able to get out of bed. Lying to her, telling her I was marrying Vivienne, had been unbearable. But the real agony had come later, when I'd gone to Vivienne's apartment and found Talia's room empty.

The walls had been bare. The carpet clean with vacuum tracks. The coconut and citrus scent already fading.

Vivienne had found me in that room, standing in the middle of the space. Lost and heartbroken, knowing I'd never see Talia again. Knowing that the blame was mine.

I'd stood in that empty room for hours, reliving the breakup. Hearing the lies that had spewed from my mouth. Wondering how she could have believed them so easily.

I have feelings for Vivienne I can't keep ignoring.

She's the one.

I'm asking her to marry me.

Utter filth to drive Talia away.

I'd never forgive myself for those words. For those lies. But standing in that empty bedroom, I'd promised myself that if I ever had the chance to make it right, I'd tell Talia the truth.

After she'd basically kicked me out of her place last night, I'd spent the midnight hours tossing and turning on the couch. Replaying the conversation. Reliving the shame. Realizing how livid she was with Vivienne.

When I'd finally given up on sleep, I'd spent the morning tidying up the apartment and cleaning the already clean gym. Six miles on the treadmill hadn't helped clear my head. Neither had a shower and lunch before I'd climbed in my truck to head into town.

The sun streamed through the clear sky. The river rambled over smooth rocks beyond the road. A beautiful January day in Montana.

Had coming here been a fool's dream? Had it all been in vain? Seven years I'd spent wishing for this chance.

Had it been doomed from the start?

Talia was right. She'd deserved the truth seven years ago. But the threats Arlo had made still echoed in my mind. Talia's safety was everything. That was why I'd lied, not because I hadn't believed she could handle the situation. But instead of sharing the burden, I'd shouldered it.

Another mistake.

There was more to tell Talia. More to explain. But Vivienne had begged for the chance to do that herself. It was part of this arrangement.

Vivienne wanted to tell her side of the story, and I'd

promised her that opportunity to try.

So I would keep Vivi's secret—our secret—unless it meant losing Talia. Then Vivienne would have to deal with my broken promise.

My phone rang, Vivienne's name flashing on the truck's center screen. "Hi. Where are you?"

"Almost there." She had a smile in her voice. "Ten, fifteen minutes."

"Drive safe. There's still some snow and ice on the roads outside of town."

"Jasper is driving and he's being very careful," she said, then lowered her voice. "Did you, um, talk to Talia?"

"Yeah."

"And? How'd it go?"

"Not great."

She sighed. "She hates us, doesn't she?"

Did I think Talia hated me? No. She was angry, but hate? I doubted Talia would have had sex with me at the gym if she hated me. Not that I'd share that detail with my ex-wife. But did Talia hate Vivienne? Maybe.

"She needs time to let it sink in," I said. "And she needs the whole truth."

"You didn't tell her, did you?" Vivienne asked. "You promised."

"I know. I didn't tell her."

"Thank you." Vivienne had her own wrongs to right. I wouldn't steal that moment from her unless I had no other choice. "Still want to meet at the hotel?"

"Yeah. I'm going to grab a coffee, then I'll see you there."

"Okay. Bye."

My fingers tapped on the wheel for the rest of the drive into town, the nervous energy needing an outlet.

Today was another beginning. It would be okay, right? This wasn't a horrible decision. I was doing the smart thing by moving us here.

My self-assurances landed flat.

Please don't let this be a mistake.

I made it to town and parked close to the hotel before jogging across the street and walking three doors down to Eden Coffee. I needed more caffeine if I was going to make it through the rest of the afternoon and evening.

A group of teenagers clustered at the counter when I strode inside, kids probably enjoying the last day of winter break before school started again tomorrow.

Would she like this town? Would she like the gym? I'd been so focused on getting the place in decent shape I hadn't let myself worry over those questions. But she was almost here and now nothing I'd done seemed like enough.

The furniture I'd bought was nice but it wasn't super expensive. The bedroom was half the size of what she had in Vegas. There was a single movie theater in this town, and it was nothing like the eighteen-screen cinema close to our neighborhood.

"Does the movie theater here have peanut M&M's?" I asked the teenager in front of me in line. She loved getting a large popcorn and dumping in a box of peanut M&M's.

"Huh?" The teenager looked me up and down.

"Never mind," I muttered.

We'd sneak candy into Quincy's theater if necessary. We'd have a good life. A simple life.

And maybe, if I could score just one more miracle, that life would include Talia.

The teenagers shuffled out of the way, their arms laden with pastries and lattes.

"Americano, please," I told the barista, glancing past her. Was Lyla here? But if Talia's sister was working today, she wasn't out front.

I'd just fished a twenty from my pocket when a hand clamped down on my shoulder. I turned, my face splitting into a huge grin when I saw Jasper at my side.

"Hey." I gave him a quick hug and back slap. "You were fast. Thought I'd see you at the hotel."

"I dropped off Vivi so she could get checked in, then parked. Figured I'd find you here and I need some coffee too. That was a long-ass drive."

"Tell me about it." I chuckled. "It's good to see you. Thanks for coming. And thanks for driving up with Vivi. I felt better knowing you were in the car too."

"You don't have to thank me."

I nodded. "Yes, I do."

"We're really doing this?"

"We're really doing this. Back to the basics. On everything. Life. Training."

He smirked. "You're too old and too rich for basics."

"Probably." I laughed. "But it's worth a shot."

"Could I get a black coffee?" he asked the barista.

I glanced to the door, ready to get to the hotel. "Vivienne said ten or fifteen minutes. You made fast time."

"Anxious to get out of that car," he said, taking his coffee from the barista and giving me a nod of thanks when I paid for the cup. "How's it going with Talia?"

"Not great," I admitted as we walked outside and headed across the street. "But the fight's not over yet. I'm not giving up."

"This is where she grew up?" He glanced around, taking in all of Main. "It's quaint. Definitely not like Vegas."

"Which adds to the appeal."

"Think you'll get restless in a town this small?" he asked.

"Nope." I'd never cared for neon lights and swanky crowds. Traffic was a pain in the ass and there were too many bad memories in Vegas. "Glacier National Park is close. This summer we'll have to go hiking. There are a couple bars on Main, one on each end. Not exactly a nightclub on the strip, but they've got cold beer. Maybe I'll take up fishing." I'd never been fishing.

"I'm in for the hiking and cold beer. Not sold on the fishing but ask me again later."

"Will do."

Jasper would only be in Quincy temporarily. He'd found a vacation rental to stay in while he helped me train, an A-frame cabin on the outskirts of town. After the fight was over in March, I expected him to stay in Vegas while I returned to Montana. Not sure how that would work for future training but I'd keep him on as my trainer for as long as he wanted the job.

Jasper's Yukon was parked next to my truck. I quickened my steps as we approached the hotel, eager to get inside.

We were just about to the hotel's front doors when two women rounded the corner of the brick building.

I came to a dead stop.

Shit. Lyla hadn't been in the coffee shop, because she'd been with Talia.

Why wasn't Talia at the hospital? She'd said last night she had a twelve-hour shift today. She shouldn't be downtown. She *couldn't* be downtown, not yet. I didn't want her bumping into Vivienne, especially after how she'd reacted last night.

"What?" Jasper stopped when he realized I wasn't moving. Then he followed my gaze as Lyla and Talia passed by the hotel's front doors, walking our way.

Talia glanced up, and the moment her blue eyes met with mine, my heart skipped. Pretty sure it always would where this woman was concerned.

She was dressed in scrubs and tennis shoes. Her black coat was zipped up and her hair was in a ponytail. Her stride changed, slowed for a couple of steps, then she closed the distance between us. "Hi."

"Hi." *Stay inside, Vivi. Stay inside that hotel. Please.*

Talia and I stared at each other, the rest of the world becoming a blur, hazy on the edges.

"You okay today?" I asked.

She lifted a shoulder. "I don't know. I'm mad. I'm frustrated. It's a lot to take in."

And there was more. "Can we talk? Tonight? Please." I wanted to at least warn her that Vivienne was in town.

"Okay. I'll be at the hospital until seven."

"I'll come over around eight."

Jasper cleared his throat, and I tore my eyes from Talia's. He and Lyla were studying us both.

Lyla was scowling. The glare she sent my way was the one I'd expected from the start. Talia must have told her about me. Thank fuck. I'd rather be an enemy than a nameless stranger.

"Talia Eden, meet Jasper Vale," I said. "My trainer and friend."

He held out a hand, shaking hers. Then did the same for Lyla. "Jasper."

"Lyla." She smiled for him, but when she faced me again, that icy glare was back. Lyla could rake me over the coals later.

When we weren't within fifty feet of Vivienne.

"Tonight?" I asked Talia again.

She nodded, then she and Lyla took a step, ready to pass us on the sidewalk.

Except a voice rang out from behind them. The hotel's door was pushed open by a little girl.

My little girl.

"Daddy!"

Kadence streaked down the sidewalk, her chestnut hair streaming behind her as she raced my way with a beaming smile that had lit up every one of my dark days.

I thrust my coffee into Jasper's free hand just in time to catch my daughter as she launched herself into my arms. "Hi, little bug. Oh, I missed you. So, so much."

"Missed you too." She hugged me so tight around my neck it was a chokehold.

There were eyes on us, but I held on to Kadence, breathing her in. Never again would I go this long without her. The daily calls and FaceTimes hadn't been enough.

I kissed her temple, then set her down, crouching so we were eye to eye. "How was the trip?"

"Really, *really* long."

"Where's your mom?"

Kadence hooked a thumb over her shoulder. "Inside."

I glanced past her, not seeing Vivienne. "Does she know you came out here?"

"No, but I saw you from inside the windows, so I thought it was okay."

"Kadence, you can't leave a building without telling her."

"It was an accident."

That was her excuse for everything these days. *It was an*

accident. We'd be working on the difference between accidents and mistakes.

I touched her cheek and stood, holding out my hand for hers. If Vivienne noticed Kaddie was gone, she'd freak.

"Let's go inside." I was about to take a step, when I saw Talia's face.

The color had left her cheeks. Her eyes were wide and her mouth parted, shock etched on her beautiful face.

"What's wrong?" I asked.

Talia stared at Kadence like my daughter was more of a surprise than anything I'd told her last night.

Wait. Hadn't she known about Kaddie? I'd talked about my daughter, hadn't I? I was sure I'd mentioned her. Our conversations streamed through my mind too fast to analyze but the sinking in my gut was telling. Mostly, we'd talked about the past. I'd been focused on explaining the time *before* Kaddie was born.

I'd just assumed Talia knew. She had to know.

How many times had I googled Talia over the years? How many times had I gone to the Quincy Memorial Hospital's website just to look at her photo in the staff directory? How many times had I pulled up her Instagram account to look at the profile picture?

At some point in seven years, she'd done the same for me, right?

My social media accounts were public because my manager and agent had encouraged me to build a following. To have a presence. Most of my photos were of me in the gym, training, but every now and then, I'd add something personal.

And usually those photos or stories were of Kadence.

If Talia didn't know about my daughter, that meant...

She'd blocked me out completely.

"You didn't know," I murmured.

Talia didn't so much as blink.

Fuck.

CHAPTER 12

TALIA

His daughter was adorable. She'd lost her front baby teeth and there'd never been a more precious toothless smile.

A daughter.

He had a daughter.

I put my hand over my heart, pressing hard because it hurt. Oh, God, it hurt.

"I'm sorry," Foster said. "I thought you knew."

His daughter tugged on his hand. "Daddy, are we going?"

"Yeah." His eyes were full of more apologies but he didn't say another word as he let her drag him toward the hotel. The trainer, Jasper, followed.

A daughter.

Foster and Vivienne had a family.

"Talia." Lyla touched my elbow.

I couldn't speak. I couldn't breathe. I couldn't move.

When would this stop? Was this some sort of sick joke? His way to torture me?

Lyla moved in front of me, forcing me to make eye contact. "What can I do?"

I shook my head and managed to choke out, "Work. I need

to go back to work."

"Okay." She looped her arm with mine, taking a step and pulling so hard I had no choice but to walk away.

I'd taken a late lunch break today and come to the coffee shop to talk with Lyla. We'd decided to go for a walk around downtown because her barista, Crystal, was sweet but she gossiped constantly. Neither Lyla nor I trusted her not to eavesdrop.

So my sister and I had wandered downtown, behind the coffee shop and around the hotel, while I'd told Lyla everything Foster had revealed last night.

The underground fights. Arlo's blackmail. The money. My suspicion that Vivienne had been in love with Foster from the beginning, so she'd gone along with her father's scheme.

She'd won Foster. And not only had she gotten to claim the title of wife, she'd also given him a beautiful daughter.

A daughter I'd once dreamed of having.

"Goddamn it." Tears flooded my eyes as we crossed the street, and I furiously blinked them away.

"Well, I'll give Foster credit for something," Lyla said as we rounded her building for the alley where I'd parked my Jeep. "He's brought you out of your emotional shell."

I slowed my steps, forcing her to do the same. "What? I don't have an emotional shell."

"Don't you?" She gave me a sad smile.

"Seriously? You're saying this to me today?"

"You're right. Forget I said anything."

Unlikely. "Just because I'm private doesn't mean I have an emotional shell," I snapped.

"I didn't say that to pick a fight." She held up her hands. "Not that we ever fight. Not that you ever fight with anyone. Or cry with anyone. We're twin sisters and the last time we had a decent argument was in high school."

My jaw dropped.

"Sorry. Bad timing. I just... I can't help but think that since he's come to town, you have been more open with me in days than you have in years."

"You're praising him for breaking my heart?" I shook my head, as frustration bubbled inside my chest. "Are you trying to make me angry?"

"Um, no? Just stating an observation."

"Unbelievable." I stomped away, digging my keys from my coat pocket.

"You're just proving my point!" she called to my back.

I lifted a hand and flipped her off.

"See?"

I spun around, walking backward for a few steps. "You wanted a good fight. You have one now. Don't call me for at least two days."

Lyla shrugged as an infuriating smile spread across her face.

"Three days," I barked, then turned and stormed around the corner toward my Jeep. I slammed the door too hard and smacked my hand on the wheel. "Ouch. Damn it."

Thanks to my sister, at least I wouldn't be crying when I got to the hospital.

An emotional shell? How could she say that? I laughed and smiled and joked all the time. I was happy. I was a blissfully content person.

My molars ground together as I drove to work. I stormed into the locker room to stow my coat and keys, then washed my hands before heading down the hallway, ready to drown myself in work for the next few hours.

"Hi, Rachel," I said as I stopped at the nurses' station. "Just wanted to let you know I'm back."

She was seated behind the counter, eyes glued to a computer screen. Her gaze flicked my way before she glanced to the wall clock over her shoulder. "Long lunch?"

Don't call her a bitch. Don't call her a bitch. I forced a smile. "Just the hour. Like usual. Please let me know when my two o'clock appointment gets here."

"Don't I always?" Rachel returned her attention to the screen and hummed my dismissal.

This woman's attitude had frayed my last nerve. But what was I supposed to do? Tattle on her? That would only make it worse.

This wasn't Lyla's coffee shop. If my sister had issues with an employee, she could fire them, put out a help-wanted sign and have a new barista within two weeks.

Rachel, for all her personality shortcomings, was a good nurse and manager. Fighting with her would do nothing for me. So I walked away.

"Because I'm a freaking professional," I muttered to myself.

Dr. Anderson came walking down the hallway, dressed in his usual khaki slacks and white lab coat the same color as his hair.

"Hi, Dr. Anderson."

"Hi, Talia."

Talia. I called every doctor at Quincy Memorial *Doctor.* And they called me Talia. The nurses did too. Not just Rachel, everyone.

No one called me Dr. Eden. Why? Was I not worthy of that title? Was I not worthy of the respect? Was that why Foster had hidden the truth about the underground fights and the blackmail? Was that why Dad had confronted Foster at the gym instead of letting me handle it?

Did everyone see me as weak? Incapable?

"I'm taking off for the day," he said. "Heading out early so I can take my wife out to dinner. It's our anniversary, and I'd like to swing by the jewelry store for a little something and the grocery store for flowers."

"Happy anniversary," I said, faking more smiles and polite conversation even though I just wanted to go hide in the supply closet. "Where are you going to dinner?"

"Knuckles."

"Good choice. Though I'm biased." Not really. Knox's restaurant was the best in the state. And I was in the mood to fight anyone who disagreed.

"Are you all set here?"

"Yes. I've got a couple of routine checkups this afternoon. Otherwise, I'll do the rounds and handle anything that comes up."

"Excellent. Dr. Murphy is in the ER until seven. Then Dr. Herrera is on call tonight if you need any help."

Dr. Murphy. Dr. Herrera.

Doctor. Doctor. Doctor.

"Would you mind checking in on a few patients for me this evening?" he asked.

"Not at all."

Dr. Anderson gave me a quick summary, then with a dip of his chin, took off for the day, leaving me on my own.

The hospital didn't have the budget or demand for a doctor on-site twenty-four seven. We staggered the day and evening shifts, working varying schedules. There was at least one doctor in the building from seven in the morning to seven in the evening. On days like today, when we had scheduled appointments, one physician would be in this wing with patient and exam rooms while the other was in the emergency room for walk-in traffic.

When I'd first started my residency, all of my shifts had coincided with Dr. Anderson's so he could supervise and observe. As my mentor and teacher, we'd worked cases together. But as I'd progressed through that first year, he'd given me more freedom.

Now, three years in and so close to taking my exams and getting my license, I often worked the late afternoon and evening hours alone. It had become my favorite time at the hospital.

Mornings were hectic. The lunch hour was usually too short. But by four or five o'clock, after the nurses' rotation and the appointment window closed, it was peaceful.

My final appointment was with a woman who'd come in for her yearly exam and a mammogram. After saying goodbye, I left her to get changed while I wandered down the hallway, away from the exam rooms and through the doors that led to the patient rooms for those staying overnight.

The scent of garlic and tomatoes and pasta filled my nose as I passed a nursing assistant carrying a food tray. Dinner tonight must be spaghetti.

I stopped at the third door on the left, knocking before I pushed it open. "Hey, Dante."

The teenager lying in bed looked as miserable as he had yesterday. "Hey."

On his table was his own tray of food. The plate was shielded with a metal lid and the glass of milk covered with plastic wrap. "Spaghetti is the best dinner of the week. Need some help with it?"

"I guess," he mumbled.

I went to the sink to wash my hands for the hundredth time today, then helped him uncover the meal. "How are you feeling?"

"Like I have two broken legs and a broken arm."

I handed him a fork for his unbroken arm. "Could be worse. You could have a broken neck."

"Yeah." Dante poked at his pasta.

"How's your pain?"

He glanced at the white board on the wall where the pain scale was depicted on the bottom. "Three."

"Call if it gets above a five."

" 'Kay," he muttered. "My mom is pissed."

"It's her job as your mother to be pissed."

Dante had come into the ER yesterday with a myriad of broken bones. He was a sophomore in high school. He and a buddy had spent New Year's Day together. They'd decided to go sledding off Dante's roof into a snowdrift in the driveway. He'd taken the pioneer voyage, which had landed him in the back of an ambulance, destination: Quincy Memorial.

Dr. Murphy had been in the ER yesterday. The fractures had been clean, so he'd set the bones and put them in splints for the night. Then today, after another set of X-rays to make sure everything was aligned, they'd put him in casts.

He was staying tonight for observation, but tomorrow, he'd be on his way home.

Dante's dad was a firefighter in town. His mom was an accountant. Dante was the oldest of five kids, and according to Dr. Anderson's recap earlier, his parents were swapping shifts here at the hospital. His mom was due any minute.

"Want to watch some TV while you eat?" I asked, picking up the remote.

"My mom said I'm not allowed to do anything until I've lain here and thought about the idiocy of my ways."

I pulled in my lips to hide a smile. "And have you? Thought about the idiocy of your ways?"

"Oh, yeah." He nodded. "I'm a dumbass."

"Everyone makes mistakes."

He nodded toward his legs. "This is a big mistake."

There were far worse things in a human body to break than bones. "You'll heal. Don't worry. Good as new in no time."

The corners of his mouth turned down. His dark eyes flooded. "I'm going to miss basketball season."

"I bet Coach Payne will let you sit on the bench and cheer for your team." The high school basketball coach was one of the nicest people in Quincy and he loved his players.

Dante sighed. "Yeah. I guess."

"Eat your dinner," I said, turning on the television. "I'll tell your mom that a little TV time was doctor ordered for stress relief and pain management."

The tears in his eyes only seemed to multiply as he swirled some spaghetti around his fork.

Poor kid. He'd learned a hard lesson this week.

"Mind if I sit with you?" I asked, checking my watch. There was always work to be done, but I'd stick around until his mom got here.

"That's cool." He shrugged and ate another bite.

I pulled up the guest chair. "What do you feel like watching? ESPN? Disney? Cartoon Network?"

"ESPN."

I scrolled through the guide and found the right channel.

Dante's attention was instantly rapt on the small screen and the sports news recap.

ESPN wasn't a channel I watched, mostly because I didn't have the desire to keep up on professional sports. But also because it came with too high a risk of seeing Foster on television.

Dante's mother had been right. We should have left the TV off.

Like the universe knew I was tuned in, the announcers changed the topic from football to the UFC. The show cut to an interview where a reporter was holding a microphone to a man's face.

The man was wearing a pair of sweats and a tank top, his muscled arms covered in tattoos. Between the beeps they used to cover his curse words, he was talking smack about a fight.

"Scott Savage is going to kick that *beep* boy's ass. You *beep* hear me? He's old. Man needs to hang it up. Scott Savage is sending him into retirement."

"This guy is such a douche," Dante scoffed. "He always talks about himself in the third person. With both his names. Who does that? I hope Foster Madden kicks his ass."

This—Scott Savage—was Foster's opponent for his upcoming fight? I hated him already. *Cocky bastard.* "Me too."

Foster's face came on the screen, for just a minute, as the announcer recapped the fight date and each man's stats.

Foster, on ESPN.

It was surreal to see him on the screen. I'd always believed he would achieve great things. I'd believed in him so hard that the loss of that faith had only multiplied the emptiness when he was gone.

I dropped my gaze to the floor and tuned out the television.

It was easy, like placing a pair of earmuffs over my ears.

He had a daughter.

A lovely girl who was a mirror of Vivienne, from her chocolate eyes to the shade of her hair—brown with red streaks that glowed like copper strands under the sun.

My hand came to my heart. No matter how hard I pressed, the ache wouldn't go away. Tears welled in my eyes.

Kadence. Cute name for a cute kid.

A name I would have known had I looked him up.

Maybe I should have looked him up years ago. But I definitely should have done my research when he'd arrived in Quincy. Before I'd let him into my home. My body.

Oh my God, I was an idiot. Such a fucking idiot.

Of course they had a kid. Kids? Did they have more than one child? They'd been married long enough to have a family.

Foster and Vivienne. And Kadence.

The Maddens.

My heart twisted again.

"Uh, are you okay?" Dante was staring at my profile, fork hovering above his plate.

"All good." I lifted the remote and notched up the volume. Then I wiped the corner of my eye and sat straighter, staying until his mom breezed into the room, not caring a bit that he was watching TV while he'd had his dinner.

The ache in my chest lingered through the remainder of my shift. When I stood in the locker room, staring at the tally marks on the inside of my locker, the pain only grew.

What was the point of keeping track of good days? Should I erase the lines? Should I toss the marker in the trash? I'd been so determined to win over the nurses, my colleagues and our patients. To prove myself.

They didn't even call me Dr. Eden. Maybe I hadn't earned it.

I pressed my fingers to the marks, hesitating for a moment, before swiping them away. Then I pulled on my coat, slammed the locker closed and exited into the cold, dark night.

The streets of Quincy were quiet. Tiny snowflakes floated from the sky, catching the beams of my headlights. When I reached the turn off Main that would lead me home, I hesitated, almost continuing straight. Almost driving to the ranch for the night to sleep at Mom and Dad's.

But I turned, knowing that Foster's truck would be parked in front of my house.

It was.

The man himself sat on my porch's top stair.

After pulling the Jeep into the garage, I trudged inside, my footsteps as heavy as my heart. Flipping on the lights as I made my way to the front door, I slipped outside and joined him on the stair. We sat with our elbows on our knees, gazes aimed forward.

My anger from last night had faded. Or maybe it was just masked with this numbness. Shutting down seemed like the only way to keep from feeling too much.

It might have been peaceful, sitting in the night, sheltered from the snow. There were no streetlamps in my neighborhood. The only light came from the homes, golden and cheerful and warm. I was the only single person who lived on this block. Every other house belonged to a family.

It might have been peaceful.

Except tonight, I'd never felt so alone.

"Where's your daughter?" I asked.

"With Vivienne at the hotel." He dragged a palm over his

beard. "I thought you knew."

"How would I know?"

"Figured you'd looked me up at some point."

"Never."

Foster's frame deflated. "Never."

Never. The severity, the magnitude, of that word seemed as endless as the night sky above.

"Kadence starts school here tomorrow."

I sat up straighter. "What?"

"That's part of why I'm here. I don't want her growing up in Vegas. I don't want her part of that world."

"So you came here? To *my* world?"

"Quincy is where you are."

Foster had come to Montana for me. I'd known that for weeks now, but tonight, it hit differently. He hadn't just moved himself. He'd moved his daughter. His family.

"You told me that if I heard you out and I still wanted you to leave, that you'd go. You weren't going to leave, were you?"

He met my gaze. "Never."

Never.

"I have never been, and never will be, in love with Vivienne," he said. "I have never stopped loving you."

"Foster—"

"And I never will."

My hand came to my chest for what felt like the hundredth time today. I pressed and pressed and pressed. But it did nothing to stop my heart from cracking. Jagged lines began to split, right down my center.

There was a reason I hadn't dated. There was a reason I hadn't moved on with my life. Why I didn't have a husband or family of my own. Why I was married to my career.

His *never*s mirrored my own.

That's why this hurt so much. I'd given him my heart and never taken it back.

I stood from the step, making my way to the sidewalk, then I stepped into the snow on the yard, my tennis shoes sinking into the fluff. The ice slipped beneath the hem of my pants, melting against my skin.

This fresh snow had added a perfect layer of white, like the powdered sugar Lyla sprinkled on her pastries.

I was careful with my steps, doing my best not to leave unneeded marks in the pristine surface, then lay on my back, legs straight with my arms at my sides.

Scrubs weren't exactly snow gear. My legs were instantly cold, but I didn't care. I made a snow angel, raising my arms and sweeping out my legs, all while I kept my eyes locked on the few stars that dared shine past the clouds.

Foster followed, joining me on the snow. He lay still for a few moments, his eyes on the heavens, until his legs moved. Then his arms. He made his own angel, then gave up the sky to stare at my face.

"How old is she?" I asked. "Your daughter?"

"There is more to say than I said last night."

"Answer the question."

Deep down, I knew the answer, or had a rough idea. I was a doctor in a small town, which meant I saw a lot of kids in exam rooms. Kids needing their yearly checkups. Kids getting shots for kindergarten. Kids with bumps and bruises. Kids who had lost their front teeth, usually around the time they were six or seven.

Foster blew out a long breath, the wisps floating over the snow around us. "She turned seven last month."

Seven.

We'd been apart seven years. Which meant if the girl's birthday was in December, Vivienne had been pregnant before I'd left.

"I never cheated on you, Talia."

Another never.

Was I a fool to believe them?

"Will you let me explain?" He reached for me, his cold fingers clasping around mine. "Please."

I didn't answer. I tugged my hand free and stood, leaving Foster in the yard as I went inside.

• • •

When I woke the next morning and peeked out the window, our snow angels were gone. Erased by the storm and the inches of snow that had fallen overnight.

Erased, like they had never been.

I cried for an hour before I went to work.

I wanted the angels back.

CHAPTER 13

FOSTER

I glanced at the clock on the microwave. "Shit. I'm late."

"Here." Jasper opened the fridge, grabbed a bottle of water, tossing it my way. "Tomorrow."

"Tomorrow. Will you lock up before you go?" I caught the bottle, waved, then jogged for the door, not waiting for his reply as I hustled outside and into the truck.

Jasper had been here since nine this morning, whipping my ass into shape. In Vegas, we'd start our days earlier, around six and end around lunch. But in Quincy, our training hours would be dictated by Kadence's school schedule.

So Jasper would come at nine, after I dropped Kaddie off at school, and we'd end by two, giving me just enough time to take a quick shower before heading into town to pick her up.

Today was the first official day of training since I'd moved, and Jasper hadn't held back. After an intense cardio and calisthenics rotation, we'd spent two grueling hours in the ring doing takedown drills. All to get ready for this fight with Scott fucking Savage.

Normally, just thinking that asshole's name would give me a surge of adrenaline. A thrill at the idea of putting that mouthy piece of shit in his place. But my head, my heart, wasn't in it. Something Jasper had commented on numerous times today whenever he'd caught me staring off into the distance, thinking about Talia.

It had been six days since we'd made snow angels in her front yard.

I'd given her time, foolishly hoping that she'd come around. She hadn't. Every day that went by, my hopes faded.

The only bright part of the past six days had been Kadence.

My phone rang as I drove, Vivienne's name popping up on the screen. "Hey."

"Hi. How was training?"

"Long day," I said. "I'm running a little late."

"That's okay. I'll just wait." Vivienne wanted to be on the phone when I picked up Kadence. If she couldn't be here in person, this was the next best option.

"You doing okay?" I asked.

"I hate this. I miss her. Phone calls aren't enough."

"I know exactly what you mean. It's temporary."

She sighed. "I know but it still sucks."

Last week had been a short week at school. Vivienne had stayed in Quincy, making sure Kaddie was settled into the apartment. They'd slept together in the bedroom and unpacked Kaddie's suitcases, filling her closet and drawers. They'd hung up some photos on the walls and tried to make it like home.

Then Vivienne had left on Saturday. We'd driven her the two hours to Missoula to the airport, and after a tearful goodbye, she'd flown to Vegas while Kadence and I had driven home to Quincy.

She'd cried for almost an hour of that trip. And I'd been

helpless to distract her since I'd needed to keep my eyes on the road.

For Vivienne's next trip, I'd charter a plane so she could fly directly to Quincy and land at the small, local airport that offered no commercial flights. At least that would save us all the drive.

"Are we making a mistake?" she asked.

"I hope not." I blew out a long breath. We were trying to be good parents. We were trying to make the right decisions for our daughter. Quincy held the promise of a wonderful life and childhood.

"Is she doing okay?"

"She's good, Vivi. Misses you too."

"It's temporary," she repeated. "I'll be there soon."

While I was here with Kaddie so she could start school, Vivienne was in Vegas. She was packing up the house so we could put it on the market. She'd sell Angel's. She was planning a wedding.

She was moving on from Arlo's blackmail too.

"Look, before I pick Kadence up, I need to talk to you about something," I said.

"Okay. What's up?"

"I have to tell Talia the truth. The whole truth." Including Vivienne's side of the story. If Talia had let me explain the other night, I would have.

"No. You promised me."

I clenched my jaw. "I'm losing her, Vivi. I can't lose her."

"I'll come this weekend. Can you just wait? Please?"

Fuck. "Fine."

"Thank you."

"Yeah," I mumbled.

The rest of the drive to town was in silence. I joined the parent pickup line, inching forward in the line of cars. Then there was my girl, jogging toward the truck, her backpack bouncing and her coat looped over an arm.

It was twenty-three degrees outside.

"Hi, Daddy." She smiled as she climbed into the back seat.

"Hi. Why aren't you wearing your coat?"

She groaned. "It's not that cold."

"Kadence Rose Madden," Vivienne said. "Wear your coat."

"Right now?" Her eyes pleaded as she settled into her booster seat.

"No, just buckle up." I cranked the heat, even though I was still burning up from the gym.

"Tell me all about your day, honey," Vivienne said.

"It was good, I guess." Kadence touched the side of her hair where the strands were shorter, hidden mostly unless you knew where to look.

The movement had become a habit of hers, one that made me wince.

"What was for lunch?" I asked as I pulled away from the school.

"Pizza."

"I like pizza. Was it good?"

"It was okay."

"Did you make some friends?" Vivi asked.

Kadence just shrugged. "Sorta."

I studied her through the rearview. Her eyes were on her lap. My beautiful girl with a beautiful spirit who was learning too young that people, especially other kids, could be cruel.

There was only one elementary school in Quincy. One middle school. One high school. Kadence would graduate with most of the kids she'd met last week. In a smaller community, I hoped she'd have the chance to build closer relationships with her classmates. That Vivienne and I could get a better read on parents. That we'd learn who to trust.

And who not to trust.

"Okay, Vivi, we'd better let you go," I said, slowing as the hospital came into view in the distance.

"You'll call me later, right?"

"Yeah."

"Bye, Mommy," Kadence said. "I love you."

"I love you too." Vivienne sniffled. She'd be crying after we hung up. And I suspected that her plan to stay in Vegas until summer would soon change. She wouldn't last six months this far away from our daughter, no matter how often she visited.

I pulled into the parking lot at Quincy Memorial, spotting Talia's Jeep in its usual spot. No matter what was happening between us, I always wanted to see her. I'd gone too long without her in my life. But today, part of me hoped we didn't bump into each other. For her sake, not mine.

It would be easier for Talia to see Kadence after Vivienne explained this weekend.

"Homework tonight?" I asked Kadence as I parked the truck in a visitor spot.

"Spelling words. But I know them all."

I twisted to give her a wink. "I'm sure you do."

She winked back.

I snagged her coat, then held her hand as we walked through the hospital's entrance. One day, Kaddie wouldn't want me to hold her hand, so I held it as often as she'd let me.

We checked in at the reception desk, then waited in the lobby until a nurse called us back. She took Kaddie's weight and measured her height before setting us up in an exam room.

"So this is just a well-child check?" the nurse asked as she took Kaddie's pulse.

"That's right."

A flyer had come home in her backpack Friday that first and second grade basketball was starting soon. Kadence wanted to play and since we were moving here—had moved here—she'd need a doctor. So I'd called and made an appointment with a Dr. Anderson.

Not Talia. Not yet. But someday.

This was the beginning of another round in the fight. My tactics so far had been futile. So it was time to back off, try another strategy.

Give her space. Let her contemplate the past from a different angle.

Talia had spent seven years thinking of me in a tainted light. She needed to adjust to this new hue.

The truth.

"Any concerns?" the nurse asked.

"Nope." I shook my head.

"Great." The nurse typed a few things into the computer, then stood. "Dr. Anderson was just finishing up with another patient, then he'll be in shortly."

"Appreciate it." I nodded as she slipped out of the room.

Kadence started swinging her legs on the exam table, the tissue paper under her butt crinkling.

"Want to read a book while we wait?" I asked, pointing to the basket of books on the floor.

"Nah."

The wallpaper was a hot air balloon pattern. There was a display case of Hot Wheels hanging on one wall. A jar of lollipops sat beside the sink next to a jar of tongue depressors.

"What should we have for dinner?" I asked Kaddie.

Before she could answer, a knock came at the door.

It wasn't Dr. Anderson who walked into the room.

Talia. My heart skipped.

She was wearing her scrubs and a white lab coat with a stethoscope draped around her neck. Her silky hair was up in a ponytail, the ends draping over a shoulder.

"Hi." She gave me a tight smile. "Dr. Anderson was held up and asked if I could do Kadence's checkup."

"Of course." I held my breath as she came into the exam room, closing the door behind her.

"Hi, Kadence." She extended her hand to my daughter. "I'm Talia."

"Hi." Kaddie gave her a shy smile, totally oblivious to the flash of pain on Talia's face when their hands touched.

Thankfully, that was the only time Talia looked bothered. She conducted the exam, chatting with Kadence and asking her questions about school. Professional and compassionate. Exactly the type of doctor I'd always known she'd make.

"Mrs. Edwards is a really nice teacher," Talia said. "Don't tell anyone I told you this, but she's the best first-grade teacher. You're lucky."

Kadence smiled, glancing in my direction.

"Okay, we're all done." Talia sat on the rolling stool, shaking the mouse on the computer. "Did you already get your flu shots?"

I nodded. "We did."

"Then you're all set." Talia hadn't looked at me once since she'd started the exam. Her focus had been entirely on her patient.

Fine by me. I could have kissed her for all the kind smiles she'd sent my daughter. Kaddie deserved that attention.

"Say thanks," I told my daughter.

"Thank you, Talia."

"Dr. Eden," I corrected.

Talia had earned that title. In this building, we'd use it.

"Dr. Eden," Kadence repeated.

Talia looked at me for the first time, and there was something in her expression I couldn't read.

"What is it?"

"Nothing." She waved it off. "The exit is down the hallway and to your left."

"Wait." I stood before she could disappear. "Can I have a minute?"

"Um—"

"Great, thanks." I motioned for Kadence to hop off the exam table. "Put on your shoes, then just hang in the hallway for a minute, okay, little bug? I just need to talk to Dr. Eden for a second."

As soon as Kaddie was out the door, I eased it closed. Then I framed Talia's face in my hands and, before she could stop me, sealed my lips over hers. One lick of my tongue against her lower lip and she whimpered, opening for me.

I slanted my mouth over hers, sweeping inside. God, she tasted good. The best in this damn world. Fire raced through my veins as her tongue tangled with mine. Her hands came to my arms, clutching tight.

We couldn't be over. Not yet. Not if she kissed me like this.

I kissed her fast and deep, then let her go.

Okay, so maybe I wasn't giving her space.

"What was that for?" she asked, stepping away. Her hand

floated to her lips, not to wipe my kiss away, but to touch it.

"To say thanks."

"For an exam?"

"For being kind to Kadence. This has been a hard year for her."

"I was just doing my job." She made a move for the door, but I snagged her hand before she could escape.

"I remember everything you ever told me about Quincy. How people left their homes without locking the doors. How the town was decked out in the school's colors whenever a team made it to a championship. I came here for you, Tally. I'll stay for you. But I came for Kadence too. Because I'd do anything to give her your childhood instead of mine."

Talia studied my face for a long moment, then nodded, tugging out of my grasp to open the door. Except she had to rear back when another woman, hand raised to knock, nearly collided with her. "Oh, sorry, Rachel."

"Talia." Rachel's lips pursed in a thin line. "I'm not a babysitter."

"We were just—"

Before Talia could finish explaining, Rachel sneered and walked away.

What the fuck?

Talia's shoulders fell in defeat. She masked it quickly, smiling at Kaddie before walking away.

What the hell was that about? Kadence was standing against the wall, not moving, not causing trouble, just waiting like I'd asked. No babysitting necessary for the two minutes it had taken to kiss Talia.

"Let's go." I held out my hand and took Kaddie's, leading her toward the exit. But before we pushed through the door that would take us to the lobby, I glanced over my shoulder just in time to see Talia jogging to catch up.

She had Kaddie's coat in her hand.

We'd both forgotten it.

"Here." She handed it over, then took a step back. Then another.

"Thank you, Dr. Eden." I dipped my chin.

There was that strange expression again. Almost confusion. "Nobody, um...calls me Dr. Eden."

"Do you not like it?"

"No, I don't mind. I guess I'm just Talia here. Most people in Quincy have known me since I was a kid."

"So?" They could still treat her with the respect she'd earned.

She lifted a shoulder. "Bye, Foster."

"Dr. Eden?" I stopped her before she could turn away.

"Yeah?" The corner of her mouth turned up. If she liked hearing me call her Dr. Eden, I liked saying it. I was damn proud of what she'd accomplished.

"You'll never be *just Talia*. Not to me."

Those sparkling blue eyes lit up. And as much as I hated to lose the smile on her face, I didn't mind a bit when she gave it to Kadence instead.

"See you around, Miss Madden."

Kaddie giggled.

Talia laughed.

And just like that, I was back in this fight.

ROUND 4

CHAPTER 14

TALIA

You'll never be just Talia. Not to me.

In the four days since Foster and Kadence had come to the hospital, I'd replayed his words a hundred times. A thousand. And every time, my heart ached a little less. My anger faded a little more.

Time was healing.

So were truths.

"Good night," I told the nurse at the reception counter in the hospital's lobby as I strode past her desk. "Have a great weekend."

"You too, Talia," she said with a wave.

Should I correct her? Should I ask everyone to call me Dr. Eden? No. That would only make it awkward. And for what? My pride? My ego? All I wanted was for people to trust me as their doctor. Their colleague. I didn't need the title.

But I also wouldn't mind it.

Funny how the only person who'd insisted on calling me Dr. Eden had been Foster. A man who knew me intimately. A man who had whispered my name while being inside my body. But he'd insisted on calling me Dr. Eden. He'd insisted Kadence do the same.

Was that why I'd kissed him? Or because when it came to Foster, I had no control?

God, that kiss. A woman could survive on a kiss like that each day. Just thinking about it made my heart flutter. Resisting him was impossible.

Foster Madden had a presence as powerful as a thunderclap.

I was the woman who'd always loved his wild storm.

What were we doing? For so many years, my next steps had been planned. The path stretched before me so long that I hadn't worried about what was waiting at the end.

Undergrad. Med school. Residency. The end of the road was in sight. The years had passed in a blur. What next?

What about Foster?

Over and over, I'd replayed what he'd told me about Arlo. About Vegas and the fights. About being trapped. He'd said there was more to discuss. There was.

Kadence.

Foster had promised he'd never cheated on me with Vivienne. Was it foolish to believe him? For a week, I'd searched my heart for doubts and come up empty.

Who was that little girl? The better question wasn't who... but whose? If not Foster, then who was her father?

I drove away from the hospital and headed downtown, parking in the lot behind the hotel beside my brother's truck.

Knox had texted me earlier tonight to see if I wanted to eat at Knuckles. Maybe he'd heard that Lyla and I were currently not speaking to each other. Or maybe Lyla had told him about Foster.

I'd been avoiding my family for a week because I didn't want them playing mediators between Lyla and me. But it was time to show my face, and when it came to my siblings, we all picked favorites.

Mateo was mine. But since he was currently flying planes in Alaska and relatively out of touch, I was going to my second favorite—Knox. Even though *his* favorite was Lyla.

I walked inside the hotel, having traded my scrubs in the locker room for jeans and a navy sweater.

Eloise was at the front desk with the phone sandwiched between her shoulder and ear so she could type with both hands.

I tapped the counter and waved so she'd know I was here.

"One minute," she mouthed.

Leaving her to finish the call, I walked to the sitting area next to the lobby's fireplace and stood beside the hearth, soaking in its warmth.

This hotel had been in our family for generations. Mom had managed it when I was younger, working here while Dad handled the ranch. But in recent years, Eloise had claimed The Eloise as hers. Fitting.

There was a vanilla candle burning on the coffee table, the scent mingling with the fire. Smoke and sweetness. The holiday decorations had been taken down, but she'd kept the small golden lights wrapped around the windows that overlooked Main.

Eloise had probably lit this fire herself so the lobby would be cozy and welcoming on a cold January night. This was her hotel, even if her name wasn't officially on the deed quite yet. My youngest sister had grown into one hell of a businesswoman.

Footsteps sounded behind me and I turned. Maybe Eloise could join us for dinner— My smile dropped.

Vivienne.

Seeing her was inevitable. I'd known this moment was coming. That didn't make it easier. What was she doing here at the hotel?

"Hi." Her voice was shaky as she stopped behind a couch.

She looked grown up. I guess I probably looked the same. Her chestnut hair was shorter than it had been in college, falling past her shoulders. Her face was just as beautiful, the features more defined. Her Chanel bag was slung over a shoulder. Her coat was from Prada. She looked stunning and rich and every bit a famous UFC fighter's wife—ex-wife.

A flare of rage, of bitterness born from betrayal, caused my muscles to tense. I fisted my hands, my spine rigid.

She touched the leather, then took her hands away, tucking them into the pockets of her coat only to take them out again and put them back. She should be nervous. "It's good to see you."

I arched an eyebrow.

Foster had been blackmailed into this marriage. But what was her excuse? She'd known how much I'd loved him. How many nights had we spent in our apartment, laughing and gossiping? How many times had she teased me for having hearts in my eyes?

And she'd taken him. She'd taken my place.

Vivienne opened her mouth, then closed it, struggling for words. She might not have them, but I did.

"You were my best friend. I told you more than I told my twin sister. I *loved* you. How could you?" Without waiting for her answer, I strode from the fireplace, keeping my eyes locked on Eloise still at the front desk.

"Talia, please." Vivienne stepped closer, her hand stretching out.

I shied away, not wanting her to touch me.

"I'm sorry."

"Everyone is sorry these days," I said.

"No one more than Foster." Her shoulders fell. "He's always loved you. Always. He regretted everything that happened. Hate me if you need to. But not him."

"Defending your husband?" I hated that she could claim that title.

"Please let me explain."

"Everyone has apologies and explanations. I'm so sick of explanations that come seven years too late. Fuck you."

Her pretty face paled.

Damn it. An icky feeling crept beneath my skin. I wasn't mean. I didn't like being mean. So it was time to go because I was angry, and I'd say things that would only make us both feel worse.

"I was pregnant," Vivienne blurted.

So much for my escape. I faced her, crossing my arms over my chest. "Obviously. I met your daughter."

Vivienne stepped closer, glancing over her shoulder toward the door before lowering her voice. "Kadence isn't...she isn't Foster's biological child."

Relief. Sweet relief that my guess hadn't been wrong. That Foster hadn't cheated. But who? If not Foster, then who? It was on the tip of my tongue to ask, but I kept my lips locked together.

"Kadence doesn't know," Vivienne said. "She doesn't need to know. Foster is her dad. She loves him. He loves her. And he loves you. If you still have feelings for him, please give him a second chance."

The pleading in her eyes made me uncross my arms.

"He used to talk about you," she said. "All the time. Especially in those early years. Talia this and Talia that. It was like he wanted to say things out loud so he wouldn't forget how much you liked strawberry ice cream or having Bravo on in the background while you studied. How you'd only wear his T-shirts to bed and hum along with the hair dryer."

Foster had talked about me while I'd tried my hardest not to even think his name.

"I'd get so jealous," Vivienne said.

"Because you were in love with him."

"No." She scoffed. "No offense, but gross. Foster is my best friend in the world but he might as well be my brother. Maybe if I hadn't known that he'd already given you his heart, that would be different. But it never was. I don't love him."

"Then why were you jealous?"

"Because he will love you for his entire life. Whether you forgive him or not. That's why I'm jealous."

A lump formed in my throat. "He broke me."

Vivienne nodded. "I'm sorry. I'm sorry for what my father did. I'm sorry I didn't recognize the monster in him sooner. I'm sorry for my role in it too and not pushing harder to change the situation. I'm so sorry, Talia. I wish we could go back. Do better. But that's why he's here. To fix our mistakes."

She loved him. Maybe not a romantic love, but the love of family. She would plead Foster's case, drop to her knees and beg, because she loved him.

She'd had years to love him. To be his friend. Vivienne knew him better than I did. She wasn't the only one who was jealous.

"Hey." Eloise appeared at my side, a smile on her face.

I tore my gaze from Vivienne and hugged my sister. "Hi."

"What's up?" She glanced between Vivienne and me, probably trying to figure out why I was talking to her. Maybe Vivi was a guest here again.

"Just chatting," I said. "I'm having dinner at Knuckles."

"Oh, fun." Eloise pointed toward the reception counter. "I'm manning the front desk for a few more hours, otherwise I'd join you."

"I'll bring you a dessert," I told her, then cast one last glance at Vivienne.

She had tears in her eyes. Maybe she'd thought an apology would erase the past. Maybe she was right. But not tonight.

So I took a step away, walking with Eloise to the desk, where I left her to work while I continued to Knuckles.

Knox's restaurant was bustling, like it was most Friday nights. Conversation and laughter filled the room from wall to wall as I followed the waitress to a booth Knox had reserved for me. The dark and moody atmosphere fit my own.

"Can I get you anything besides water to drink?" she asked.

"Wine. Red. Any red in any big, big glass."

She laughed. "You got it, Talia."

"Thanks." I stripped off my coat and slid into the booth, sinking into the seat and closing my eyes.

Too harsh. I'd been too harsh to Vivienne. Though I wasn't the one who'd married her best friend's boyfriend.

The table shifted and I opened my eyes, expecting my brother.

But it was Foster who took the opposite side of the booth. My heart leapt. It always leapt, the traitorous organ.

"What are you doing?"

He answered by plucking the wine list from where it was propped against the brick wall.

"Foster," I drawled.

"Talia."

I glanced over my shoulder. Were Vivienne and Kadence nearby?

"They went out to dinner together. Vivienne is visiting for the weekend before she heads back to Vegas."

"And you're not joining them?"

"Nope."

The waitress returned with my wine, startled by Foster's presence. "Oh, I'm sorry. Knox said he was eating with you tonight."

"He is—"

"Not." Foster gave her his most charming smile. "Change of plan. I'll have red wine too. Whatever Talia's having."

"Foster," I warned, but he ignored me.

"What is your special tonight?" he asked the waitress.

She rattled it off, then after he ordered one for us both, she left us alone, probably to inform Knox that I had a date.

"You're exhausting." I took a long gulp from my wineglass.

He smirked, reaching across the table to take my free hand in his. "Vivienne said you talked."

"I was mean to her." *Shit.* "And now I feel guilty."

"She'll be okay." His thumb stroked my knuckles. "What did she tell you?"

"She told me about Kadence."

"Good." He sighed, like that was the answer he'd hoped I'd give. "It was important to her that she be the one to tell you."

"Why?"

He threaded his fingers through mine, staring at them like

he'd forgotten what it looked like to have our hands intertwined. "We both have regrets. Vivi carries a lot of guilt because it was her dad who put us in this position."

"What happened with her and Arlo?" Vivi had called him a monster in the lobby, but when I'd lived in Vegas, she'd adored him. "She said she was pregnant. Who is—"

"Me. I am Kadence's father. She is mine." There was an edge to Foster's voice before he swallowed hard, clearing his throat. "And she is not mine."

The waitress appeared at that moment, delivering Foster's glass of wine. He nodded his thanks, then took a sip. All while he kept his hand clasped with mine.

I didn't try to take it away. At the moment, he looked like he needed it.

"Vivienne was five months pregnant when you left. When Arlo blackmailed me after that fight."

"Five months?" I searched my memories for any signs. She hadn't been showing, which was normal that early with a first pregnancy. And Vivienne's style had trended toward boho chic with flowy tops and layered pieces. I couldn't remember her being sick. I couldn't remember her dating anyone.

"She was seeing a guy. They met at the gym, but I didn't know him. I guess he came in and out, was there for a short time. Probably because it was a well-known fact that if anyone touched Arlo's daughter, they were dead."

"It was?"

"Oh, yeah." Foster huffed. "Only a guy with a death wish would have chased Vivi at Angel's. Arlo wanted that to be her safe place. If anyone looked at her too long, one of us would run the guy off."

"But not this one."

Foster shook his head. "She kept it quiet, and he stopped coming to the gym. She said it was casual, mostly they'd meet and hook up. Then she got pregnant. Got scared. She wasn't sure how to tell anyone, including this guy. I guess he'd made some comments about not wanting kids."

"Oh." Vivienne had been going through all of that while we'd been living together. What kind of friend was I that I hadn't noticed? "She didn't say a thing to me."

"She kept it a secret from everyone. I think she was working up the courage to tell this guy first. She went over to his place one night to tell him but walked into a bad situation. This guy had a roommate. The roommate's girl was mouthy. Vivi said she was a lot of drama. Vivienne heard this commotion in the apartment, so she peeked inside. Her guy and his roommate were taking turns punching and kicking this woman."

I gasped. "Oh my God."

"Vivienne went straight to Arlo. It was the week of my fight."

"It was because of the baby that she married you, wasn't it?" I'd assumed she'd been in love with him.

"Vivi's guy was in a gang."

"What gang?"

"The kind where members end up dead more often than not. The kind with close connections to drug cartels."

I gaped. "And Vivienne didn't know?"

Foster shook his head. "Not a clue. Not until after Arlo laid it out. When she told him she was pregnant and told him what she saw at that apartment, Arlo went ballistic."

"And that's when he decided you were going to get married."

"Yeah. He had me by the balls. So he just kept twisting. Arlo wanted Vivienne safe. He wanted her to have money.

Security. And yeah, she could have moved in with him. Arlo could have watched out for her. But why, when I was a long-term solution with enough earning potential for her, the baby, and him on top? He wanted his daughter married to the man of his choosing. He saw her fear and the chance to take control, so he capitalized on it."

"Why would Vivienne agree?" She could have told Arlo to go to hell and not married Foster.

"She was terrified. She wanted to keep the baby. And Arlo, that manipulative son of a bitch, took everything he knew about that gang and threw it in her face. Made sure she wasn't just scared, but petrified. Told her that if she didn't marry me, this guy might figure it out. Might try to hurt her before she could have the baby. That the best way to avoid it was to make the world think this kid was mine."

The cost? My heart. "Do you think it was true? Do you think this guy would have hurt her?"

"Maybe. More importantly, Vivienne believed it. So she went along with her father's wishes. Arlo knew I'd never hurt Vivi. He knew I could provide for her, and if I was his son-in-law, it was just another way to shove those hooks deeper into my spine."

"And the guy from the gang? What about him?"

"A month before Kadence was born, he showed at the gym looking for Vivi. He was stoned out of his damn mind. Reeked of booze. I told him I married her. Lied and said we'd been hooking up for years."

"He believed you?"

Foster shrugged. "We never saw him again. About two years ago, Arlo came to the gym with an obituary."

"He died."

Foster nodded. "Two gunshot wounds to the chest."

I tensed. "Who knows about this?"

"Me. Vivi. Jasper. Arlo." He blew out a long breath. "And you. I'd like to keep that list as short as possible."

Because Kadence was his daughter and he wouldn't lose her.

"Someday Kaddie will need to know," he said. "But even then, it won't change the fact that I'm her father. She is *my* daughter."

"She is your daughter." Just like Drake was Knox's son, even if it wasn't Eden blood in Drake's veins. He was ours. Like Kadence was Foster's.

"So Arlo convinced Vivienne to marry you," I said. "But if that guy believed you and disappeared, why didn't you get your marriage annulled? Or why not after her ex died? Why did she stay married to you?"

"Arlo never let either of us forget the cards he was holding. He reminded Vivienne that he'd ruin my career if we got divorced. He'd paint me as a criminal, and since Kadence isn't mine, he'd file a custody suit to take her away. Claim that Vivienne was unfit."

"Could he do that?"

Foster shrugged. "It would have been bullshit, and we would have fought it. But it would have been a fucking mess regardless. And the person who would have suffered the most was—"

"Kadence."

"Yeah." He gave me a sad smile. "Vivienne and I weren't willing to risk her happiness simply to test Arlo. He never let go of the strings. Every year he just wound them tighter."

"What do you mean?"

"Besides ruining me, he never let me forget what he could do to you."

My eyes bugged out. "Me? I was gone."

"Maybe from Las Vegas." Foster tapped his heart. "But not here. Arlo saw it plain as day. I couldn't risk it."

So Foster and Vivienne had played into Arlo's hands. Everyone had stayed quiet until the day he'd died.

My head was spinning again. Swirling around the truth, trying to make sense of what I'd convinced myself since leaving Vegas. Maybe there had been a better way. A path that wouldn't have been so hard for us all.

Would I have done differently in Vivienne's place? Or Foster's?

There was no way to know.

"I don't know what to say to all of this." Maybe I should have been livid. But damn, I was tired of being angry. I was tired of being hurt and confused. I didn't have the energy for any of it tonight. "I wish you had told me."

"What if we forgot?" Foster asked, his thumb caressing my hand. "What if we forgot the past? What if we forgot the world, just for tonight?"

"I'd like to forget. Just for tonight." The words slipped past my lips. The smile that stretched across Foster's face made them worth it.

The waitress appeared, two plates in hand with Knox's famous cheeseburgers and fries. She set them down, forcing Foster to release my hand. "Anything else?" she asked.

"Ranch," Foster said. "Please."

He didn't like ranch. But I did.

I grabbed the bottle of ketchup, twisting open the cap, just as Foster lifted the tomatoes off his plate and put them on mine.

"You could have ordered it without tomatoes."

"But you like them." He didn't. But I did. "Do you remember our first date?"

I laughed. "You mean the time you ambushed me at my favorite diner? Your tactics haven't changed."

"It worked for me then." He chuckled, the light in his eyes dancing. "Figured, why not try again?"

We'd been flirting at Angel's for months. It had gone on so long that I'd begun to think I'd misread everything between us because Foster hadn't once hinted at a date.

Instead, he'd just taken it. In true Foster fashion.

He'd found out from Vivienne that I liked to study at this fifties-themed diner not far from our apartment. The booths were spacious. It was rarely busy. And even though the smell of grease would stick in my hair so badly I'd have to shower whenever I got home, the scent reminded me of home. Of coming home from school to find Mom in the kitchen, frying burgers for dinner because Dad always said he could eat a cheeseburger for every meal for the rest of his life and die a happy man.

Foster had slid into my booth at that diner one night, exactly like he had tonight, and we'd talked for hours. We'd been nearly inseparable from that moment on.

"I want to start over, Tally."

It sounded so easy. So simple. Foster and me, starting fresh. "Do you really think that's possible?"

He shrugged. "Why not? Unless you're afraid to try."

"Are you baiting me?"

Foster smiled, arrogant and assured. "Is it working?"

I fought a smile and took a drink of my wine. Maybe. Maybe it was.

CHAPTER 15

FOSTER

"Fuck, it's cold." Jasper rubbed his hands together, blowing on them as he bounced on his toes in the ring.

"I need to buy more space heaters." I rubbed my temples. If only this headache would go away.

But it wouldn't. Because the headache was directly tied to my furnace—the furnace that had quit working five days ago. I'd come home from my dinner with Talia to a freezing cold gym.

I probably should have expected it with how hard the damn thing had been running since I'd bought this place. I should have had someone inspect it earlier.

The guy who'd come to look at it Saturday had laughed, saying I was lucky it had worked this long.

There was no repairing it. If this had been Vegas, I probably would have had a new one that same day. Except this was Quincy and they'd needed to order a replacement because the two they had on hand were spoken for. My furnace wouldn't arrive until Friday.

So for the past five days, I'd been heating the gym and apartment with electric space heaters.

"Of course this doesn't happen in the spring or summer," I told Jasper. "Has to happen on the coldest damn week of the year."

The high today was forecasted to be three. Three fucking degrees above zero.

"My toes are numb," he grumbled.

"Mine too." Most of the heaters were in the apartment, making sure it stayed warm enough for Kadence. The ones out here were barely cutting the chill. The gym was simply too big and the temperature too low.

"I'm not cut out for Montana," he said.

I scoffed. "I'm not sure I am either."

This morning, I'd taken Kadence to school dressed like a marshmallow in her bibs, puffer coat, boots, hat and mittens. The snow was a novelty for her, part of the adventure. But even she'd complained about the cold, and on the ride to school this morning, she'd been sullen and quiet.

"Okay." I rolled my shoulders and jumped up and down, gearing up for whatever else Jasper had planned for today's training session. We'd been at it for hours, each of us pushing hard simply because if we were moving, we weren't freezing. "What's next?"

"I want to practice some sweeps. I've been studying videos from Savage's previous fights and I noticed a pattern in his later rounds. When he gets gassed, he sinks into his heels. Might be an opportunity to sweep for a takedown."

"All right." I cracked my neck and got into my fighting stance, arms raised.

Jasper mirrored my position, facing off.

I stopped worrying about the cold. I stopped thinking about anything outside of this ring. I focused on my opponent, ready to jab, fake a kick by raising my knee, then sweep my lead leg against his, hoping to get him off-balance.

Except before I could move, the chime of my phone filled the air.

"Ah. Sorry." I rushed to the side of the ring. The school's name flashed on the screen. "Hello?"

"Is this Foster?" a woman asked.

"Yes."

"This is Denise, the school nurse. I've got Kadence with me and she's got a 100.3 fever."

I'd started ripping off my shin pads before she'd even finished her sentence. "I'll be right there."

"What's going on?" Jasper asked as I hung up, taking off the other shin pad.

"Kadence is sick. I gotta go."

"What can I do?"

"I don't have any kids Tylenol." *Fuck.* "Or a thermometer."

Why hadn't I bought any medicine, just in case? I ducked between the ropes, rushing to the apartment to pull on a hoodie and a pair of sweats over my shorts. When I came out with keys, Jasper was pulling on his shoes, dressed similarly to me.

"I'll hit the store and get supplies. Meet you back here."

"Thanks." I nodded and jogged for the door.

The outside air was a frigid slap to the face, the wind biting into my skin, so I quickened my steps, blasting the heat in the truck as I sped into town and whipped into the school's parking loop.

Kadence was waiting by the front desk with the nurse when I burst through the front door.

"Hi, little bug." I dropped to a knee and pressed one palm

to her forehead while the other took the backpack off her shoulders and slung it over mine. "Not feeling good?"

She shook her head.

I glanced up to the nurse. "Do I need to check her out or anything?"

"We'll take care of it. Feel better, Kadence."

She forced a smile, looking like she was about to cry. Guess her mood this morning hadn't been about the cold, but about feeling crappy.

But she'd made it nearly through the whole day. Why hadn't she told me she wasn't feeling well? Or made the school call me sooner?

"Let's go home." I picked her up, thanked the nurse, then carried my girl to the truck. When she was buckled in her seat, I pressed a kiss to her temple and hurried to the driver's side.

"Daddy?" she asked as I pulled onto the road.

"Yeah?"

"Am I gonna miss school tomorrow?"

I glanced at her through the rearview mirror. "I don't know. Depends on how you're feeling. Why?"

The corners of her mouth turned down. "We were supposed to have a popcorn party."

"Is that why you didn't tell me you were feeling icky this morning?"

Her chin dropped. "It's Maggie's birthday today and she brought cupcakes."

My sweet girl.

I felt awful that she was missing fun and so fucking happy that she wanted to be at school, that she was making friends. "If you miss it tomorrow, I'll get you popcorn, okay? The most important thing is we get you feeling better."

She slumped against the door, and by the time we made it to the gym, she was asleep.

Jasper hadn't made it back from the store yet, so I carried Kadence inside, stripping off her coat and getting her into bed. Then I dug my phone from my pocket and called the first person who came to mind, hoping like hell she hadn't changed her number.

"Hello?" Talia answered.

"Hey."

"Foster?"

The surprise in her voice was another punch in the gut. "You deleted my number."

"Oh, um...yeah."

She'd erased my contact info while I'd kept hers safe and memorized her 406 number just in case. That was on me, not Talia. And at the moment, I didn't have time to worry over past mistakes.

"Kadence is sick. She's got a fever."

"What temp?"

"It's 100.3."

"Have you given her anything?"

"Not yet." I stalked to a window, searching down the road for Jasper's Yukon. "Should I bring her to the hospital? I'm starting to freak out."

"Has she never been sick before?"

"Yeah, she has. But I don't do good with this stuff. Vivienne is the calm parent."

There was a jingle in the background, like she'd picked up a set of keys. "I'll be over in a minute."

"You're not working?"

"Not today. See you in a few."

The air rushed out of my lungs as I ended the call. Then I paced the apartment, calling Vivienne next, and when she didn't answer, I left a message.

Every time I passed a space heater, it was too hot. When I got close to a window or the doorway, it was too cold.

Kadence hadn't once complained about the apartment or the gym. My girl was a trooper. But her room was small, and despite Vivienne's efforts to hang photos and decorate, it wasn't home. This place wasn't a home.

"Hi." Jasper walked into the apartment with a plastic grocery sack in one hand. I was so stuck in my head I hadn't noticed him drive up.

"What the hell was I thinking living here?" I threw an arm in the air. "I should have a house. A real home with two bedrooms and a goddamn working furnace."

"Maybe you should crash with me for a few days until they get the heat working."

"I'm going to call the hotel." The A-frame he'd rented was nice, but it was small and there wouldn't be room for all three of us. It wasn't much bigger than this apartment. "Thanks for offering. And for going to the store."

"Anytime."

I dragged a hand through my hair, my eyes cast to the bedroom. "I hate it when she's sick. I feel helpless."

"She'll be fine." Jasper put the bag on the counter just as a car door slammed. We both glanced to the window, watching as Talia hopped out of her Jeep. "Looks like you called in reinforcements."

"Yeah."

"Holler if you need anything." He walked out of the apartment, his voice low as he greeted Talia.

"Hi." She stepped across the threshold and my lungs filled with air. I could breathe again.

"Hi. Thanks for coming."

"Sure." She walked straight for the counter, rifling through the bag Jasper had brought. "You haven't given her anything yet, right?"

"No, not yet."

"Okay." She worked efficiently, pouring some red medicine into the tiny plastic cup. Then, with the thermometer in hand, she went to the bedroom, sitting on the edge of the bed as she coaxed Kadence awake. "Hi, Miss Madden. Your dad says you're not feeling so good?"

She shook her head. "Uh-uh."

"Can you sit up for me?"

Kaddie obeyed, her eyelids droopy.

Talia took her temperature, still high, then helped Kaddie drink down the Tylenol. Then she tucked my daughter into bed before we retreated to the kitchen.

"Thank you," I said, easing Kadence's door closed. "Vivienne was always in charge of this sort of thing. I get a little worked up."

"And she is...not here?"

"She's back in Vegas. It's not an ideal arrangement, but it's only temporary. She'll move sooner or later, but we wanted to get Kadence into school here as soon as possible."

"Ah." Talia nodded, pulling the sleeves of her coat over her fingers. "It's chilly in here."

"The furnace broke." I scrubbed my hands over my face. "It won't be fixed until Friday. I've been trying to stick it out, but I'm going to call the hotel. See if they've got a room." Time to tap out.

"I'm sure whatever bug she has isn't related. She's in a new school. New friends come with new germs."

"But the cold can't be helping. It's drafty and cramped. If she's still sick on Friday, I want her to get some rest, and if they're putting in a new furnace, it will be loud. And to be honest, I'm sick of sleeping on the couch."

Talia glanced at the couch and the blankets I'd folded on a seat this morning.

"Know anyone who has a place for rent?" I asked. "Or for sale?"

"It's January. Quincy doesn't exactly have a booming housing market, especially in the winter."

I sighed. My asshole of a realtor should have told me about the condition of the gym. Or I should have asked for a virtual walk-through. Maybe if he'd known I was bringing my daughter to live here, he would have warned me against it. Damn, I should have bought a house.

"You guys should come stay at my place," Talia said.

"Huh?" I blinked. Had I heard that right? "Seriously?"

"You can stay at the hotel if you want, but you'll need a kitchen. I happen to have a kitchen and two guest bedrooms. I'll also give my realtor a call, see if she has anything on the market."

I was still stuck on the invitation. "You'd really let us stay?"

"If you want." She shrugged. "But if you'd rather stay here, then—"

"Ten minutes." I held up a hand, already moving toward the bedroom. "Just give me ten minutes to pack some stuff."

"How about you let her sleep?" Talia dug her keys from her coat pocket. "Come over when she wakes up. I'll stop at the store and grab some soup for dinner."

Was this a dream? " 'Kay."

"See you in a bit." She waved and headed out, leaving me stuck in place. Then I glanced around, really looking at the apartment. It was a far cry better than what it had been. It was clean and tidy. But there was no life here. This was fit for a bachelor, not a little girl.

And if Talia was willing to let me be closer, I'd jump at the chance. For me and for Kadence.

While Kadence slept, I moved around the apartment, packing quietly. Vivienne called and checked in, and after we talked for a few minutes, I made sure the space heaters were plugged in and close to the sinks, with one in the bathroom, so hopefully the pipes wouldn't freeze. There was no other choice but to leave them running, even if I wasn't here. But if the building burned down, well... I wouldn't be heartbroken.

It was nearly dark outside by the time Kadence stirred from her nap. I had her suitcase and my own packed and loaded into the truck, so all I had to do was carry her outside and buckle her into her seat.

"Where are we going?" She yawned, cuddling her favorite green blankie.

"We're going to stay with Talia for a little bit. Until we get the heat working at the gym."

"Okay." She yawned again, not voicing a single word of protest. Not that I'd expected one. She hadn't complained about the gym but she hadn't complimented it either.

The lights of Talia's house were a welcome sight when we parked on the street. So was the woman standing on the porch, ready to wave us inside.

I took Kaddie in first, leaving her with Talia, while I hurried to bring in our bags. Then I closed the door behind me, toeing off my boots, before following the sound of voices into the kitchen.

A bar separated the kitchen from a dining nook. Kadence was sitting on a stool, her attention on Talia as she moved around the room, ladling soup from a pot on the stove into a small bowl.

Maybe it should have been awkward, the first night as a guest in her home, but as Talia served our dinner, the three of us ate chicken noodle soup and it felt like something we'd done a hundred times.

But that was Talia. That was us. Even when she was angry or frustrated with me, it hadn't been awkward. We were too in tune with each other. We flowed, always had.

After dinner, Kadence took a warm bath before settling into the guest bedroom. Talia checked her temperature and gave her another dose of Tylenol. And when my daughter was dressed in her favorite pink dinosaur pajamas, I brushed out her damp hair and curled beside her in bed, waiting until she was asleep before easing out of the room.

Talia was in the kitchen, the dishwasher running and the leftovers stowed away. The wind had picked up after dinner, whipping snow against the house. "Is she asleep?"

"She's exhausted." I yawned, rubbing the back of my neck. The kink I'd gotten from too many nights on the couch felt permanent. "I hope she can rest."

"Me too. Your room is next to hers. I'll be upstairs if you need anything. Just make yourself at home."

I nodded. "Appreciated."

"See you in the morning." That scent of coconut and lime filled my nose as she walked by, heading for the staircase.

I drew in a long breath, holding it in my nose, forcing my

feet to stay exactly where they were.

She hadn't invited me here tonight for anything but a decent place to stay. And as much as I wanted to follow her upstairs, to find out what color sheets she had on her bed, I stood at the counter, gripping the edge tight. It wasn't until I heard the sound of a door closing upstairs that I wandered down the hallway to the bedroom next to Kaddie's.

The bed was plush and warm as I slid beneath the covers. Given how many restless nights I'd had lately, I should have conked right out. Instead, I listened to the wind howl and stared at the ceiling. What was Talia dreaming about tonight?

A light turned on, casting a glow toward my open door. I shoved out of bed, wearing only a pair of boxer briefs, and padded toward the kitchen. Talia stood at the sink, filling a glass of water.

The sight of her made my mouth go dry.

She was wearing an oversized T-shirt that had once been dark green, but after countless washings, the color had faded over time. Her back was to me, but she didn't need to turn. I already knew what was on the front of that tee. It barely fell past the curve of her ass. Her toned legs were bare. Her hair was pulled up in a messy knot, a few strands escaping down the long column of her neck.

Fuck, but she was perfect. There would never be another woman, only Talia, wearing one of my old T-shirts.

Maybe she'd deleted my phone number. But she hadn't tossed that tee.

"Couldn't sleep?" I asked.

She startled, turning to face me and pressing a hand to her heart.

"Sorry." I stepped into the room, loving the flare of lust in her eyes when she took in my naked chest. "I wondered where that shirt went."

Her gaze dropped, taking in the distressed white shamrock on the front. "Your lucky tee."

"My lucky tee." I walked right into her space, not giving her a chance to object as I framed her face with my hands. "Thief."

"You abandoned it in my drawer."

"Then I guess I'll have to steal it back." I crushed my mouth to hers, wrapping my arms around her.

Talia rose up on her toes, her tongue tangling with mine as I swept into her mouth, savoring her sweet taste with a hint of mint toothpaste.

God, this woman. She tasted good. Felt good. I held her tighter, one arm over her shoulder while the other came around her ribs. Pinned.

She did the same, holding me so tight it was like she didn't ever want to let go. There was no space between us as I hefted her up, setting her ass on the counter. Then I kissed her deeper, leaving no corner of her mouth untouched.

Fire spread through my veins. She lifted her legs, wrapping them around my hips to haul me closer.

My cock throbbed as it pressed into her core, wanting so badly to sink inside. The only thing between us were her panties and my boxers. I groaned down her throat. I swallowed her whimper. Every stroke of her tongue, every nip of our lips, I fought the urge to bury myself in that wet heat.

Talia clung to me, her fingertips leaving crescent indents in my back as she swirled her tongue against my own.

She'd always loved to dig her nails into my back. I'd always wanted to have those marks tattooed on permanently. Maybe now I would.

Another night, I'd worship her body for hours. Another night, when my daughter wasn't sick and asleep down the hallway.

Tearing my mouth away, I dropped my forehead to hers as we both panted for breath. "Talia."

"Don't let go." Her arms cinched tighter.

"Never," I whispered, holding her with my face buried in the crook of her neck, until finally she relaxed her arms, and I helped her off the counter.

Her lips were swollen. Her face was flushed and her hair was coming loose from its tie. Wearing my lucky tee, she was perfect.

"Why'd you really invite us to stay?" I asked, pushing a lock of hair off her forehead.

She touched my beard, lightly, like she was trying to decide if she liked it or not. "I don't know."

"Do you regret it?"

"No." She ran her thumb over my bottom lip, then slipped past me, glancing back when she was on the opposite side of the room. A safe distance, out of my reach before I changed my mind and hauled her to bed. Smart woman. "Good night, Foster."

"Good night, Tally."

CHAPTER 16

TALIA

I stared at the blank face of my locker. No tally mark today. The last time I'd marked a good day was when Foster had brought Kadence in for her checkup. That had been nine—*no*—ten days ago. Were my standards for a good day too high?

There was a flu running through town and it had made people especially irritable, staff and patients included. It was probably the same bug that Kadence had picked up at school.

I snagged my keys and tucked them in my pocket before leaving, more than ready to get out of the hospital. It was dark outside as I drove the Jeep toward home.

Toward Foster and Kadence.

I still wasn't sure what had come over me yesterday when I'd offered to let them stay at my house. A break in my sanity? Except it had been so...easy.

In college, Foster had all but moved into my apartment. My place had been bigger and nicer than his, and Vivienne hadn't minded his company. He'd fit into my life seamlessly.

Having him in my home was as comfortable as wearing one of his old T-shirts to bed.

I'd walked into the kitchen this morning to find him

waiting with a cup of coffee poured with my favorite creamer.

He'd kissed my cheek goodbye, and I hadn't asked if they'd be there when I came home. I just knew they would. As much as I wanted him to stay, maybe he did too.

I didn't linger in the garage but rushed inside. He stood at the kitchen counter in the exact place where he'd kissed me last night.

The image of him in only those boxer briefs sent a throb to my core. And, God, the way he'd held me.

Foster had held me like I was his tether to the earth.

There wasn't much I wouldn't do to have him hold me like that every day.

Even forgive.

Maybe I already had.

"Hi," I said, coming into the room.

"Hey." He turned and smiled. "How was your day?"

When was the last time I'd come home to someone asking me about my day? Years. It had been Foster. Because I hadn't lived with anyone since Vivienne. I hadn't realized how lonely my life had become. Even here in Quincy, with family members in every direction, it wasn't the same as coming home to a person of my own.

"What's that look?" he asked.

"Nothing." I shook it off. "Do I have time to change and take a quick shower?"

"Fifteen minutes." He pointed to the oven's timer.

"Be right back." I jogged up the stairs, stripping out of my scrubs and putting them in the hamper. Then I tied up my hair into a messy bun and hopped in the shower, hurrying to scrub the day from my skin.

Dressed in a pair of joggers and a long-sleeved tee, I made

it back to the kitchen with five minutes to spare.

"Tell me about your day," Foster said.

"Meh. I've had better. Everyone has been grumpy lately. It usually happens this time of year. Short days and long nights make for cranky hospital staff. And I had a patient yell at me." In my defense, he'd yelled at both nurses before I'd walked into his exam room, so at least I'd had company.

"What?" He stood taller, his expression instantly murderous.

"It's not the first time, nor will it be the last." I laughed. "Unclench that jaw, killer."

A grin stretched across his sexy mouth. "I forgot how much I like it when you call me killer."

I liked it too. "It smells good in here. You didn't need to cook."

"Don't mind. Besides, my diet is about to get strange as I gear up for this fight."

"Do you have to cut weight?" At six foot three and already ripped with muscle, it wasn't easy to trim pounds. I'd always dreaded that part before his fights, when he'd work so hard and eat so carefully to make sure he hit a number on the scale.

"A few pounds. But not much." He stepped closer, his hand coming to my face. His thumb brushed across my cheekbone. "Sorry about your day."

"It's okay." I leaned into his touch. "What about you? Where's Kadence?"

He jerked his chin toward the living room. "She's commandeered your TV."

"How's she feeling?"

"Better. No fever since last night."

"Good." I closed my eyes, savoring the tingles across my skin. Then his mouth was on mine, just a brush of his lips that left me wanting more.

I rose up on my toes, except before I could deepen the kiss, the timer on the oven dinged.

He growled against my mouth, then stepped away to swipe an oven mitt off the counter and yank open the oven door. Then he took out a sheet pan with chicken and potatoes and green beans. "Want to get Kadence?"

"Sure." I turned, ready to head to the living room, but froze.

Kadence was standing in the doorway, watching.

"Oh, hi." *Shit.*

She had her eyebrows knitted together, probably because she'd just watched her dad kiss me.

Foster's heat hit my back. Then his arm was around my shoulders, hauling my back to his chest. "We talked about you today."

"Me?"

He hummed.

That was it. That was his explanation. A hum. Then he let me go and clapped his hands. "Okay, sit down and let's eat. Kaddie, what do you want to drink?"

"Milk," she answered, walking to the dining room table, where he'd already set out napkins and silverware.

"Tally?"

"I, um…water. I can get it."

"Grab me one too, love."

Love. Never babe or honey or darlin'. The only endearment he'd given me was *love.*

Foster breezed past me, carrying two plates to the table.

I unstuck my feet and got our drinks, taking Kaddie her milk first. As we sat together, I waited for a bit of discomfort or awkwardness after that kiss. But Foster just cut up Kaddie's chicken, then tore into his own meal, which was twice as big as he'd plated for me.

"Daddy said you're like Dex," Kaddie said, her mouth full of food as she talked.

"Who's Dex?"

"Mommy's boy—no, wait." She looked to Foster. "What's that word again?"

"Fiancé."

I choked on a potato.

"Tally." Foster flew out of his chair, rounding the table to smack me on the back.

I coughed and waved him off, dislodging the food and chewing it. Then I swallowed it down with a gulp of water before staring up at him still hovering by my side. "Vivienne's fiancé?"

"Dex."

Kadence nodded. "Dex."

"Dex," I repeated.

Foster winked, then returned to his seat. "Kadence missed a popcorn party at school today, so after dinner, we thought we could watch a movie and have popcorn. You in?"

"Um, yeah. I like popcorn."

"Me too." Kadence gave me a small smile as she chewed.

"Your dad said you were feeling better." I pressed my palm to her forehead, just to see for myself that she wasn't warm.

"Daddy said I still have to stay home from school tomorrow."

"Probably a good idea. Just to make sure you're rested." I shifted my attention to Foster. "Any word on the furnace?"

"The guy called me earlier. Said it's all ready for tomorrow. Then we'll be out of your hair."

Kadence mumbled something under her breath as she stabbed a green bean.

"Speak up, little bug," Foster said. "What's on your mind?"

"Do we have to go back to the gym?" she whined. "This place is way better."

I pulled in my lips to hide a smile. She wasn't wrong.

"Yeah." Foster sighed. "We have to go back."

"But not until the weekend," I blurted. I wanted another day of coming home from work to a full house.

"Yesss." Kaddie did a little dance in her chair.

And when I met Foster's gaze, those blue eyes were shining, crinkled at the sides. Happy.

We finished our meal, entertained by Kadence's recap of the show she'd watched today on Netflix about a dragon prince. I did the dishes while Foster took Kadence in for a bath. Then we settled on the couch, Kadence in the middle, bundled in a blanket with the bowl of popcorn in her lap. She only made it through an hour of the movie before she fell asleep.

Foster stood, bending to sweep her into his arms. Then he padded down the hallway, melting my heart when he kissed her hair. He emerged just moments later, rolling his shoulder.

"What's wrong?" I asked.

"Just a knot."

"Sit down." I pointed to the floor in front of me and crossed my legs on the couch.

He obeyed, blowing out a deep breath when my hands came to his shoulders. Then he moaned, a low, deep rumble from his chest that rekindled that pulse in my center. He let me massage the knot for a while, and when my hands stopped moving, he relaxed even deeper, stretching out so that his head was on the couch.

"So..." My fingers played with the ends of his dark hair. "Dex."

"Dex," he breathed. "Good guy. He loves Vivi. He's sweet to Kadence."

"And Vivienne is engaged? You just got divorced."

"They've been together for two years."

My jaw dropped. "What? She cheated on you?"

Foster chuckled.

"Why is that funny?"

He shifted and stood, holding out a hand. "Come here."

I unfolded my legs, taking his hand to help me up. But instead of leading me somewhere, like the kitchen, which was farther away from the hallway just in case Kadence woke up, he swung me into his arms.

"Dance with me." His lips brushed my forehead as he started to sway. Two counts and his foot landed on mine. "Shit. Sorry."

I laughed. "You're still a hopeless dancer."

For a man who moved like lightning in the boxing ring, he couldn't dance to save his life.

He smiled against my hair. "I haven't had a lot of practice."

"You didn't dance with Vivienne?" The question came out too fast, before I could mask the envy in my tone. "Never mind. I don't want to know."

Maybe she hadn't loved him. Maybe he hadn't loved her. But she'd been his wife. And he, her husband.

"I've never danced with Vivienne."

It eased the sting. She'd had nearly everything else, but at least this was mine.

"What did you talk about with Kadence today?" I asked as he danced us in a slow circle around the living room.

"That you're my Dex."

"Not exactly the same if Vivienne is marrying Dex."

He hummed. Another hum without an explanation to follow. "Dex and Vivi have been together for a long time, but he's just recently met Kadence. We didn't introduce them until after the divorce. But she knows that Vivi loves him. She knows that Vivi and I will always love her, even if we're not married."

"Was the divorce hard on her?"

"Yes and no. Yes, because it means we've had a lot of change. Yes, because it happened right after Arlo died, and like it or not, he was her grandfather. No, because the first time she saw Dex kiss Vivienne, Kadence came to me and asked me why I never kissed Mommy like that."

I leaned back to study his face. "You didn't kiss Vivienne?"

He stopped moving, locking his eyes with mine. "Not on the mouth."

But they'd been married for seven years. How was that possible? "Earlier tonight, when you kissed me in the kitchen, Kadence saw us. She had this look on her face."

"She's piecing it together."

That Vivienne loved Dex and that was why she kissed him. That Foster loved me.

Kadence was connecting the dots.

"Vivienne is my friend," Foster said. "Nothing more. I don't kiss Vivienne. I am not in love with Vivienne. And I have never had sex with Vivienne."

This time, it was me who stepped on his foot. "W-what?"

"We didn't have a marriage, Talia. We had a prison sentence. When she got with Dex, I didn't see that as cheating, because she's only ever been my cellmate."

His companion.

So if he hadn't been with Vivienne, then who? Anyone?

"I waited a long time for you, love. I'll wait as long as you need. *You* are mine." And he was here in Quincy to claim me.

"I don't—" How did I say this? "I, um—"

"Don't tell me." Foster put his finger over my mouth. "The idea of you with another man... I can't think about it. I can't hear it. So don't tell me."

There was nothing to tell.

Pathetic, right? He'd broken my heart into a thousand pieces, and I still hadn't been able to move on. I hadn't been able to let him go. Instead, I'd concentrated on school and work, blocking out even the idea of someone new because deep down, no one would ever be Foster.

I wrapped my hand around his wrist, pulling it away from my lips. "There hasn't been another man."

His eyes narrowed. "What?"

Saying it again was too hard, so I shrugged.

"Fuck." Foster's hands came to my face, his fingers threading into my hair as he dropped his forehead to mine. His entire body sagged, like he'd just let go of seven years' worth of worry.

"Say something," I whispered.

"How many?"

"How many, what?"

One of his hands unthreaded from my hair, his fingertips skimming over my cheek. The sparks beneath his touch spread as he trailed lower and lower, over my collarbone and to the swell of my breast. Then he skimmed my ribs, dropping past my hip until he brushed my thigh and moved those fingers between my legs, pressing hard enough for me to gasp.

"Orgasms."

I wasn't sure who moved first. It might have been him, capturing my mouth. Or it could have been me, throwing my arms around his shoulders and climbing his body like a damn tree.

The lights were ignored. The TV was left on Kadence's movie. And the world was forgotten as Foster carried me through the house.

My legs wrapped around his waist as his tongue twisted with mine. His leg bumped into the coffee table as we skirted the living room. My ass brushed the banister when he started up the stairs. He stopped halfway, angling his mouth as our kiss became frantic.

A groan rumbled from his chest. A moan escaped my throat as I tore my mouth away.

"Bed. Hurry." I clung tighter to his shoulders as he rushed us up the stairs, glancing both ways. "Left."

He strode down the hallway, his mouth finding mine again.

My back hit a wall, his body trapping me in place as he devoured. Until I was breathless and tugging at his shirt. Foster hauled me off the wall and stepped into my bedroom, kicking the door closed behind him.

Three steps and we were falling onto the bed, his weight hitting mine as his arousal pressed into my core.

Another moan. Another whimper. Our mouths remained fused as our hands roamed, tugging and pulling to get each other out of our clothes.

My shirt was gone first, yanked over my head and thrown over his shoulder. His T-shirt came next, pulled from behind his neck with corded arms and tossed to the floor. Jeans. Pants. A bra. Boxers. Panties. Piece by piece, they made their way to the floor until there was nothing but Foster's naked heat against my skin. And the wet sear of his mouth as he dropped kiss after kiss on my body.

His tongue dipped into my navel as he kissed along my belly, lower and lower until he was just above the place where I needed him most.

"Did you touch yourself thinking of me?"

"Yes." I threaded my fingers through his hair, urging him lower, but he didn't move. He licked a path across my belly.

"Tell me how."

I let go of his hair, ready to touch myself, but he batted my hand away. "Foster."

"Tell me, Talia." The rasp in his voice, rough and thick, made me shiver. "What did you do first?"

"I'd touch my clit."

He kissed my hip bone, then shifted, leaning on his side as he touched my clit. "How?"

"Slow at first." I panted as he did the same. "Just light."

He hummed. "Then what?"

"Then I'd go lower."

Foster moved his hand, his fingers dipping into my soaked folds.

"Yes," I hissed. "More."

He obeyed, my voice becoming his command.

"Back to my clit," I breathed.

Except this time, instead of doing it with his finger, he shifted, his hands going to my knees. "Spread."

I was wholly exposed, the cool air skimming my sensitive flesh. Until his tongue was there, lapping at my wetness. "Oh, God, baby."

"Fuck, you taste sweet, Tally." He fluttered his tongue against my clit, causing my back to arch off the bed.

My moan filled the room, my legs trembling.

This man and his wicked tongue. He licked me again, a

growl vibrating against my skin. And then he dove in, like a man starved, and feasted. His beard rubbed against the sensitive skin on the inside of my thighs. His tongue was relentless, licking and sucking until I writhed beneath him.

"Foster." I clutched the bedding at my sides, my legs spreading even wider.

"You're mine, love. Say it."

"I'm yours."

"That's my good girl." He slipped a long finger inside, stroking that sensitive spot, and I came apart.

A loud moan, entirely uncontrolled, came from my throat and he reached up, covering my mouth with his palm.

Pulse after pulse, the orgasm crashed into me as stars broke behind my eyes. Foster's tongue never stopped, not until I collapsed on the bed, spent and boneless.

"There's one," he murmured, kissing the inside of my knee.

I smiled, my eyelids too heavy to open.

"Look at me," he ordered as he hovered above me, his elbows bracketing my head. His hips settled into the cradle of my own, his cock pressing into my sensitive flesh. Then he waited until I opened my eyes, his darkened gaze waiting.

"I love you." He rocked against my core. "Fuck, but I love you."

My heart stopped.

I opened my mouth, a surge of panic rising, when there were no words to say.

I loved him. I'd loved Foster for what felt like my entire life. I just...

Why couldn't I say it?

He ran his knuckles along my cheek, then he hummed. A hum that said it was okay. That he understood. That he'd be here when I was ready.

I lifted off the pillow, my mouth finding his. Then I flicked my tongue against his, tasting myself. One thrust of his hips and he buried himself to the root, stealing my breath. I stretched around him, meeting his strokes, needing more and more and more.

Every need, Foster anticipated. Every touch, he drove me higher. Until I clawed at his back, my nails digging deep, and shattered.

He buried his face in my neck, pouring his own release inside of me. After the haze cleared, he wrapped me in those strong arms and held me, twisting us so I was draped across his chest.

"Say it again," I murmured, sleep creeping in at the edges.

"I love you."

This time it was me who hummed.

Maybe if he said it over and over, I'd be able to say it back. Maybe if he said it over and over, I'd stop thinking about the years we'd missed.

Maybe if he said it over and over, I'd stop worrying that love wasn't enough.

CHAPTER 17

FOSTER

Jasper's gloved fist connected with my face.

My head whipped to the side, a burst of pain spreading through my cheek. *Motherfucker.* That was the third time he'd hit me today.

"What's with you?" He jabbed again. "You're distracted."

"Sorry." I worked my jaw, moving around the ring. My hands were up to guard my face, but yeah, I was distracted.

Jasper dropped his arms to his sides and frowned, pulling out his mouthguard. "Are you going to be able to do this fight with Savage?"

"I don't know," I admitted, taking out my own mouthguard and tucking it in the waistband of my shorts. "Fuck, I don't know. My head's not in it."

No, my head was at Talia's house, along with my heart.

It had been nearly a week since we'd left her place. Kadence and I had packed our things and returned to the gym on Saturday. The furnace was new, the heat working perfectly and quiet as a mouse compared to the old one.

We'd spent last weekend in the apartment, cleaning and lazing around. Kadence had made slime from a kit I'd picked up at the grocery store. Jasper had come over on Sunday with pizza and we'd watched football on the couch while Kaddie had played her Nintendo Switch. It might have been an enjoyable, relaxing weekend.

Except, as my daughter had pointed out, Talia's house was way better than the gym.

And I missed her.

I hadn't seen her since we'd left her place. We'd texted. Yesterday, I'd been so desperate to hear her voice I'd called her after Kaddie had gone to sleep.

This was progress. Good progress. We were taking it slow. Talking. Texting. Rebuilding what I'd broken.

So why couldn't I shake this feeling that everything was about to fall apart? That I'd lose her again?

The doubts had made it nearly impossible for me to focus on anything, including this upcoming fight.

"Maybe this has to be the last one," I told Jasper.

He raised his eyebrows. "You want to retire?"

I shrugged and walked to the corner, picking up my water bottle and taking a long drink. "Honestly? Maybe. I'm not getting any younger. Montana is a hell of a long ways from Vegas. It's been easier out here to detach."

And that was the problem. Because the last thing I wanted to do was fly to Vegas. Maybe that was why I couldn't shake this feeling. I had this fear that if I left Montana, I'd lose Talia.

Jasper dropped to the mat to stretch. "You told me when you came up here that you needed something to fight for. A reason. You've always needed that. Some specific motivator to latch on to."

That was exactly my problem. I had enough money to last a lifetime. I'd won the belts. My name was synonymous with victory. What now?

My fight wasn't in Vegas, not anymore.

My fight was here, for Talia's heart.

"What happens if you lose?" Jasper asked.

"I'll be pissed." Maybe I didn't need to win, but that didn't mean I enjoyed losing.

"You need to ask her to go with you."

"Who? Talia?"

Jasper nodded. "You're worried about leaving here, aren't you?"

"Get out of my head."

He chuckled. "I get it. You came up here, threw everything into this place. You put it all on the line, hoping she'd take you back."

And she had. Sort of. Probably. I'd told her I loved her and she hadn't been able to say it back. There'd been some hesitation, indecision, in her eyes. But she just needed time.

"What's your point?" I asked.

"If Talia is here, your head will be here. So it's pretty obvious. You've got to convince her to come to Vegas and be there for the fight. I'm guessing that if your girl is sitting front row, there's no way you let her see you lose."

Fuck no. I wouldn't let her see me lose. A grin stretched across my face. "I'm not paying you enough."

He laughed. "No, you are not. Did you see the temperature this morning? Five below. I'm not made for five below."

"Come on." I walked over and extended a hand to help him to his feet. "It's my turn to punch you in the face."

"Not a chance." He smirked, putting in his mouthguard. Then he walked to the timer we kept in the ring. As soon as the beep sounded, Jasper lifted his hands. "Five minutes."

A full round.

It was like a fresh wave of energy had infused my body as we faced off. My head snapped into place, everything beyond this ring becoming a blur. And that uneasy feeling was gone.

I'd bring Talia to the fight. I'd beat Scott Savage if only to see Talia's face when I emerged the victor. Then we'd come home. We'd come to Montana. And if I had another contract in me, I'd negotiate it. And if not, well…retirement would be a damn nice consolation prize.

Jasper faked a kick, raising his knee fast. But before he could throw a jab–reverse punch combo, a move I'd seen him do a hundred times, I did my own fake like I was going to do a round kick, but shifted my hips in a flash, changing the kick to a hook.

My foot tapped him on the side of the head, just a touch before I pulled it away. Then it was my turn to smirk. "See? I'll be fine."

Scott Savage was a brute. He didn't have my speed or technique. I preferred to fight on my feet, and my biggest worry was that he'd get a lucky takedown and we'd spend most of our fight grappling on the mat. Even then, I could take him.

I'd be relying on my training. Years of boxing. Years of Brazilian Jiu-Jitsu. And I'd be relying on my heart. Because Jasper had nailed exactly what I needed.

If Talia was sitting front row, no way I'd let her see me lose.

Jasper and I danced around the ring, both light on our feet. When the timer beeped at the five-minute mark, we were both sweating and breathless.

I was headed for the corner to get another drink when the door opened, a gust of cold air sweeping inside. Then I had to press a hand to my chest to keep my heart from leaping out as

Talia walked inside.

She'd come to me for a change.

I fucking liked that. A lot.

"Hi." She waved and walked toward the ropes. "Am I interrupting?"

"No." I crouched down, waiting until she was close enough. Then I hooked my finger under her chin and pulled her in for a soft kiss. "Hi."

"I didn't know if you'd be training or not." She glanced over my shoulder. "Hey, Jasper."

"Hey." He jerked up his chin.

"I don't have to stay," Talia said, lowering her voice. "I wasn't working today and—"

"You missed me."

Her cheeks flushed. "I missed you."

"Missed you too, love."

Talia's gaze raked down my bare chest. "I forgot about this."

"About what?"

She waved a hand toward my body. "You. How sexy it is when you're fighting."

Good thing she thought it was sexy. Hopefully that would make her accept my invite to Vegas. "Kiss me."

She obeyed instantly, rising up on her toes. And instead of a brush of our lips, I reached through the ropes, fisted the lapel of her coat, and held her to me as my tongue swept inside.

Jasper's throat cleared behind us but I licked and sucked and didn't let Talia go until her cheeks were thoroughly flushed.

Talia bit her bottom lip, trying to hold back a smile.

"Think that's my cue to leave." Jasper walked past us, laughing as he climbed out of the ring. Then he went to a bench, snagging his sweatshirt. He tugged it over his head before trapping his sweaty hair beneath a baseball hat. With his shoes on, he walked for the door. "Have fun, you two."

"You doing okay?" I asked as Jasper left.

She lifted a shoulder. "I'm fighting with Lyla. Sort of. I don't know. But I haven't talked to her much and it's weird."

"What happened?"

"Oh, it's nothing. Sister drama." Was it nothing? Before I could ask, she changed the subject. "In other news, my mom wants to meet you."

"I'd like to meet her too."

"It might be awkward."

I shrugged. "Awkward won't last forever. They'll get used to me eventually."

"Yeah." There was hesitancy in her voice. Either she didn't want me to meet her family.

Or...she still didn't believe I'd stay. She doubted me.

Unease swam in my veins like a poison.

The Talia from before hadn't held back. She'd given me her all. Trusted. Believed. That woman was still in there. Somewhere. And somehow, I had to coax her out. Prove to her this was real.

"What time do you need to get Kadence from school?" she asked.

I shoved my fears aside, glancing at the clock. "About an hour. Why?"

"You need a shower." She raised an eyebrow, then walked away, out of my reach. By the time she'd strutted to the apartment door, her winter coat was on the floor. One hand worked free the zipper on her hoodie, shaking it from her arms and dropping it on the floor. And when she reached behind her back to unclasp her bra, I leapt over the ropes, jogging to catch up.

My hands went to her hips, shuffling her toward the bathroom as my mouth latched on to her pulse, giving it a good suck.

"Foster." She moaned, reaching back, her fingers threading into my hair.

"Get these off." I flicked at the hem of her jeans. "Now."

She freed the buttons and shimmied them down her hips as I shoved my own shorts to the floor, kicking them away.

My cock sprang free, throbbing as I pressed it into the crack of her ass.

Talia hissed, arching into me.

"Are you wet for me?" My hand drifted over her hip, across her belly. I dipped into her folds. *Soaked*. "You're fucking soaked."

I dragged my fingers through her wetness, spreading it across her pussy. The moment we crossed the threshold to the bathroom, I swung her around, hoisting her up and planting her on the countertop.

My electric toothbrush toppled off its charger. A brush clattered into the sink.

I shoved Talia's knees apart, hooking my hands beneath them to drag her to the edge of the surface, her hands coming to my shoulders to hold on tight, and then I lined up at her entrance and thrust home.

"Fuck," I groaned as she clenched around me. "You feel so good. So fucking good."

She cupped her breasts, her rosy nipples hard and begging for my mouth.

So I bent and sucked, pulling out to thrust inside.

"More," she breathed. "Harder."

"Tell me you missed me again," I said, kissing across her

chest to her other breast.

"I missed you," she whispered as I sucked her nipple. Hard.

I let that bud pop free from my mouth and stood tall, reaching between us to place my thumb just above her clit. "Come to Vegas with me. For my fight."

Her eyes flew to mine. "What?"

"My fight. Come with me."

She leaned in, her lips seeking mine. "Do we have to talk about this now?"

Before she could kiss me, before I lost my nerve, I shied away and nodded. My thumb moved closer to her clit but still didn't touch. "Say yes."

"Foster." She wiggled but I had her trapped.

"I need you with me, Tally. Come." Slowly, I eased out, teasing her with just the tip. When her eyes were locked with mine, I eased forward, inch by inch, until I was buried deep. So deep that maybe she'd realize nothing would tear us apart. Not again.

A shudder ripped through her body, her inner walls fluttering around my length.

My thumb grazed her clit before I pulled it away. "Say yes and I'll give you exactly what you need."

"Yes." She swallowed hard, her hands digging into my shoulders. "Yes."

"Good girl." I pulled out, then slammed forward, earning a hitch in her breath. Then I circled her clit with just the right amount of pressure to make her limbs tremble.

Talia's hands moved to the counter, her arms braced as her head lolled to the side. Behind her, her hair flowed in rhythm with my thrusts. Her lips parted, and with each piston of my hips, I earned a quick inhale. Her breasts swayed, those nipples impossibly hard. Perfection. She was fucking perfect.

"Look at us. Look at me fucking you." Shifting my hand out of the way, I rocked us together, my cock disappearing into her body. I watched her take me inch by inch. And when I was rooted to the hilt, I met Talia's gaze. "You and me. It's always been you and me."

She took my face in her hands, hauling my lips to hers. The kiss was short. She tore away, panting as I picked up my pace. Then she cried my name, her mouth open and against mine, as her orgasm broke. She pulsed, harder than ever before, those inner walls squeezing me like a fucking fist.

"Tally. Yes." My body tightened, that build in the base of my spine, until I snapped. I released inside of her, clinging to her as she clung to me. And when we were both spent, I pushed that silky, dark hair away from her face and let myself drown in those beautiful blue eyes.

"You'd better get in the shower," she said, breathless, her fingertips stroking my beard.

I wrapped my arms around her, our bodies still connected, and held tight. "One more minute."

One minute turned into two and finally I eased out, reaching to the shower to crank on the spray.

Except the faucet only dribbled a weak stream into the tub. "What the hell?"

Talia hopped off the counter, peering past my shoulder. "Um, that's not good."

"Son of a bitch." I stalked out of the bathroom, buck naked, and out of the apartment.

The utility closet was in between the locker rooms. They'd been cleaned, but otherwise, I'd ignored them, concentrating on the gym and apartment. The rooms weren't large, and since

I had the bathroom in the apartment, they were pointless at the moment.

Talia followed in my wake, dressed in her bra and panties and shrugging on her sweatshirt as she rushed to catch up.

The noise hit me first, the sound of water hitting a floor. My floor. I was stepping through the door, turning for the men's side and the source of that trickle, when my foot splashed in a puddle.

"You've got to be fucking kidding me." I waded through the water, so warm it was nearly too hot, until I reached the utility closet. I yanked open the door.

Water poured from the bottom of the hot water heater.

"For fuck's sake." I stretched past the cylinder, reaching for the shut-off valve. Once it was twisted and off, I stood and pinched the bridge of my nose.

"Oh, shit." Talia met my gaze. "I'm sorry."

I tipped my head to the ceiling. Would it cave in next? When would the disasters end?

"How would you feel about a couple of houseguests?"

CHAPTER 18

TALIA

Foster strode into the kitchen, his dark hair disheveled and sticking up at odd angles from how many times he'd dragged his hands through it in the past few hours.

"She asleep?" I handed him a glass of wine.

"Yeah." He took a drink and leaned against the counter. "What a cluster."

I nodded my agreement and sipped from my own glass.

The afternoon and evening had been chaos. We'd taken every towel he had at the gym and built a blockade to stop the water from leaving the locker rooms. Then he'd raced into town to pick up Kadence while I'd stayed at the gym, calling both plumbers in town—both of whom were on other jobs. Thankfully, one of them had agreed to leave the new build he was working on and come over.

By the time the plumber had arrived, Foster had returned with Kadence. She and I had packed as much of her stuff into the back of my Jeep as possible, then tossed all of Foster's clothes into suitcases.

After they'd shut the water off to the gym, Foster had emptied the pantry and fridge into a cooler, then we'd set off for my house, stopping to grab burgers on the way home.

"That place is falling apart," he said. "We're jumping from one disaster to the next. If it was just me, I'd deal. But with Kaddie here now, it's not fair to her."

"You can stay here."

He sighed. "Please don't take this the wrong way. But I don't want Kaddie to feel like a guest. She needs a home. She needs her own room where she can make a mess and leave the bed unmade and just be seven. I can't tell you how much I appreciate you letting us crash. But…"

"It's not home." But it could be, right? All I had to do was hand him a key.

He'd accepted any invitation I'd extended. Given the way he'd held me earlier, kissed me, Foster had missed me this past week as much as I'd missed him.

Except I didn't offer to let them move in. Something was holding me back. The same something that had kept me from telling Foster I loved him.

"Why did you buy the gym and not a house?" I asked.

"A lot of reasons." He blew out a long breath. "I thought it would work temporarily. We could stay there for six months, maybe a year. I honestly didn't think it would be so bad. The photos the realtor showed me were, uh, misleading."

"Ah." Without asking, I knew which realtor he was talking about. Definitely not one I'd recommend. "Maybe if the furnace and the water and everything was working, it would work. You've done a nice job cleaning it up."

"Still should have bought a house. But I was waiting, I guess. I wanted to get here and just… I wanted to get here."

"You wanted to see how it went with me."

His eyes softened. "Yeah."

"You said you weren't going to leave. No matter what I said."

"Which is true after I saw you that first night. But I wasn't entirely sure what to expect before I got to Quincy. Christ, I've never been so nervous driving into a town. The whole trip from Vegas I was a wreck. Judging from what I could find online, I knew you weren't married. It didn't look like you had a boyfriend, but I wasn't sure."

"What if I had?"

"Then he would have had competition."

The corner of my mouth turned up. "So you bought the gym instead of a house."

"Seemed like a smart move. One property that I could offload if needed. But I should have started shopping for a permanent place before Kaddie got here. That was my mistake. I thought it would be good enough, but she deserves better."

"It's not that bad, Foster. It just needs some upgrades."

He took a long gulp of his wine, then rubbed a hand over his beard. "She was so happy when I picked her up from school today. The whole trip to the gym, she just talked and talked about these two friends she made. Even knowing I was going back to clean up a mess, I didn't say a word about the water until we were parked outside. I didn't want that smile to dull. It's been hard to coax them out of her lately."

"Because of the move? Or the divorce?"

"Both. The moment Arlo died, Vivi and I knew change was coming. Finally. We could live our own lives. Maybe it was a mistake, but we thought it would be better to accelerate as much of it as possible for Kadence."

"Rip the bandage off."

"Just get to the other side." His eyes softened. "Get to the good stuff."

Me. I was the good stuff.

"Vivienne needed to stay in Vegas."

"To sell your house and Angel's." It dawned on me that he'd also mentioned she'd been planning a wedding. I'd assumed it was for a client or something. But no. She was planning her *own* wedding.

"Vivi and Dex want to get married there. It's home for her. She's giving it up for me because I want to be here. But I think she needs time to say goodbye. And Dex has been dragging his feet."

"He doesn't want to move?"

"Not really." Foster shrugged. "I don't know the specifics. Haven't asked. But she mentioned that it's been a point of tension. Regardless, Vivienne wants Kadence to be close to me, and I'm not leaving. She made it clear to him that their future is in Montana. He'll get on board."

"She'd really sacrifice her home, her life in Vegas, just so you could come to Quincy for me?" That seemed unbelievable. Selfless. Not at all the person I'd made Vivienne out to be over these past seven years. Maybe she wasn't the enemy after all.

"Like I told you, she has a lot of guilt about what happened. She wants me to be happy. But especially, she wants Kadence to have the best life possible. We saw this as a chance to get her out of a bad situation."

My forehead furrowed. "What bad situation?"

Foster jerked his chin for me to follow him to the dining table. And when we were seated, he leaned back in his chair to glance down the hallway, probably to make sure his daughter wasn't eavesdropping.

"Kaddie's preschool also offered kindergarten. She had a

lot of friends and she knew the teachers. So we kept her enrolled there last year while Vivi spent months researching schools for first grade. We applied at the best private schools in the city. We did interview after interview. And we got into our top pick. Quality teachers. Rigorous curriculum. They encouraged extracurricular activities like sports and music. It was exactly what we were looking for. Thought it would be great."

A sense of dread crept into my bones. "It wasn't."

"It was a nightmare." His jaw ticked. "The kids in Kaddie's class were brutal. There's no other way to describe it. These were first graders. I didn't think we'd have to worry about bullies until middle school. High school if we were lucky. But first grade?"

"What happened?"

"We didn't catch it soon enough. Kaddie was coming home grumpy every day. It was so unlike her. We thought it was just because of school in general. Longer hours than the preschool. More intense learning. Bigger class size. None of her friends from kindergarten were there. She was the new kid. We thought it would pass. It didn't."

I covered his hand with my own. "That's a normal rationale for any parent."

"Is it? That's my little girl. She was miserable, and I dismissed it. I thought it was because she wasn't getting an afternoon nap." Foster's voice was hoarse as he spoke, filled with regret.

"It got to the point that when I asked Kaddie if she had fun at school, she'd tell me she hated school. Every morning, it was a fight to get her ready. She'd hide under her bed in her pajamas. We assumed it was because she had to wear a uniform and hated the skirt and tights. Again, our fuckup because we should have pushed harder, earlier, to dig into what was really bothering her. We'd ask and she wouldn't explain. When we finally found out, it was a damn mess."

"What happened?"

"Kaddie didn't talk about friends. She'd been going to the school for months, and she didn't talk about friends. But she'd talk all about her teacher. She loved her teacher. And the teacher loved her. During a conference, we asked her teacher how she was doing and how she behaved. Teacher said Kadence was an angel. That she was bright, maybe a little shy, and she had this intense focus on her schoolwork. Something the teacher had never seen with a first grader before."

"That's a good thing, right?"

"Kaddie focused on her schoolwork because it was her way to escape the other kids. She blocked them out by reading books in the corner alone."

"Oh." My heart broke.

"She came home with a Halloween party invite. Vivienne and I were overjoyed. Like, finally, she's making friends. She's settling into this new school. So we took her to the party. The parents were hosting it at their own house. This massive house. They'd rented inflatable jumpers. They had a pool. A clown. Food for an army. There were people everywhere, kids dressed in their costumes. I was talking to a few of the other dads, just hanging out while the kids chased each other around. Then I heard this ear-splitting scream."

"Kaddie."

He nodded. "I've never run faster in my life. I found her surrounded by a group of girls. One of them had a lock of her hair in her fist. She'd yanked out a chunk of my child's hair."

I gasped. "Oh my God."

A sheen of tears filled his eyes. He turned his hand over so we were touching palm to palm. "They were laughing at her. She was crying on her knees, her hand to her hair in pain, and they were laughing at her."

"Oh, Kadence." I wanted to sneak into her bedroom and wrap her into a hug. "That's why she touches the side of her head, isn't it?"

He nodded. "Every time she does it, I want to scream."

I hadn't seen Kaddie do it much, but every once in a while, she'd touch her hair. Like she was touching an old wound.

Sort of like how I'd touch my heart.

"After that, it all came out," he said. "She told us how the other girls had been mean to her since the beginning of the year. They'd tease her and snicker behind her back. They told her that if she tattled on them, they'd lie and no one would believe her because she was poor and they were rich."

My jaw dropped. "What?"

"I don't know why they thought that. The goddamn school has a net worth requirement. Whatever. But Kaddie believed them. Maybe because I've never been one to flaunt my money. We lived in a nice house, but it wasn't ostentatious. I bought a new vehicle every year but it was a GMC truck, not a Ferrari. That's not my style. Never has been."

No, it wasn't. Which was part of why I admired him. Foster had become incredibly successful. He could have easily spent his fortune to make up for what he'd lacked in his childhood, but he wasn't the type of man to squander money. Hell, the man had bought a fixer-upper gym in Quincy.

He reminded me of my parents in that way. Their wealth was immense. Mostly land and capital interests, like the hotel. But they didn't flaunt it. And they'd taught us all to save our money.

That the good things in life don't come with a price tag.

"I'm sorry."

"Me too." He gave me a sad smile. "The school was apologetic. Maybe they thought I'd go public and rake them over the coals for allowing it to happen. They put her in a different classroom. They sent home daily reports on how she was doing. It was better. But..."

"Still not great." Kaddie had probably run into those other girls in the hallways or at recess.

"It was first grade. What was going to happen when these kids moved up to high school? She'd be with the same girls for years. I just... I couldn't ask her to endure it. So a new school was inevitable. Then Arlo died two weeks later and suddenly instead of that new school being in Vegas..."

"You looked into Quincy."

"Everything changed. For the better." He laced his fingers through mine. "Tally, she got in the truck today and all she talked about were her friends. How they're all doing basketball when it starts and how Maggie asked if she could go sledding over the weekend. How Maggie's mom was going to call me tomorrow."

There was so much hope, such joy, in his eyes.

Never in my life had I been prouder to live in Quincy.

Sure, our town had its problems. I'd had a few run-ins with kids in school. That was inevitable. But our community was strong. And if Kadence needed a safe place, she'd find it here.

"I know the gym isn't a forever spot. She needs a real home. So tomorrow, I'll call a realtor—a different realtor—and start hunting. Find her a place."

"You're a good dad, Foster."

He lifted a shoulder. "This year, I've felt like a failure more often than not. But damn, I'm trying."

This man would put everything on the line for the people he loved.

And I was on that list.

Foster drained the rest of his wine, then set the glass aside, standing and extending a hand. "Dance with me."

I took his hand, letting him lead me into the center of the kitchen, where he swept me into his arms. We made it a whole three turns before his bare foot stepped on mine.

"Sorry."

I laughed. "It's okay."

He held me closer, swaying more than stepping. "You sure you're okay with us staying for a bit?"

"It's all good."

"We could check into the hotel."

"This is better." I pressed my nose into his chest, drawing in his woodsy scent. "Kids need room."

"And what do you need?"

I tilted my head back, meeting his eyes. "You."

All I'd ever needed was him.

Foster dropped his lips to mine for a kiss. The lazy strokes of his talented tongue weakened my knees, and he swept me into his arms, cradling me against his chest as he carried me upstairs for the shower we hadn't taken at the gym.

CHAPTER 19

FOSTER

"That's it?" I asked my realtor as I eased the truck to a stop in front of Talia's house.

"Inventory is low."

Low? Based on the email she'd just sent with the exact same listings she'd sent the week before, inventory was practically nonexistent. "Yeah."

"Sorry, Foster. February is a tough month for listings. But it will pick up in the spring."

"Not your fault." I couldn't exactly blame her for this situation. It wasn't like she could conjure a decent home for Kadence and me out of thin air.

"For what you're looking for, I think a new build will be your best option."

"Yeah. Will you start sending me lot listings?"

"Absolutely. I'll warn you there isn't much."

Of course there isn't. "Appreciate it." I ended the call and stared down the street. "Damn."

This realtor was Talia's recommendation because I sure as hell wasn't going to use the same guy who'd sold me the gym. Over the past two weeks, I'd all but memorized the available listings in a twenty-mile radius.

My top options were a modular that from the outside looked in worse shape than the gym. Or I could buy a tiny, two-bedroom house on the outskirts of town next to the highway and the garbage dump.

Which meant once we left Talia's, it was back to the gym.

Or maybe…

I stared at Talia's house. The green siding was the color of desert sage. The brick at the base of the house was the same they'd used for the covered porch's stairs. The afternoon sunlight caught on the dormer windows upstairs. And beyond the wooden front door was my girl.

Two weeks we'd been here. Each night, I told Talia that I loved her before she fell asleep in my arms. Two weeks and she hadn't hinted at saying it back. Two weeks and there was still something holding her back.

It had only been two weeks. Two weeks in the scope of time was nothing. But two weeks spent dwelling on my fears had twisted me into a knot.

Not even the brutal training regimen with Jasper had helped erase the mountain of tension in my gut.

Talia hadn't made a single comment about Kadence and me moving out. Not one. She also hadn't asked us to stay after the gym was back to normal.

Was it too soon to move in together? Probably. Except I was ready to take leaps into the future. Talia was shuffling baby steps. She was keeping up a shield, a wall invisible to most.

Not me.

Sure, things between us had been incredible. Any other man wouldn't worry. But I knew Talia Eden better than I knew myself. And this just…it wasn't like the days before.

The days when I'd lived for her next breath and she'd survived on my heartbeat.

I shoved out of the truck and made my way inside, stomping the snow off my boots before tugging them off.

"Talia," I called.

"In here."

Down the hallway, she was in Kadence's room with a laundry basket on the bed and a clean shirt in her hands. "I would have done that."

"I don't mind." She smiled as I came to stand beside her, dropping a kiss to her mouth before plucking a pair of jeans from the pile and folding them into a square.

"How was your day?"

"Quiet." She'd worked all weekend and had today and tomorrow off. "It was nice to catch up on housework. How was the gym?"

"Fine. Jasper's determined to kick my ass every day until the fight." Which was coming in less than a month. The nerves were beginning to creep in. The anticipation.

We'd worked out for hours today, mostly practicing grappling techniques. Then we'd done cardio, the treadmill and stationary bike, until I'd been ready to drop to my knees. But that was my strategy. No opponent would outlast me. I'd be in better shape than any man I'd met in the ring.

"You smell good." Talia leaned in and pressed her nose to the sleeve of my shirt. "Did you shower?"

"Yeah. The plumber finished up yesterday."

"Oh, that's great."

Did she say that because now that the water was back to rights, we could leave her house?

"What's wrong?" She stared at the frown tugging at my mouth.

"Nothing." I gave her another kiss and went back to the laundry.

The plumber who'd come in to check on the water heater had replaced it quickly enough. But in the process, he'd found a pipe that was rusted and in bad shape.

I was done with these goddamn emergencies, so I'd told him to replace it. Of course it had been the main pipe leading to the apartment, so he'd had to rip out a decent section of the wall to get it fixed.

While he'd been making repairs, I'd also hired an electrician to assess the building. The last thing I needed was an electrical fire. The wiring was old but worked, though the electrical panel was outdated and overloaded.

All problems that had all been overlooked, or missed, by the property inspector my realtor had arranged. And by me, because I'd been in such a damn hurry to move, I hadn't thought twice.

The electrician had fixed the panel. I'd slapped some sheetrock over the holes the plumber had left behind. Tomorrow, I'd add wall spackle and eventually paint. Today was the first day when no one had been at the gym but Jasper and me.

"We can probably get out of your hair tomorrow," I said, holding my breath.

Her hands stopped folding. "Oh."

"Unless you don't want—"

"That will probably be—"

We spoke over each other, then stopped.

"You go," I said.

"Do you want to leave?" She worried her bottom lip between her teeth.

"Do you want us to stay?"

There was such vulnerability in those blue eyes, like she was scared to admit what she wanted.

Tell me. Please. Just tell me. Come on, Tally. Let go.

"Stay for a little longer."

It wasn't everything, but it was something. I hauled her into my arms, pressing my nose to her hair and breathing her in. "Okay. A little while."

"Do you think Kadence will care?"

I chuckled. "Uh, no."

She'd asked me on the way to school this morning if we could live at Talia's until we found our own house. Part of that was because we'd learned that her friend Maggie was just a block away, and last Saturday, we'd let them have a playdate.

But the other part was Talia.

My daughter was falling in love.

I envied her that. What I wouldn't give to go back to the beginning, when Talia and I were strangers, and experience the magic of falling in love with her all over again.

She let me go and went back to the laundry, the two of us folding it in comfortable silence. I stowed everything in the drawers while she hung up Kaddie's sweaters in the closet. When I finished before her, I sat on the edge of the bed, watching as she moved.

Talia would make an amazing mother. Did she want kids of her own?

I wanted more kids. I wanted to watch Talia grow with our child. I wanted a life of us chasing them around and then, once they were asleep, sliding into bed beside her until the end of my days.

"Do you want—" I stopped myself. Too soon.

"Want what?" she asked.

"Want to come with me to pick Kadence up?"

"Sure." She hung up Kaddie's last sweatshirt, then I followed her from the bedroom, taking the basket to the laundry room while she pulled on a pair of tennis shoes. The black leggings she wore today were molded to her long, toned legs and the curve of her ass.

My cock twitched behind my jeans. This woman had no idea how I craved her, every moment. But I didn't dare touch because if we started, I wouldn't stop. And we needed to get to the school.

When Talia reached for a coat on the hook in the entryway, I snatched it first. "You forgot the rules."

She rolled her eyes. "Oh, did I?"

"Clearly." I held out the coat for her to slip it over her arms.

"Always the gentleman."

"For you." I'd forbidden her once from putting on her own coat when I was in the room. Or opening a door. Or twisting the lid off a jar.

"I can do this, you know?" she said as I zipped her jacket up to her throat.

"For all his faults, my dad is always a gentleman." Even though I'd always insisted on doing the little things for her, I'd never told her why. "Even when he is furious with my mom for losing two grand in a night, he treats her with respect. Opens doors. Holds out her coat. Pulls out her chair."

I hadn't learned much from Dad—mostly what not to do— but that had been one of the good lessons.

"It's not about taking away your independence," I said. "I know you can zip up your own coat. Open your own doors. But it's a way for me to give back to you just a fraction of what you give to me."

Her eyes softened. "Foster."

"Let me."

"Okay."

"Thank you." With my finger under her chin, I pulled her closer for a kiss.

Her hands came to my chest as she rose up on her toes, opening for me to slide inside.

Fuck it. My hands went to her ass, my palms molding to her curves as I squeezed. Damn these leggings.

Talia moaned, her arms sliding around my neck.

With a quick hoist, I had her up and pressed against the door. Then I pressed my arousal into her center, letting her feel how much I wanted her. How insatiable I was when it came to her.

I was seconds away from shoving those leggings down and giving her a hard and fast fuck when my phone vibrated in my pocket. "Ignore it." I kissed her again.

But the vibrating continued, and damn it, we didn't have time, so I tore my mouth away with a growl.

Talia laughed, wiping my lips dry with her thumb. "We're getting carried away."

"With you? Always."

She giggled and unwound her arms as I set her on her feet. Talia didn't reach for the door. She waited for me to adjust my aching cock, then open it for her. And she did the same when we reached the truck, letting me hold the door as she hopped into the passenger seat.

I took her hand in mine as we drove across town to school and took our place in the pickup line.

"Who called you?" she asked.

"Oh." I dug out my phone, having forgotten about it. I hit

the missed call notification, the ring of the phone filling the cab. "It was Vivi."

"Hi," she answered. "Did you pick her up yet?"

"No, just waiting in line."

"Okay, good. I wanted to talk about something before she got there."

I glanced at Talia, pointing at the console. Did she want me to tell Vivienne she was here? But she shook her head. "What's up?"

"I'm coming up tonight."

I blinked. "Tonight?"

"There's a six o'clock flight that gets into Missoula around midnight. I'll just stay there and then get up early to drive over in the morning."

"All right." This was days earlier than we'd planned, but if she wanted to come to Montana before the weekend and see Kadence, I wouldn't argue. Kaddie would be overjoyed. "Everything okay?"

"I hate this, Foster." The click of a zipper, like a suitcase closing, sounded in the background. "I hate this."

"I know you do, Vivi."

"I'm not missing her first basketball practice."

I chuckled. "It's only practice. You'll be here for the first game."

"And I'll be there for the first practice too."

"Okay. She'll be thrilled."

"Don't tell her I'm coming. I booked a last-minute flight, and I don't want her hopes up, just in case it falls through."

"Why didn't you just call the charter company and change your flight?"

"I tried, but something about needing to submit a flight

plan twenty-four hours in advance. I don't know. I just... I'm not waiting. I can't keep doing this. It's too hard." Her voice cracked and tears would be next.

"Don't cry."

"I'm not crying."

"Yet."

"Yet." A sniffle came. "I wanted to give you time with Talia. I know she doesn't want to see me. But I miss Kadence. I miss her so much it hurts."

I glanced over at Talia. There was understanding on her face. She didn't speak up but she gave me a slight nod. "Talia understands. Come. Be here. We can all watch the first basketball practice."

"Thanks." Vivienne blew out a long breath. "How's it going with you and Talia? Did she say she loves you yet?"

Oh fuck.

Talia's eyes widened for just a moment, and then she looked to her window, her jaw clenched tight.

Fuck. Fuck.

"Here comes Kadence," I lied before Vivienne could say another word.

"Ack." A muffled thud came through the speakers. "Let me call you right back as soon as I get in the car. I almost dropped my phone trying to load my suitcase."

"Okay." I ended the call and the silence that followed in the truck was suffocating. *Fuck.*

I should have told her Talia was here. I shouldn't have called until Kadence was here to be a buffer.

Talia wouldn't look at me. She kept her eyes aimed out the window and her shoulders curled in, like she wanted to disappear.

Thankfully, it didn't take long for Kadence to rush toward the truck. Talia had braided Kaddie's chestnut hair this morning but after a day of school and recess, some wisps had come loose around her temples.

She was smiling as she came to the truck, looking over her shoulder to yell, "Bye!"

It should have sent my heart soaring. Except the emptiness on Talia's face was excruciating.

"I'm sorry," I whispered as Kaddie tossed her backpack into the truck, plopping into her seat. Then I focused on my daughter. "Hi, little bug."

"Hi, Daddy. Hi, Talia. Guess what?" Kadence spent the drive home telling us about an assembly they'd had today, where a guy named Radical Roy had come to the school to demonstrate different science experiments.

When we got home, Talia disappeared to her room with the excuse that she had her own laundry to do.

I gave her space, not wanting to push a discussion with Kadence around to hear. Dinner was tense at best. Even Kaddie noticed Talia was quiet, giving kind, but short answers whenever my daughter asked a question.

Talia didn't meet my gaze once. When it was finally time for bed, I wasn't surprised to come out of Kaddie's room and find that Talia had escaped once more upstairs.

I checked the locks. Shut off the lights. Then climbed the stairs.

Her bedroom door was closed.

"Talia." My knuckles tapped on the face. No answer. I twisted the handle and walked in anyway.

She was sitting on the bed, her knees drawn to her chest. There was a book beside her but she was staring out the window into the darkness beyond. "You talked about me."

"She asked how we were doing. I was honest."

Talia's hands fisted. "That's not her business."

"You're right. It's not. But I didn't do it to hurt you. To gossip about you. She's just…my friend. I've shared my life with her these past seven years. And it's a habit that I'll have to break."

"What else did you tell her?"

"Nothing. I swear. It was a two-minute conversation. I told her we were staying here while the work was being done at the gym. I wanted her to know that we were sleeping together in case Kadence mentioned it. She asked if we were serious. I said yes. She knows I'm in love with you. That was the extent of the conversation."

Talia's gaze shifted my direction. "That's all?"

"That's all." It was just bad fucking luck that Vivienne had phrased her question that way earlier. Because I hadn't admitted that while I'd said *I love you,* Talia had yet to say it back.

"I don't know how to feel about her." Talia's shoulders slumped.

"That's fair." I closed the door behind me and walked further into the room, rounding the bed to sit beside her feet.

"I'm not mad. Not really." She sighed. "I'm just confused. A little hurt. And jealous. I hate that you can tell when she's about to cry, and that when she has a problem, you're who she turns to. And I know I shouldn't be jealous. But I am."

God, it was good to hear. Not that I wanted her to suffer, but jealousy was something. A feeling, good or bad. It was something.

I took her hand in mine, peeling her fingertips away from her palm, then pressed it against my chest. "She never had my heart."

"She had seven years."

"And I'll give you seventy." If that meant I'd have to live until 101, I'd do everything in my power to give her that time.

"I'll get over it," she muttered.

Yes, she would. Eventually she'd realize that what I shared with Vivienne was nothing compared to what we had. Tonight, I'd remind her.

So I picked up where we'd left off earlier.

And stripped those leggings from her body.

CHAPTER 20

TALIA

Kadence streaked across the gym floor, racing for Foster's open arms as her ponytail streamed behind her. Her brilliant smile was contagious. "Did you see me?"

"I saw you. You did awesome." He kissed her cheek and twirled her around before setting her on her feet so she could launch herself at Vivienne.

"You made three baskets." Vivi peppered her daughter's face with kisses. "I'm so proud of you."

Kaddie giggled, and when Vivienne let her go, she looked up at me, her pretty brown eyes dancing.

"Way to go, cutie." I held out a hand for a high five. "You were a superstar."

First-grade basketball was by far the sweetest sporting event I'd ever seen. The girls had chased from one end of the court to the other, all clumped together as whoever had the ball attempted to dribble. Most shots thrown toward the hoop didn't come close to the rim. But Kaddie had nailed three layups.

The team they'd played was the first-grade boys, and I'd been thrilled when the girls had been hailed victorious. There weren't many other teams for the kids to play and next weekend they'd take on the other first-grade girls' team.

The following week, they'd play the second graders. Then in a few weeks, we'd drive Kaddie to one of the neighboring towns to play their team. That was the life of small-town sports. Parents committed to road trips. And along the way, they bonded with each other.

Maggie rushed up to Kadence, the two girls giggling and whispering as Maggie's mom waved at us all. "Bye. See you at practice next week."

Foster jerked up his chin as Vivienne waved back. And I simply smiled, not sure how I fit into this mix.

"Hi, Talia." A woman I'd gone to high school with walked by with her three kids in tow. One of them was on Kaddie's team.

"Hey, Lindsey."

We hadn't been good friends in high school, but when your graduating class consisted of fifty-three people, you didn't get to be very choosy with friends.

Three other people passed, all saying hello to me as they made their way to the exit.

After the last one passed, I turned to Foster, his eyes waiting.

"What?" I asked.

He threw his arm around my shoulders, hauling me into his side to kiss my temple. "You know everyone."

"Not everyone. But almost everyone."

He chuckled. "Thanks for coming today."

"Of course." Even with Vivienne here, there was no way I'd have missed Kaddie's first game.

"Okay, what's next?" Vivienne asked, her hand clasped with her daughter's.

"Ice cream." Kaddie jumped up and down. "Can we get some? Pretty please?"

"Um..." Foster let me go, crouching to talk to her at eye level. "I'll have to pass on ice cream. No sugar for Daddy right now."

What? No sugar? That was news to me. He'd had one of Mom's chocolate chip cookies last night when she'd dropped off a dozen.

Mom had been not so subtle about her impromptu visit. She'd wanted to scope out Foster, but she'd been sweet. And he'd flattered her from the moment she'd stepped through the door to the moment he'd insisted on escorting her to her Cadillac because the sidewalk had been icy.

Maybe that was why he'd eaten a cookie, for my mother's approval. Or maybe this diet of his was just an excuse to keep interactions between Vivienne and me to a minimum.

Sitting with her at practice earlier in the week and through today's game hadn't been horrible. But oh, it had been awkward. So, so awkward.

Vivienne and I had spent countless hours talking when we'd lived together, but now, I just... I didn't know what to say. So I'd opted for nothing. She'd followed my lead.

And Foster was in the middle, trying to engage with us both but not one more than the other.

So awkward.

"We can get ice cream," Vivienne told Kadence. "Then hang out at the hotel and go out to a special dinner."

"Do you really have to leave tomorrow, Mommy?"

Vivienne sighed. "Unfortunately. But I'll be back soon."

The smile on Kaddie's face dimmed.

If Vivienne missed her daughter, the feeling was mutual.

Since Vivienne had arrived five days ago, the two had been nearly inseparable. Foster had spent some time at The Eloise visiting with them. I'd had to work late the other night and he'd taken them to dinner.

"Okay, then we'll get going." Vivienne moved close to Foster, standing on her toes to kiss his cheek.

I stiffened.

It was so automatic, so natural, like she'd done it a hundred times. Because she had. That flare of envy raged, but I refused to feed it. A kiss on the cheek was nothing, right? Just a friendly peck.

Vivienne's gaze darted to mine and her eyes widened. Apparently she'd read the jealousy on my face. "Sorry. I, um... habit. That's not really appropriate anymore."

"It's fine," I lied.

Foster's hand found mine, squeezing tight. Reassurance that we'd get through this. We'd figure out how to coexist for Kadence.

He gave his daughter another hug and kiss. "See you in the morning? Have fun with Mommy."

"Bye, Daddy. Bye, Talia."

"Bye, Miss Madden."

She gave me her toothy grin like she always did when I called her *Miss Madden*.

"Good to see you." Vivienne gave me a look so full of pleading, of apology, it only made the awkwardness worse.

If she kept silently begging for forgiveness, and if I kept holding up my hand, it would always be uncomfortable. Someone—*me*—had to give.

"Have a safe trip home." I'd be at work by the time she left tomorrow.

They left first, leaving Foster and me with the stragglers in the gym. It would be time for the high school game soon. My parents were coming into town to watch, even though they didn't have any kids playing. But that was Quincy.

We loved our kids.

"You okay?" Foster asked.

"I don't want it to be awkward."

"It won't last. Give it time."

Time. "Yeah," I muttered.

"Come on." He took my hand and led me from the gym.

"Where are we going?"

"I'm hungry."

"You're hungry. But you said no to ice cream?"

He bent to speak into my ear. "That's not the dessert I'm after today, love."

A shiver rolled down my spine as he quickened his steps.

Maybe there were some benefits to Vivienne hogging Kadence this week. Without having to be confined to the bedroom, Foster had gotten creative. The gleam in his eyes made my pulse race.

The long hours he'd been putting in training lately had turned his already sculpted body into a work of art. Those arms. That cut V around his hips. The rippled abs and that ass so firm I could sink my teeth into it.

I was hungry too.

"Drive fast."

• • •

Hours later, after Foster and I had finally torn ourselves from each other to shower, my hunger for him had turned into actual hunger. And rather than cook, we'd come downtown to eat at Knuckles.

Knox wasn't working tonight. He was home with Memphis and Drake. It wouldn't be long until they had another addition to their family and Knox was already trying to cut his hours at the restaurant to help out at home.

His absence was part of why I'd suggested Knuckles for dinner. The rest of my family was likely at the basketball game. The visit from Mom last night had gone well, but I was taking introductions slow.

Everyone knew our story, thanks to Lyla's big mouth. Dad had filled in some of the gaps too. While they were likely talking about us, I was keeping Foster to myself for a little longer.

Enjoying our bubble.

"So tell me about this fight," I asked as he poured me a glass of wine.

"It's a title defense."

"This Scott Savage is challenging your championship?"

"Yep. That's been all my fights lately. About one match, maybe two, a year. But once this one is over, I'll have time to decide if I want to retire or keep going. If I decide to keep going, I'll need to take a fight within eighteen months so they don't pick an interim title fighter."

"What's that?"

"Basically a placeholder. They do it for fighters who get injured. Give them a certain amount of time to get back in the Octagon. But if eighteen months pass, then it bumps to twenty-four. If I don't fight within that two-year period, then my middleweight champion title gets stripped."

"Oh." Stripped seemed like such a harsh word. "Do you want to keep fighting?"

"Honestly?" He reached across the table, taking my hand

and lacing our fingers together just like the last time we'd eaten here. "I don't know."

"You still love it, don't you?"

"I do." He nodded. "But the events are a lot of pomp these days. You'll see. It's unreal. The press is ruthless. You've got guys like Savage who just run their mouth and that shit irritates the hell out of me. So much so that I don't even do much press these days. I'm lucky in that regard. The media still likes me."

"What if they didn't?"

"It's a show. At the end of the day, what matters most to the people in charge is selling pay-per-view fights. For guys like Savage, the media eats up his ego and trash talk. For me, I've built a reputation as someone quiet."

"Polar opposites," I said.

"Exactly. I'm lucky because it works. The media loves to speculate about me and what I'm not saying. There's a lot of rumors going around right now about why I'm in Montana. I ignore most of it, but that phone call I took earlier while you hopped in the shower? It was my manager. He gives me a regular rundown of what's going on, but mostly leaves me alone unless it gets out of hand."

"Is it out of hand?"

"Nah. It's nothing. There's just more speculation than normal because this is the last fight on my current contract."

"Ah." I took a drink of wine. "What are the rumors?"

"That I'm injured. That I'm secluded to try some new fighting techniques at high altitude. I'm in rehab for emotional stress."

I laughed. "Seriously?"

He shrugged. "From the divorce."

"Oh." To the world, Foster and Vivienne had been a real

couple. It was another layer to this complicated mess. Would people compare us on social media? If Foster retired, would they blame that on me, the new woman in his life?

"I ignore it, Tally. You should too."

I hadn't gone on social media much lately. Other than looking at Foster's Instagram, I hadn't done much exploring. Maybe I should. Or maybe it was best to take his advice. Whatever I found would probably make me mad.

"Do you want to retire?" I asked.

"Maybe." His gaze drifted to the table as he stared unblinking at the rim of his water glass. He'd stopped drinking wine this week. "I need a reason to fight. That's always been the case."

"Not just for the sake of winning?"

"It's not enough. Not for me. In the beginning, I fought to prove myself. To Arlo mostly. To my parents. And then, after it all fell apart, I fought because it would keep Vivienne and Kadence safe. Provide them a life. Now that Arlo and his shackles are gone, it feels...different."

The pained expression on his face was like a punch to the ribs.

Loss. Regret. An athlete looking back at his career and realizing it was coming to an end.

"I'm sorry," I whispered.

He gave me a sad smile. "Don't be. At the moment, you're my motivation."

"That's why you want me to come."

"I need you there. I need to see your smile when it's over, win or lose. But mostly, if this is the end, the last fight, then I want to win it for you."

"You'll win."

"Even if I don't, I won the fight that matters."

"Your title fight?"

He shook his head. "You. You are the biggest fight of my life."

Oh, how I loved him.

I was endlessly in love with Foster Madden.

So why couldn't I say it?

Since I couldn't form the words, I just held his hand tighter. "You won. You know that, right? You won."

Foster's entire body sagged, like he'd been waiting to hear those words.

There was no way I could walk away, not now. There was no way I'd be able to let him go.

He lifted my hand, pulling it farther across the table, forcing me to stretch as he brought my knuckles to his lips. That was it, just a kiss.

But I saw the love in his eyes.

I hoped he could see it in mine.

The waitress arrived with our food, setting it in front of us. Salmon and rice for Foster. Pasta carbonara for me.

"About Vivienne," I said, needing to talk about what had happened earlier. "I'm not trying to make it hard on her."

"I know that. She does too."

"When will she move here?"

"The original plan was this summer. After the wedding. She wants to sell Angel's and the house. But these trips back and forth are getting old. She hasn't mentioned it, but I'm thinking she'll bump up the timeline. That said, she's going to run into the same problem that I have with this real estate market."

"Then I guess you'd better stop house hunting. Save the good homes for her."

His fork fell from his grip, clattering to his plate. "What are you saying?"

What I'd wanted to say earlier this week but had hesitated to. Why hadn't I asked them to move in when we'd talked about it over Kadence's laundry? Why could I do it now?

Maybe Vivienne's visit, maybe that envy, had spurred me on. Now I could say that I shared his address too.

"I don't want you to leave," I said. "I like coming home to you at night. I like waking up with you in my bed."

"You tell me this now? In public? When I can't show you what it means to me?"

My cheeks flushed. "You already had your dessert."

"There will be seconds." His voice dipped to a gravelly rumble. "You sure about this? Living together?"

Yes. No. This was all happening so fast, but at the same time, it felt natural. Like this was always meant to be.

My parents would probably have a few words of caution, Dad especially. My brothers would hover and my sisters would invade personal boundaries.

"Well, hello." Eloise chose that moment to slide into the booth at my side.

"Um, hi. What are you doing here? I thought you had the night off."

"She's with me." Lyla took the empty space beside Foster, giving me a blank stare.

I mirrored the look and took a drink.

"You two need to stop fighting." Eloise rolled her eyes.

"We're not fighting," Lyla and I said in unison.

Yeah, we were fighting.

"I figured you would be at the high school basketball game," I said.

"It was a blowout," said Eloise. "We were up by thirty points at halftime, so we decided to come over for a bottle of wine and some food."

Foster moved over in the booth, making more room for Lyla. "Join us."

"We're on a date," I argued.

He ignored me. "Want some wine? I'm not drinking and Talia won't finish this bottle alone."

I pursed my lips in a thin line, but arguing was pointless. So I shifted toward the wall to make space.

"We don't have to stay," Eloise said. "We'll just see you tomorrow."

"What's tomorrow?" Foster asked.

Lyla and Eloise shared a look before they stood.

My stomach dropped. That was the look of an invasion. "Not tomorrow," I blurted. "Kadence has been with her mom all week and I don't want a bunch of people over on her first night back." It was a flimsy excuse but I prayed it worked.

"Oh, good point." Eloise frowned. *Phew.* "Then next weekend."

"No—" Before I could finish my objection, she and Lyla strode toward the empty table the waitress had set for them across the room. *Damn.*

"What was that about?" Foster asked.

I grabbed the bottle of wine to refill my glass because I'd most definitely be drinking it. "The bubble."

"What bubble?"

"*Our* bubble. It's about to burst."

CHAPTER 21

FOSTER

"I wish Matty was here," Talia said for the second time since we'd left the house. "He's always good about breaking tense moments."

"Stop worrying." I took her hand from her lap and brought it to my heart. "This will be fun. Right, Kaddie?"

"Right," my daughter answered from the back seat.

Talia closed her eyes and breathed, like she was saying a silent prayer. "You never told me exactly what my dad said to you that day he came to the gym."

"It doesn't matter. He was kinder to me than I deserved."

"What do you mean, Daddy?"

"Nothing." I glanced over my shoulder at Kadence, giving her a wink before focusing on the road.

After Lyla and Eloise had stopped by our table last week, Talia had called her parents to discuss whatever the Edens had planned behind our backs. And instead of allowing *the invasion*, as Talia called it, she'd convinced them to host dinner at the ranch. There was more space for everyone than at her house—our house.

She'd joked that by having it at the ranch, we could escape

if things went badly. But dinner would be fine. No matter how much flack her family gave me, I'd bear every word. They probably wouldn't scream and shout or toss me out into the snow.

Yeah, there might be a few uncomfortable moments, but we'd deal.

Maybe after a family dinner, she'd stop holding back. Even after she'd asked me to move into the house, there was still that undercurrent of doubt.

Talia, holding back, barely, but enough to make it noticeable.

Me, wondering if this was our new normal.

I didn't hate it.

I didn't love it either.

"Left up here," Talia said, pointing to a turnout off the highway.

I eased off the gas, careful with the brakes. It had snowed lightly all day but the temperature had hovered just above freezing, so the flakes had melted on the roads. The sun was dropping toward the horizon and the water on the road was beginning to freeze. Driving home after dark would be slow, and I suspected the roads in town would be an ice rink.

Talia had suggested we leave early enough to see the sunset at the ranch.

"This is...wow," I said, taking it in.

The sun cast orange and golden beams over the snow-covered meadows. It limned the tips of the evergreens on the foothills. It highlighted the towering mountains, their jagged peaks covered in white. Those mountains had a way of making a man feel free, yet insignificant at the same time.

"Pretty, isn't it?"

"Gorgeous."

Talia had described the ranch to me and shown me pictures. But words and photos didn't do it justice. They missed the raw nature of the landscape and its rugged beauty.

"This is all part of the ranch?" I asked as we drove beneath an archway.

"Yep. It stretches along the mountains for miles. There's a path that runs from one end to the other. This summer, I'll take you around. We could even go riding."

"Riding horses?" Kadence asked. "Can I go too?"

"Of course." Talia twisted to give her a smile. "I'll teach you both how to ride."

"Maybe I could even have my own horse someday," Kaddie said.

"Maybe." If a horse or pony would keep her smile in place, if it was something Talia and she could bond over, I'd buy her a hundred.

At the end of the lane, a large home appeared. Behind it were stables and a barn. A line of vehicles was parked outside the house.

Talia's knees bounced as I pulled into a space beside another truck.

"Hey." I put my hand on her knee, my thumb stroking over her jeans. "This is your family. They'll support you."

She nodded and met my gaze. "I know. I just..."

Wanted them to be nice to me.

Something she wouldn't voice with Kadence listening.

"It's all good." I hooked my finger under her chin, pulling her across the console for a kiss before unbuckling her seat belt. Then I hopped out and walked to their side of the truck, opening both of their doors. "Kaddie, do you want to carry in the drinks?"

"Sure." She looped the tote bag full of drinks, juice boxes and sparkling waters over her arm while I snagged the bottle of wine and bouquet of flowers for Anne.

Talia's mother had been a sweetheart when she'd dropped by the house last week with cookies. I was on a strict diet. No processed foods, no refined sugar leading into this fight. I wouldn't risk not making weight.

But when she'd offered me a chocolate chip cookie, I'd eaten two, not only because they were delicious, but also because I'd wanted to earn whatever favor I could. Maybe Anne could help convince Harrison I wasn't an awful choice for his daughter. And tonight, no matter what we were having for dinner, I'd clear my plate. I'd already warned Jasper he'd have to push me to the max tomorrow in training.

Talia led the way up the porch stairs to the front door. I held Kaddie's hand, making sure she didn't slip. Before we could knock, the door swung open and a tall, broad man filled the threshold.

He looked like a younger version of Harrison, with Talia's blue eyes and the same dark hair. Griffin. Her oldest brother.

"Hi." He kissed Talia's cheek, waving us into the entryway. "You're going to want to hang out right here for a minute."

"What?" Talia asked. "Why?"

"Trust me."

Voices carried from deeper in the house, not all of them cheerful.

"Foster, meet my brother Griffin," Talia said. "Griff, this is Foster and his daughter, Kadence."

"Hey, Kadence. Nice to meet you, Foster." Griff extended a hand, shaking mine.

"You too." I waited for a glare or for him to size me up.

We were about the same height and build. But he looked like the type of man who hadn't built those muscles in a gym like me. He'd done it through physical work on this ranch, and I respected the hell out of that.

The sideways glance, the warning stare, never came. Either he didn't know about me or I had an unexpected ally.

"What's going on in there?" Talia pointed down the hall as she unzipped her coat, letting me help take it from her shoulders.

"Let's see." Griffin held out his fingers, tapping each as he rattled off his answer. "Eloise invited a guy with her. Why she thought tonight would be the night to bring a date, I have no idea. But the guy she brought knows Winn."

"How?" Talia asked.

"Because Winn got called down to the grocery store two days ago. The general manager caught this idiot stuffing a cucumber down his jeans."

I laughed. "You're kidding."

"Can you arrest someone for— Nope." Talia held up her hand. "That's the wrong question to ask first. Why is Eloise seeing a guy who would stuff a cucumber down his jeans?"

"No idea. Apparently they met at Willie's a few weekends ago and have gone on a couple dates." Griffin sighed as the arguing down the hall got louder. "Pretty sure she's dumping him."

"That's disgusting!" a woman shouted. "Why would you do that? It defies the common rules of basic hygiene. And that's not how you treat produce!"

Kadence looked up to me with wide eyes.

I squeezed her hand twice, a silent okay.

Griffin shook his head. "Eloise couldn't have worse taste

in men."

Which meant I wasn't on the bottom of the list. *Score.* Eloise had just become my favorite of Talia's siblings.

Footsteps pounded our way. A lanky guy in a beanie kept his eyes aimed at the door as he rushed outside. Thirty seconds later, an engine revved and headlights flashed as he disappeared.

"Cucumber man?" Talia giggled.

Griffin nodded. "Yep."

I expected the noise to lessen now that Eloise wasn't shouting, but the commotion continued. The voice that rose above the others sounded like Anne's but I couldn't be sure given I'd only met her once.

"What's wrong with Mom?" Talia asked.

"She thought it would be fun to FaceTime Mateo so he could 'join the family dinner.' " Griffin chuckled. "He's at a bar, drunk off his ass at the moment. Which Knox and I thought was hilarious. Mom? Not so much. She snapped at me when I told Mateo to have another shot. And then she started in on a lecture that he'll never remember come sunup."

Talia craned her neck, picking out other voices. "And what's Lyla pissed about? Other than me?"

"Lyla's pissed at you?" Griffin asked.

Would Talia tell her brother why she was fighting with her twin? Because she hadn't explained it to me.

"It's nothing." Talia flicked her wrist.

Guess I wasn't the only one in the dark.

"Oh. Well, Lyla's fighting with Knox." Griffin blew out a long breath. "Since Mom is talking to Mateo, she asked Knox to season the steaks. Lyla's in a mood because she insisted on doing it herself. But according to Knox, she was doing it wrong and... I don't know. I just want to eat a steak tonight. With or without seasoning."

Me too. Steak was diet approved.

Beneath the adult voices was a baby's cry.

"And Hudson doesn't feel good," Griffin said. "He doesn't want me to hold him. He only wants Winn."

"What's wrong with Hudson?" Before Griff could answer Talia's question, she flew down the hallway, probably to examine her nephew.

Griff barked a dry laugh. "Welcome to the madness."

"Is it always like this?"

"I really want to lie and say no." He took the bottle of wine from my hand and the tote from Kadence's. "Come on in."

I chuckled, helping Kadence out of her coat before taking off my own and following Griffin deeper into the house, where we found the Eden family congregated in the kitchen.

The arguing, the conversation, stopped.

All eyes swung my way.

Okay, so maybe it was a bit nerve-racking. I held tighter to Kadence's hand.

Harrison stood from the stool where he'd been seated and stalked my way, his face as hard as granite.

"Dad," Talia warned, holding a little boy with dark hair. Hudson, based on the rundown of family members she'd given me all week. And the woman at her side had to be Winn, Griffin's wife and the Quincy chief of police.

Harrison stopped before me, giving me the head-to-toe glance I'd expected from Griffin. But when his eyes fell on Kaddie clinging to my leg, his expression softened. He bent, giving her a warm smile. "Hi, Kadence. I'm Papa Harrison."

"Hi," she murmured.

Harrison stood tall, locked his eyes with mine and, after

three pounding heartbeats, held out his hand. "Glad you could join us tonight."

"Thank you for having us." I returned his shake.

Talia walked over with Hudson on her hip. She came right to my side and, like Kadence, leaned in close until I put an arm around her shoulders.

I kissed her hair, then smiled at Hudson, who had a thumb in his mouth. His eyes were full of tears as he dropped his cheek to Talia's shoulder.

No surprise the kid loved her.

"Foster, I hope you like boring seasonings on your steak," Lyla said from across the kitchen before she gulped from the wineglass in her hand.

"Not boring, Lyla," Knox scolded, pinching salt between his fingers over the cutting board teeming with rib eyes. "Simple."

"You guys missed my date." Eloise slumped in the stool Harrison had vacated. "He was a real winner. Is there such thing as a cucumber fetish?"

"Daddy?" Kadence tugged on my jeans. "What's a fetish?"

Harrison coughed into his fist to hide a laugh.

I pulled in my lips to do the same. When I met Harrison's gaze, there was something in his blue eyes. Acceptance maybe? I hoped so.

"Mateo." Anne barked into the phone. "*Mateo.*"

No response but the sounds of a bar—clinking glasses, a dull murmur shrouded by music from a jukebox.

"He's asleep. On. A. Bar." She huffed and ended the call.

"Oh, Mom." Griffin chuckled and pulled her into his side. "It's not that bad. We've all done it before. Hell, on my twenty-first birthday, I passed out on a bar. My friends put popcorn in my ears."

"You're not helping." She swatted his chest but hugged him before coming over to introduce herself to Kadence. "Hi, Kadence. I'm Anne. And aren't you just gorgeous. I guess you win."

"Win what?" Kaddie asked.

"You're the prettiest girl here tonight. Which means you get the biggest piece of chocolate cake for dessert."

Kaddie's eyes widened as a megawatt smile lit up her face.

"The other kids are in the living room, playing. We've got toys and coloring books. Want to check them out?" Anne asked her, holding out a hand.

"Sure." With that, Kadence was swept out of the room.

"Anne went and bought 'big kid' toys this week," Harrison said. "We can either send them home with you guys tonight or we can leave them here for Kadence to play with when she visits."

My throat tightened. Yeah, we'd be fine. We'd get there. "We can leave them here. That would be great."

"Beer?" he asked.

"Foster isn't drinking before his fight," Talia said. "We brought some sparkling waters for us and juice boxes for the kids."

"I'll get you one." Harrison kissed her cheek, then whispered something in her ear that made her smile.

The remainder of the evening was just as loud as the start. Except instead of shouting, there was laughter. It filled every corner of the house.

Never in my life had I been a part of something like this. A lively family with endless stories. With inside jokes that would stretch for miles if written on paper.

Like me, Kaddie watched with wonder as the night

progressed. I hadn't realized it until that moment, but our life had been quiet. Too quiet. Maybe that was my doing, Vivienne's too, as two parents who'd grown up as only children.

I didn't want quiet for Kaddie. She needed cousins. And siblings. Brothers and sisters who'd tease her mercilessly like they did Talia. Who'd rile her up and make her laugh until she clutched her sides.

Yeah, Kadence needed siblings.

Given how Talia fawned over her nephews and niece, maybe we'd get there sooner rather than later. Retirement was beginning to sound like a damn good idea.

After the meal, no one rushed to end the conversation. We sat at the Edens' dinner table, surrounded by empty plates. Kadence had chocolate frosting on her chin from Anne's cake. I was just dabbing it with my napkin when a phone rang.

"Sorry." Winn dug it from her pocket, then stood, pressing it to her ear. "This is Chief Eden."

Griffin watched her hurry down the hallway with worry in his gaze. "That's probably the station."

"If she gets called in, do you want to stay here?" Anne asked.

"No, I'll take the kids home. Give them baths and get them into bed."

"I'll come with you and help," Eloise said. "It's not like I have a date anymore."

Quiet descended on the room, such a stark contrast to the boisterous energy from moments ago, as we waited for Winn to return. When she did, her face was set in a serious mask. A cop going to work.

"I need to go," she told Griffin, walking to the back of his chair to kiss Emma on his lap. "I'll be late."

"Be safe," he said.

"I will." She kissed him too, then went to Harrison's chair, where Hudson was asleep on his papa's shoulder. Winn kissed her son, then her eyes shot to Talia's.

Some unspoken conversation happened, but at the end of it, Talia stood too. "We'd better head out."

"What's—" Before I could finish my sentence, her phone rang, and I knew without asking that it was the hospital. She wasn't on call. But in a town this size, that probably didn't matter.

Something had happened tonight and it wasn't good news.

Winn rushed out of the house first, her taillights gone by the time we'd loaded Kaddie into the truck. After rushed goodbyes, we made our way, slowly along the icy highway.

"What did the hospital say?" I asked, keeping my voice low because Kaddie was listening.

"An accident."

No sooner than she spoke, we rounded a corner and the flash of red and blue lights filled the night sky in the distance.

My grip on the steering wheel tightened as we approached.

"Kadence, close your eyes." Talia turned, making sure my daughter obeyed. "Keep them closed until I tell you to open them, okay?"

Kaddie whimpered. "I'm scared."

"It's okay, little bug." It was a damn lie. As we approached the scene, nothing about this was okay. Two vehicles overturned in the ditch. Metal shards and glass strewn everywhere. "Where are the ambulances?"

Talia pointed down the road, where more lights flashed. "They dispatched just a minute before they called me."

We'd beaten them to the scene. "Do you want me to stop?"

"Not with Kadence here. The EMTs know what they're doing. It would be better for me to be at the hospital when the ambulances come in."

A truck with the Eden brand on the side—Winn's—was parked at the end of a line of police cruisers. Winn was on her knees beside the driver's side door of an overturned SUV. Three other officers were crowded beside her.

On the snow, even in the dark, I could see the spray of blood.

"Squeeze them tight, Kadence," Talia said.

She began to cry, but when I risked a look in the rearview, her eyes were closed as we crept along the road.

The other vehicle was a truck. It must have rolled multiple times because the exterior was decimated, the bed twisted, the front and sides smashed until it looked like a hunk of scrap metal. There were footprints in the snow around it, but no officers.

Because there was no life to save in that truck.

Blood was everywhere.

People didn't walk away from crashes like that.

I stretched an arm across the cab, putting it on Talia's shoulder.

Like Winn, her expression was serious, her chin held high. She'd march into that hospital and face whatever came her way.

What strength she had. I walked into a ring, knowing my opponent was going to try and take me down. Talia would fight just as hard, knowing that there were some battles she couldn't win.

An ambulance whipped by, lights flashing and siren wailing. Less than a mile later, another followed. And shortly after, a fire engine.

"That's the entire emergency response team," Talia whispered.

I kept clutching the wheel and drove into town, breathing a bit easier when we reached Quincy and were off the highway. "Want me drop you?"

"No, let's go home. I need to change." She began stripping out of her coat before we'd even parked. And once I was against the curb, she flew out of the truck, jogging inside.

"Daddy, is Talia okay?" Kadence asked as I unbuckled her seat belt. My girl's pretty face was pale.

"Yes, she's okay. But there might be some hurt people tonight, so she's going to go to the hospital and make them better." Please, God, let whoever was in that SUV live. All I could picture was Kaddie in her seat, trapped beneath the weight of a vehicle. So I hugged her tight as I carried her inside.

We'd just taken off our coats when Talia came down the stairs dressed in her blue scrubs. Her hair was pulled into a ponytail. "I don't know how long I'll be."

"Just go. We'll be here."

She forced a smile at Kadence, then vanished into the garage.

Leaving for whatever horrors awaited her at the hospital.

CHAPTER 22

TALIA

After closing the curtain around my patient's bed, I stepped into the hallway and breathed for what felt like the first time in—according to the clock—twelve hours.

It was 7:17 in the morning, and I'd been on my feet all night. Adrenaline had fueled the long hours but it was waning fast and a crash was coming.

Soon. But not yet.

The hallways were nearly soundless. Two nurses sat behind the counter, talking in a hushed murmur. Everyone was whispering today. A sullen, gray cloud hovered beneath the ceiling, sucking any joy or happiness from the air.

Today would not be a happy day.

Dr. Anderson emerged from the intensive care room next door, looking as exhausted as I felt. He gave me a sad smile and came to stand at my side.

It was just the two of us now, here to tend to our patients for another few hours before we'd each go home.

Dr. Herrera and Dr. Murphy had left around three this morning to shower and sleep for a bit. They'd be back soon to relieve us and cover the normal shifts.

"How is she?" he asked, lowering his voice.

"Devastated. In shock. But she's stable. She'd like to see her kids."

"Understandable." He nodded. "The daughter is sleeping right now. Once she wakes up, let's talk about putting them in the same room. But I don't want to do it unless we're sure both are out of the woods. The last thing we need is one of them taking a bad turn and having the other there to witness it."

"Okay. And the son?"

Dr. Anderson closed his eyes. His chin quivered. In my years here, I'd never seen this man cry. He was as stoic as my father, the pillar we could all lean against.

I put my hand on his arm. "He's alive. That's what matters."

"I know." He sighed. "But last night was the hardest night of my career."

"I'm sorry."

"Me too. I think I'll put on a coat and take a lap around the building. Get some fresh air."

"Good idea." I waited until he was gone before walking toward the patient room he'd just left. The room where a little boy was sedated and asleep. Slipping past the closed curtain, I stood at the foot of his bed and studied his sweet face.

He looked peaceful. We'd let him keep that peace for as long as we could. Because he'd wake up to a nightmare.

Both of his legs had been severed in the car accident last night. And if that wasn't bad enough, his father had been killed.

Their family of four had been traveling home from a day at the ski hill in Whitefish. An oncoming truck, likely going way too fast for the road condition, had hit a patch of black ice and caused a head-on collision.

Both vehicles had rolled into the ditch.

This boy's father, as well as the driver of the truck, had been killed on impact.

Drs. Anderson, Murphy and Herrera had all focused on treating the children. The daughter had been rushed into surgery to repair a puncture wound to her abdomen. Her arm was broken and she'd have some scars that would last a lifetime.

They'd left me with the mother, who I'd revived three times in the night. A broken rib had punctured her lung. Her shattered wrist was splinted but she'd need surgery from a specialist to set the bones properly. The entire right side of her body was already turning purple, and we were monitoring her closely for any internal bleeding. Her vitals had stabilized around two this morning, and she was awake.

But those injuries were nothing compared to her broken heart.

She'd lost her husband, and when they eventually left this hospital, her entire world would be different.

A senseless, horrific accident.

All because the other driver had been high on pain pills and drunk off his ass.

Winn had stopped by around four this morning to check on everyone's status. And to pick up blood toxicity reports from the lab. I'd been with her when she'd read them. The color had drained from her face and her eyes had flooded when she'd let me see the details.

Her own parents had been killed in a car crash. Reliving it had to have been horrific.

But I knew my sister-in-law well enough to know she'd be just as stoic as Dr. Anderson. As Dad. She wouldn't collapse until she was home with Griffin.

Regardless, I'd called my brother and told him that he

needed to take the kids to Mom, then get to the police station, because his wife needed him.

The weight of this tragedy settled on my shoulders, threatening to send me to my knees. Doctors in big cities had cases like this weekly. Daily. How did they endure it?

In med school, we'd spent time shadowing doctors in Seattle. Some had been kind and accommodating to student questions. Some had been arrogant and annoyed at our presence. But there was one doctor I remembered with vivid clarity. He'd been cold. He'd had this air about him, like he'd detached from all emotion. *The robot.*

Had he always been so mechanical? Or had it been his coping mechanism?

My throat burned and my nose stung, but like I'd done for the past twelve hours, I shoved it away. My tears would not bring this little boy's legs back. Or his father.

What this family needed from me was to keep them alive. So I squared my shoulders and got back to work, checking on all three patients. Then I left the small intensive care unit and hurried to the other side of the hospital, checking on the other patients. When I finished my rounds, I returned to check on the kids and their mother. They were all resting.

The two nurses on shift had their heads bent in quiet conversation again at the nurses' station, so I walked over. When they realized I was standing in front of them, they jerked and broke apart.

"Sorry, Talia," the blond woman said. "We were just talking about, uh, Rachel."

"Rachel. Why?"

The two shared a look. Then the blonde waved me closer to whisper, "The other driver was Rachel's son."

I gasped, my hand flying to my mouth. "What?"

She nodded. "He was sort of, um...he had some addiction troubles."

Addiction troubles. How severe? Clearly, severe enough that his addiction had led him to drinking and taking too many pills. Severe enough to kill a father of two.

Today, I didn't have a lot of sympathy for Rachel's son's troubles.

"I had no idea," I said.

Rachel didn't talk to me. She didn't confide in me. We'd never been anything that resembled friends. Hell, she barely tolerated me as her coworker. No, in her life, I was a nuisance. It went both ways.

Except my heart went out to her. "Poor Rachel. I wonder if there is something we can do for her."

The nurses shared another look.

"What?" I asked. What was I missing?

"That's really sweet of you to think of her, Talia," the other woman said. "But..."

But Rachel hated me.

For years I'd been trying to win her over. And now, seeing the looks on these nurses' faces, I realized it was futile.

"If something gets organized for her, please just let me know how I can contribute. Even if it's just some money under the table."

"I can organize something," the blonde said.

"Thank you." I walked away, meeting Dr. Anderson in the hallway.

His cheeks were flushed from the cold outside and he looked to have found another burst of energy. Or he was good at faking it. "I needed that. Why don't you take a short break?

You've earned it."

"Are you sure?" I asked.

"I insist."

A walk outside might give me a boost too, so I headed for the locker room to pull on my coat. In my rush to leave the house last night, I hadn't grabbed food and since I hadn't eaten since dinner, I dug a few dollars from my purse to pick up a banana and a latte at the cafeteria.

I had my snack and a steaming to-go cup in my hand— nothing as good as Lyla's espressos, but it would do in a pinch— as I strode through the lobby toward the exit. Except a head of familiar graying-blond bun caught my attention, and I stopped short of the sliding doors.

Rachel.

What was she doing in the waiting area? Why was she at the hospital? Oh, God. Someone had told her, right? Someone had informed her of her son's death. She wasn't waiting for an update, was she?

My stomach plummeted, my footsteps leaden, as I changed directions. She sat in an upholstered chair with wooden arms and an array of magazines fanned on the table at her side.

"Rachel," I said softly, taking the seat opposite hers.

She tore her gaze from the floor and looked up. The wreckage in her red-rimmed eyes answered my questions. *She knew.* Her bun was disheveled with strands pulled free at her temples and around her ears.

"I'm so sorry," I said. "Can I get you anything? Can I call someone?"

She tilted her head to the side, blinking twice like she had no idea who I was. Then whatever fog cleared because the Rachel I knew snapped into place. The glare she sent me was laced with venom. It made the other scowls she'd given me in the past look like gentle reassurances.

"Fuck you." Her lip curled.

I tensed but stayed silent. I'd take the insults, the curses, if it helped her through the grief of losing her child.

"He worked for you," she spat. "He was one of your hired men."

At the ranch. He must have worked for Dad. Or maybe Griffin. "Okay."

"Your self-righteous brother fired him because he came to work hungover."

"Oh. I'm... I'm so sorry." What else could I say?

She scoffed. "It was after his birthday party. He'd just turned twenty-one. Half of the people out getting him drunk were your other employees. And he gets fired for a hangover? Your double standards are sickening."

Your. She kept saying "your," like I had anything to do with the operations at the ranch. I didn't keep up on the staff they hired, let alone have anything to do with firing them. But I stayed quiet, swallowing the urge to clarify.

"They claimed he was still drunk. That he'd been coming to work impaired." Her entire body began to tremble. "My son wasn't a drunk. It was a bunch of lies. Probably because your brother didn't want to pay him what he was worth."

None of that sounded like Griffin. He paid his hired men competitive salaries, usually above the local market rate. Most of the ranch staff had been there for years because of the benefits offered. But beyond that, Griffin and Dad had always treated their staff with immense respect for their hard work.

If Rachel's son had been fired, it was likely because he hadn't been doing that work.

When had Griffin hired her son? Since I'd moved home, I couldn't remember hearing that he'd had to fire anyone. He didn't always keep me apprised, but I knew my brother. Griff hated firing men. It would have bothered him enough that he'd have been noticeably grumpy about it.

Chances were that Rachel's son had been fired before I'd even moved home from Seattle. Before I'd started working at the hospital.

I hadn't stood a chance with her, had I? She would have hated me regardless, simply because of my last name.

"You walk around here like you're something special." She sneered. "When really you're just a spoiled little princess. Did you know that the hospital had to make budget changes to afford your salary? My sister worked in Human Resources. Her position was eliminated when you were hired. So were three other job openings. Positions that would have lightened the burden on *my* staff."

My mouth parted. What? "I didn't know that."

How could I have known they'd had to make cuts to afford me? I wasn't paid outlandishly. And besides, it was only temporary, right? Because Dr. Anderson would retire, and as far as I knew, they wouldn't be replacing him. That was why I was here. To learn. To train.

To be the doctor for the *next* thirty years.

That was why the board had made the decision to bring in another doctor.

Except the logic behind their decision wouldn't matter to Rachel. She was too busy hating me.

"And to think," she scoffed. "If we had actually brought in a decent doctor, maybe my son would be alive."

I flinched, the air rushing from my lungs like she'd hit me in the gut. She couldn't possibly believe that her son's death was my fault.

No, she did. It was there, in her gaze, the blame.

"We've had more deaths in this hospital since you've started than we've had in years. Because we had to hire an Eden." Rachel stood, then she was gone, leaving me in the waiting room alone, unable to breathe.

Part of me, deep down in my heart, knew those were angry words. That a mother was lashing out, and I'd been an easy target. But the other part of me, raw and vulnerable and tired and sad, wondered if she had a point.

Was I a bad doctor? After medical school, I hadn't applied anywhere but Quincy Memorial for my residency. But if I had broadened my search, would I have gotten other offers? Or would they have found me lacking?

My coffee was cold when Dr. Anderson found me in the waiting room, stuck in that same, uncomfortable chair.

"Talia, there you are. Good. I wasn't sure if you'd come in from your break yet."

"S-sorry." I forced myself to my feet. My knees felt weak. My head was spinning. "Did you need something?"

"No. Just wanted to tell you that Dr. Herrera got here, so you're free to head home. I'll see you on Monday."

"Oh. Sure." I nodded but didn't move. The grip on my coffee was shaky, and if not for the lid, it would have spilled on my hand.

"Hey." He stepped closer, touching my elbow. "Are you all right?"

"Just a long night."

"Yeah, it was. Get some rest, Talia."

"You too," I choked out.

Late last night, he'd told me that I'd saved that mother's life. That her children would get to keep one of their parents because I'd been there to treat her. He'd said it was important that he'd had Dr. Murphy's help with the boy and what a relief it had been to trust me with the mom.

I was a good doctor. He wouldn't have left me with that woman if he didn't trust me. Believe in me.

"I'm a good doctor," I whispered to myself.

The reassurance didn't stop the tears from flooding. But I blinked them away, holding it together as I collected my purse and keys from my locker, then made the drive home.

I parked in the garage, and the moment the Jeep was off, the tears fell like a tidal wave. They streamed down my face as I sobbed, my chest shaking uncontrollably.

One moment, I was clutching the steering wheel, giving my pain to the darkness. The next, the Jeep's door was open and a pair of strong arms wrapped around my body.

Foster swept me into the house, his lips against my hair as he murmured, "Tally."

It hurt. God, it hurt. My entire body was cracking in two.

He cradled me against his chest, holding tight.

While I sobbed for the lives I couldn't save.

And the lives I had.

CHAPTER 23

FOSTER

"**B**reathe," I murmured against Talia's hair as I held her in the middle of our bed. "Breathe."

She kept crying, curled so tight into my chest it was like she was trying to burrow inside my body. She cried so hard that her body spasmed with each sob. The front of my shirt was soaked from her tears. And my heart...*fuck*. My heart could barely fucking take this.

This couldn't be the first time she'd had a hard night at the hospital. Who'd held her after those nights? Who'd been here for her when it should have been me?

"Breathe, love." I needed her to stop crying. I needed her to breathe. My arms banded tighter, wishing I could take this pain and absorb it. "It'll be okay."

She nodded, her fists clutching my shirt and twisting it in her grip. "I-I c-can't—"

Stop. She couldn't stop. "In and out."

"S-sorry," she stammered.

"It's all right." I kissed her hair, kept my arms locked, until the sobs became whimpers. Her chest shook with hiccups and the flood of tears eventually ebbed.

"I'm sorry," she said, shifting out of my lap to sit on her own, cross-legged on the mattress.

"Better?" I tucked a lock of hair behind her ear and caught one of the last tears with my thumb.

"Ugh." She sniffled, wiping her cheeks dry. Then she closed her eyes, dropping her face to her hands. "Sorry."

"Why do you keep apologizing?"

"For crying."

"So?" I tugged at her wrists, pulling her hands down until I could see her face.

She dragged in a shaky breath. "I don't like crying in front of people."

"I'm not people. I'm the man who loves you. Tear stained or not."

She sighed, her shoulders slumping. Then she glanced behind her toward the open bedroom door. "Where's Kadence? She didn't see that, did she? Shit."

"She's not here. It's just us. Maggie's mom invited her over for another playdate. I dropped her off about ten minutes before you got home."

"Phew." Talia closed her eyes again. "So much for living in my emotional shell."

"Huh?" What was she talking about? "Is that some sort of doctor terminology for putting distance between you and your patients?"

"Oh, no. It's something Lyla said. It's why we got in that argument."

The argument she hadn't told me much about.

"She said I have an emotional shell." Talia sniffled. "She was glad that you came to town because since you've been here, I've shown more emotion in a few days than I have in years. Whatever that means. I show emotion all the time but apparently not the ugly ones that she wants to see. We got in a fight about it. That's why we haven't been talking."

I cupped her face, my thumb tracing her cheekbone. But I kept my damn mouth shut. She wasn't going to like that I had to agree with Lyla.

"Does this look like an emotional shell?" Talia tossed up her hand, her chin quivering again.

My thumb just kept stroking her skin as my lips stayed closed.

Talia studied my face, then her eyes widened.

Damn it. I hadn't hid it.

"You think so too, don't you?" Her chin quivered. "That I live in an emotional shell?"

"No, I don't think you live in an emotional shell." I took her face in my hands, pulling her close for a kiss. "You laugh. You tried to rip my head off the day we got it on in the ring at the gym. Joy. Affection. Confidence. You show emotion, Tally. I'm guessing what Lyla meant was that you don't always let others see when you struggle."

"That's not—"

I pressed a finger to her lips. "Case in point, you just apologized three times for crying."

Her frame deflated.

"It's my fault," I said. "I'll own it."

She scoffed. "How is my emotional unavailability your fault?"

"Because you weren't like this before." I gave her a sad smile. "Remember that time you spilled bleach on my favorite jeans? I found you in the laundry room of your apartment, bawling over a white spot the size of a dime on the knee."

"You loved those jeans. I loved those jeans. They made your ass look fantastic."

I chuckled. "And I still wore them, stain and all."

Those jeans had stayed with me a long time, mostly so I could look at that white spot and think of Talia. Too many years, too many washings, and they'd gotten so threadbare that I'd been doing yardwork one day and I'd torn through the knee. I'd had to toss them out. I'd been a miserable bastard for a week after that.

"I don't want to be closed off," she whispered.

"Drop your shield, love. Put your hands down. All the way."

"I'm scared."

"Voice your fears. Let's put them out there. Face them, together."

It took her a moment to meet my gaze. "Will you break my heart again?"

"Never." I'd die first.

"Will you leave me?"

"Never." Not willingly. Not until the end.

"Will you stop loving me?"

"Never." My love for her had no end. I'd love her in this world and the next. "Never, Tally. Never."

Tears welled in her eyes. "I love you. Only you. Always you."

Victory.

This fight was over.

"I love you, Talia Eden."

She closed her eyes, breathing like she was pulling those words into the fibers of her being, then she crawled into my lap, letting me hold her again.

I kissed her hair. "These scrubs are not the same ones you

left in last night." The ones last night had been her standard baby blue. These were teal, faded from too many trips to the laundry room.

"I had to change."

"Want to tell me about it?" I asked.

"I want to be a good doctor," she said.

"You are."

"It's easy to doubt yourself after the nights when people die."

Fuck. I held her closer, listening as she told me about the accident. About the nurse who hated her and the son who'd died.

"I'm sorry," I said when she finished.

"Me too."

"What can I do?"

"You're doing it." She snuggled closer. "I need to shower. Get some food. See Kadence. I could use a few of her smiles today."

That she wanted my daughter was, well...fuck. I didn't deserve Talia Eden.

But she was mine to keep.

"Go take your shower. Then you need to rest."

"I'm exhausted." She yawned. "But I don't know if I can sleep."

"Come on. Up you go." I lifted her off the bed and unzipped her coat. Then I helped her out of those scrubs, taking them to the hamper while she retreated to the bathroom.

It didn't take her long to shower, and when she emerged, a towel wrapped around her torso, I dragged my lucky shamrock tee over her head.

She yawned again as I steered her toward the bed. And two

minutes after I'd curled her into my side, she was out.

My arm fell asleep. I had a kink in my neck. Her damp hair soaked the sleeve and shoulder of my shirt. But damn it, I didn't move for three hours while she slept. Not until my phone vibrated in my pocket with a text from Maggie's mom saying that I could come get Kadence at any time.

The moment I shifted, Talia's body jerked. Her eyes snapped open like she was waking from a bad dream.

"You okay?"

She nodded, her eyes blinking away sleep. "How long was I asleep?"

"A few hours. You want to crash again? I've got to go get Kaddie."

"I'll come with you." She moved to roll off the bed but I gripped her shoulders, keeping her pinned to my side as I kissed her, slow and deep.

"I love you," I said as I broke away.

She smiled. "I love you."

"There's my girl." My Tally, the strongest person I'd ever met. Even after everything that had happened last night, she'd wear a smile today. For me. For Kadence.

I stripped out of my damp shirt while she blow-dried her hair. Then, still wearing my lucky tee with a pair of jeans, we took Kadence downtown for the afternoon to wander along Main and swing into Eden Coffee for drinks and a snack.

While Kaddie and I sat at a table sharing a croissant, Talia and Lyla slipped into the kitchen of the cafe. When they emerged, Talia glanced over and smiled.

Guess that meant their fight was over.

"Daddy, can we go to a movie?" Kadence asked, her lips covered in chocolate.

"Sure," Talia answered for me as she joined us at the table. "The theater here isn't as big as the ones you're probably used to. But it's pretty fun. They usually have a kids movie playing. And they make the best popcorn ever."

"Better than mine?" I huffed. "Prove it."

She laughed, musical and sweet. A laugh, unguarded and free.

No more doubts.

The three of us went to a movie. We stopped at the pizza place to pick up dinner and take it home. And after Kadence's bath, Talia and I both tucked my daughter into bed before retreating to the couch.

"How are you feeling?" I asked as she leaned into my side, putting her head on my shoulder.

"Better. Thanks for today."

"Welcome," I said. "Can I ask you something? What did you do before? If you had a rough day at the hospital, what did you do?"

"Sometimes I'd go to the ranch. Take a ride. Other times, I'd just come here."

"Alone?"

"Yeah," she murmured. "But not anymore."

"No, not anymore." I shifted, ready to carry her upstairs to bed, but the sound of footsteps came from outside a second before the doorbell rang. "Who's that?"

"A guess? Someone with the last name Eden." Talia stood. "I'm sure news of the accident is all over town."

So her family had come to check on her.

She followed me to the entryway.

Except it wasn't an Eden on the porch. I flipped the lock and whipped the door open, waving our visitor inside. "Vivienne, what are you doing here? Is everything okay?"

The latter was a stupid question.

Her face was bone white. Her eyes were bloodshot. The dark circles beneath them looked like bruises.

"I'm sorry to bother you," she told Talia. Then she glanced up at me. The moment our gazes locked, her face contorted and her eyes flooded with tears. "I'm so sorry."

"Sorry for what? For coming here?"

Vivienne was scheduled to be here next week. She'd booked a flight to Quincy to stay here with Kadence while Talia and I went to Vegas for the fight.

"No, it's...oh my God, Foster. I didn't know where else to go."

"What is going on?" My voice was too loud, but goddamn it, I was starting to worry.

Talia inched closer to my side, her hand slipping into my own. My pulse instantly calmed.

Until Vivienne spoke.

"It's Dex. He's not what he seems." She gulped. "We're in trouble, Foster. I'm in trouble."

CHAPTER 24

TALIA

"Come in." I waved Vivienne inside, shifting to make space.

Foster's grip on my hand tightened as his forehead furrowed.

"I'm sorry." A tear dropped from Vivienne's cheek, landing on the floor. "I'm so sorry."

She was on the verge of hysteria. Her fingers shook so badly she couldn't grip the zipper on her coat. She tried four times before Foster finally stepped in, helping her take off the jacket before steadying her as she struggled with her shoes.

"Did you fly?" Foster asked.

She nodded. "To Missoula. Then picked up a rental and drove here."

"You should have called me." Foster frowned. "Called the charter."

"I'm sorry." Her voice cracked. She glanced at him, then at me. Whatever she saw on our faces was enough to push her over the edge. Vivienne buried her face in her hands, the muffled sobs shaking her shoulders, until Foster pulled her into his side.

"You're worrying me, Vivi," he said, looking to me with an unspoken question in his gaze.

This okay?

I nodded.

Maybe I'd overlooked it before, or maybe I'd been too stuck in my own head to notice, but the way he hugged her was the way my brothers hugged me. It was just a hug. He gave her a strong body to lean against, nothing more.

It was nothing like the comfort he'd given me earlier. There was no intimacy in that embrace.

They were...friends.

Maybe, in time, I could be friends with Vivienne again too.

Somewhere along the way, I'd forgiven her. It had happened so quietly that I hadn't even realized it until this moment. The awkwardness might linger for a while, but I didn't hate Vivienne. I didn't resent her for the years she'd had with him.

And Foster, well... I think I'd forgiven him months ago. Around the time we'd made snow angels in my yard.

"Vivi," I said. "Do you want to see Kadence?"

She stepped away from Foster's side, using the sleeve of her shirt to dry her face. Then she nodded. "Please. Is she asleep?"

"Yeah. But you know how she is," Foster said. "We could blare heavy metal from the hallway and she'd sleep through it."

The corner of Vivienne's mouth turned up.

"I'll show you to her room," I said, leading the way through the house.

"You have a beautiful home. Kadence talks about it sometimes. She loves it here."

I smiled over my shoulder. "I'm glad. I like having her here."

We reached the doorway, and I stepped aside so Vivienne could slip into Kaddie's room. But she didn't go in. She hovered at the threshold while a different sadness—bittersweet and lonely instead of pained and desperate—filled her gaze.

"I feel like I'm losing her. Or a part of her. But if I have to share her, I'm glad it's with you." Before I could reply, she walked into the room, going straight for the bed where Kadence was curled in her blankets like a burrito. Vivienne bent and kissed her forehead, then whispered something before leaving her daughter to sleep.

Her shoulders were squared as she returned to the hallway. She sniffled but had stopped crying. "Can we talk in the living room?"

"Sure." I nodded, and when we turned, Foster stood a few feet away.

"Need a drink?" he asked.

Vivienne shook her head.

"Tally?"

"I'm okay." I walked to his side and let him take my hand, tugging me to the living room.

Foster and I sat on the couch, seated so closely that our thighs touched. And Vivienne took the seat opposite us in my favorite reading chair.

"What's going on, Vivi?" Foster asked. "What's going on with Dex?"

She sat ramrod straight, her hands clasped on her lap and her chin down. A woman who was preparing for an interrogation, ready to make her confession. "I'll start at the beginning."

For me. Foster knew their background because he'd been there. But I appreciated that she was including me too.

"Dex and I met at Angel's about three years ago. He came in with a mutual friend to learn how to box. I was working at the gym. It was all part of Dad's grand plan. He had his son-in-law for teaching and training, this wildly successful fighter Dad could claim was his protégé. And his daughter was in the office, wasting the teaching degree she'd earned to run the business side of things at the gym. It was Dad's perfect Angel's Gym family. All lies and manipulation."

Animosity crept into her tone. Vivienne glared at an invisible spot on the carpet like she was picturing her father's face.

"Thankfully, Dad wasn't around much. And he was never interested in accounting or marketing. Which meant I had the office to myself most of the time. It was perfect when Kadence was a baby."

"We set up a play area. Vivi would keep Kaddie in the office, and I was close by to help," Foster said.

"When she started preschool, it was lonely. Really lonely. Maybe that was why I didn't dismiss Dex the first time he came into the office and flirted with me. Because I was alone and, well...no one had flirted with me in a really long time."

"Did he know you and Foster were married?" I asked. Even if Dex had known it was a sham, it seemed like a bold move to chase after Foster Madden's wife.

"It was harmless." She shrugged. "And for about a year, that's all it was. Dex would come into the gym every Monday, Wednesday and Friday over the lunch hour. He'd work out. Hit the showers. Then before he left, he'd pop into the office and compliment me on my hair or my shirt or my ears or my laugh. He's handsome. I was flattered. And he made me feel wanted."

Foster sighed. There was a lot of guilt in that sigh. The reason she'd felt unwanted was because Foster had always loved me.

I put my hand on his knee and leaned in deeper. There was nothing for him to feel guilty about. He never could have been the man Vivienne needed.

Because he was mine.

"Somewhere along the way, the flirting became more serious," Vivienne said. "I can't even pinpoint when, but our conversations felt different."

"It wasn't harmless anymore," I said.

"We developed feelings for each other." A ghost of a smile pulled at her lips. "Until one day, he came in—it was a day when Foster wasn't at the gym—and asked if he could see me. He knew I was married but he said that he couldn't stop thinking about me. So we started an affair."

"No," Foster said. "Not an affair."

"Wasn't it?" she asked.

"I knew about it," he said. "I understood."

"Until today, I never felt ashamed. I fell in love with Dex, and yeah, it wasn't how I would have liked to start a new relationship, but we didn't have a lot of options, did we? But today..." She swallowed hard. "Was I so desperate to find love that I invented it? Was I so lonesome that I overlooked all of the red flags? He pursued me. Actively. He knew I was a married woman and he chased me anyway. Yeah, our marriage was a sham. But he didn't know that. Not then."

"Vivienne, if you missed it, then so did I," Foster said. "Those days he came to the gym, I knew who he was. I knew why he went to the office. You think I'd let him waltz in there if I thought he was using you?"

Vivi closed her eyes. "I think... I think neither of us knew the real Dex. Like we didn't know the real Arlo."

Foster stiffened at the comparison. "What happened?"

"Dex and I have been together for years." She didn't answer Foster's question but continued the story for me. "I didn't want to risk my dad finding out and making our situation worse, so we kept it a secret. In the beginning, Dex thought that the reason we were sneaking around was because of Foster. That we were unhappy in our marriage but staying together for Kadence. Except I couldn't have that secret hanging over our heads forever."

So she'd told him about the blackmail.

"I told Dex the truth about six months before Dad died," she said. "He wasn't very happy that I'd lied to him, but we got through it. Then Dad died and we were free."

Free. It was the same term that Foster had used.

"How does all of this lead to you coming to Montana in tears?" Foster asked. He'd been patient, letting Vivienne give me the backstory, but that patience was fading.

Vivienne's frame shrank in the chair. "Dex doesn't want to move. He's basically refused to at this point. We've fought about it so many times, I've lost track."

"You didn't tell me that," he said. "You said he was just dragging his feet."

"You needed to be here," she told him.

With me.

"He was upset about changing his job," Vivienne said.

Foster scoffed. "He works remotely for a tech company based in Houston. Nothing about his job was going to change other than the address of his home office."

"I know." Vivienne held up her hands. "But regardless, every time I brought up the move, we'd get in a fight. He didn't like that I was moving to accommodate you, even though I told him it was best for Kadence."

Foster's jaw clenched. He'd told me that Dex was a good guy, but based on the strain creeping into his body, I was thinking that opinion was changing.

"The real reason he didn't want to move is because he can't leave Vegas," Vivienne said.

"Can't?" Foster asked.

Vivienne sucked in a shaky breath, then leaned forward, elbows to knees. "Dex got in with a bookie. Put big money on a horse race and lost. I had no idea. But apparently, my dad found out."

Foster inched forward.

"Dad knew Dex and I were together. I don't know how or when he found out, but he knew. So he approached Dex about it."

"And what? Threatened him?" Foster asked.

Vivienne shook her head. "No. Dad just offered Dex the chance to make more money. Said that he'd never allow you and me to get divorced, so if Dex was always going to be my side piece, he might as well get rich in the process."

"Damn it." Foster dragged a hand through his hair. "Fights. Dex bet on fights, didn't he?"

"Yep. Dad took him to an underground fight and he's been going ever since. It started about the same time I told him the truth about the blackmail. Maybe the reason he went in the first place was because he was pissed at me. I don't know. But even knowing all that I'd told him about those illegal fights, Dex went with Dad. He did okay at first. Won most of his bets."

"Because Arlo was telling him exactly who to bet on." Foster's jaw ticked. "Fuck. Then that old bastard died."

Vivienne didn't so much as flinch at that last comment. I doubted it was the first time Foster had cursed Arlo's name.

The room went still. Vivienne didn't really need to explain. Our minds were all barreling in the same direction. When Arlo had died, Dex wouldn't have known who to bet on.

"How deep is he in, Vivi?" Foster asked.

"Almost three million dollars." She gulped. "He kept losing. Kept borrowing, promising to win big. Arlo had taught him enough about fighting, so it was just a matter of time. He was just on a losing streak."

A three-million-dollar losing streak. *Who kept giving that idiot money?* I studied Foster, waiting to see if he was going to explode. His face was granite. His stormy eyes raged. But he didn't so much as breathe, let alone speak.

"Dex sold his house. He moved in with me after Kadence came here," Vivienne said.

"That should at least buy him some time, right?" I asked. "How much did he pay off?"

Vivienne stared at the carpet again. "He, um, didn't put it toward his debt. He took that money and put it on another fight."

"Son of a bitch." Foster shot to his feet, walking to the fireplace to brace his arms on the mantel. "You're fucking kidding me."

"He bet it on your fight."

"Of course he did," Foster muttered. "Well, at least he'll likely win this one."

Vivienne winced. "He bet on Savage to win. It's two to one odds. You're favored."

So Dex had bet on Savage in the hopes that he'd get a bigger payout. Even though Foster was likely going to win.

Foster straightened. "Tell me you're joking."

"I didn't know." Vivienne's brown eyes filled with more tears. "Not until this morning. A guy came to the house and threatened Dex. I was in the kitchen, cooking breakfast. I heard shouting and banging. When I got to the living room,

Dex was kneeling on the floor. The man had a gun to his head. He said either Dex gets the money or he's dead. To give him extra motivation, he promised to kill me first. And make Dex watch."

I gasped.

Vivienne was trembling. "I packed up and left."

Foster stood frozen, staring blankly at the mantel. The muscles in his shoulders and back were bunched.

"Three million dollars?" I asked Vivienne.

"Yes." She caught a tear before it could fall. "I'm sorry. I'm so sorry. I can sell the house and give Dex my half. Sell my car. Sell Angel's. Hopefully the man who has been fronting Dex will give me time to liquidate everything, but I don't know. It sounded like they're expecting to be paid immediately after the fight."

The fight was in two weeks. She wouldn't be able to sell properties in that time.

"Who's the man Dex has been borrowing from?" Foster asked.

"Tony Sabbatini."

"Christ." He closed his eyes.

"Who's Tony Sabbatini?" I asked, staring between them both.

"A man you pay back," Vivienne said quietly. "One of Dad's nefarious acquaintances."

"I'll give you the money," Foster said. "Then we'll be done with it."

"It's not that simple." Her face paled. "Dex won't take it. I already suggested we borrow it from you."

"He's a fucking fool," Foster clipped.

"He's jealous," she said. "He won't admit it, but he's jealous of you. He said he'd rather die than live in debt to you the rest of his life."

Foster raised his chin. "That's his choice."

"Even if that means they come after me?" she asked. "I'm sorry. I know you're angry. I'm angry too. But, Foster... I love him."

Her love, and Dex's pride, might get them both killed.

My stomach knotted.

Foster's hands balled into fists. "What are you asking me to do, Vivienne?"

Her chin quivered. And though she whispered the word, it was as loud as a gunshot.

"Lose."

ROUND 5

CHAPTER 25

FOSTER

Beyond the spotless, floor-to-ceiling windows of our hotel suite, the Las Vegas strip was stirring for the day. People from around the world traveled here to revel in the sensation that was Vegas. Personally, it had never held much appeal.

I'd always been partial to the surrounding landscape, the desert scenery and the vibrant colors of sunset over the rocky plateaus. The tourists could keep the glitter and flash of these massive casinos. They could enjoy the chimes and jingles from a sea of slot machines. One night here, and I was ready to go home.

Talia's arms slid around my torso as she fit her chest to my back. She kissed my spine before pressing her cheek to my shoulder. We stood in silence, watching traffic weave through the streets and people emerge to wander the sidewalks.

We'd spent a lot of time like this in the past nine days.

Holding each other. Contemplating the future. Preparing for another fight.

I'd thought we were done. I'd thought we'd won.

But I guess there was another round after all.

"I feel trapped," I said.

"I know." Her arms tightened. "I'm sorry."

I sighed. "Me too."

"What did Vivienne say this morning?"

"Nothing. I didn't talk to her, just to Kadence before school."

It was strange not to talk to Vivienne. During our entire marriage, I could count on one hand the number of times we'd fought. We were friends. There was no passion between us. Maybe that was why it had been so easy to live together. We'd been comfortable roommates. Co-parents.

In all our years, I'd never been this angry with her. What she'd asked me to do, this position she'd put me in, was impossible.

Lose.

Like father. Like daughter.

After our conversation about Dex, I'd been so livid that I'd had to leave the living room. I'd gone upstairs, paced the length of the bedroom. When Talia had come up, she'd known that I'd been about to unravel. She hadn't questioned me when I'd left for the gym. She'd stayed behind with Kadence. And Vivienne.

I'd spent hours that night beating the hell out of a heavy bag until the red haze had cleared from my vision. Then I'd sat in the ring, alone, wondering what the fuck I was supposed to do.

History was repeating itself. It was seven years ago. And instead of Arlo Angel fucking up my life, it was my ex-wife.

Over a week later and I was still furious. Disappointed. Confused. I doubted my friendship with Vivienne would ever be the same.

I tore my gaze from the windows and turned, tugging Talia into my chest to breathe in her hair. Citrus and coconut and my girl. Did she have any idea how much I needed her? How much comfort I was drawing from her?

At least I wasn't facing this disaster alone.

"What do you need to do today?" she asked.

"Jasper and I are meeting at one. I was thinking about heading to the house, seeing what's left that I want to pack and send home. But I don't want to risk bumping into Dex."

I might kill the son of a bitch.

What if Kadence had been there? What if Tony Sabbatini's thug had broken into the house with my daughter there? What if they'd threatened her life too?

How could Vivienne even consider taking Dex's side? My muscles bunched. "Fuck, I'm pissed."

Talia let me go, putting her hand to my clenched jaw. "Let's go do something. Take a drive. Get away from the strip."

"Yeah." It wouldn't help. Nothing had helped. But I kissed her forehead anyway and let her lead me into the shower.

She'd been a miracle this week. I didn't have a lot of words right now. Everything I said seemed to come out with bite, so I'd withdrawn. But Talia had stayed by my side, holding steady.

Since I'd been a grumpy bastard, I tried to make up for it with orgasms. I fucked her against the shower wall. I worked her hard until she screamed, coming apart around my cock. Then I washed her hair and body before shutting off the water and wrapping her in a towel.

"I love you," I told her as she brushed out her damp hair at the sink.

"I love you too." She smiled at me through the mirror. "No matter what you decide, I love you, baby."

Dropping a kiss on her shoulder, I went to the closet to get dressed in some jeans and a plain gray T-shirt. Talia finished drying her hair and pulled on jeans and a black tank. Then we set out for the first floor, leaving the suite.

We'd flown to Vegas late last night. Too many sleepless nights, and I'd been exhausted by the time we'd picked up the rental car and driven to the hotel. I'd wanted to check into the suite, bury myself in Talia for a while and, hopefully, sleep.

But the lobby had been crowded. Even on a Monday night there'd been a crush, and since this was the hotel where the fight would happen Saturday, my picture was flashing on various displays. I'd signed autographs for almost an hour before we'd finally made it to the elevator.

I hadn't been in the mood last night and sure as fuck wasn't this morning, so I pulled on a hat and pair of sunglasses, keeping my chin down as Talia and I made our way outside.

When the valet spotted me, his eyes widened. Talia squeezed my hand as I grumbled under my breath. But I put on a smile, shook the kid's hand and signed my parking slip while he rushed to pick up our Tahoe.

The moment we were inside, I breathed. "I hate Vegas."

"I thought you liked it here."

"That was before I lived in Montana." I took her hand, brought it to my lips for a kiss. We swung through a Starbucks drive-thru to pick up coffee and breakfast sandwiches, then headed out of town. Away from the strip. Away from the traffic. Just...away.

It was almost two hours later by the time we returned to the city. I'd planned to head back to the hotel, but as we passed an exit, Talia pointed for me to turn off.

"Take this one," she said.

"Tally, no." I tensed. This was the exit that would lead us toward Angel's. There was no other reason for us to go this way.

"Please," she said when I didn't slow. "I want to see it."

I sighed, but I wouldn't deny her this. She'd come to Vegas for me. But maybe she had her own demons to pummel while she was here too. So I drove the familiar path toward Angel's, dread and loathing creeping into my blood with every turn. Until we were parked in the gym's lot next to a few cars.

This fucking place. Once a sanctuary. Then a jail. Not that anyone but Vivienne knew I hated this building. We'd pretended. We'd faked good relationships with Arlo.

Talia made no move to get out of the SUV, so neither did I. Instead we stared at the cinderblock wall through the windshield.

The white paint was nearly blinding beneath the morning sun. I'd always thought it was too bright a shade, but Arlo had insisted on white—inside and out—because it was clean.

Unlike his dirty soul.

Even when Vivi had convinced him to do a fresh coat a few years ago, he'd only agreed as long as she kept it white and didn't touch the wall that bordered the parking lot. That very wall had my attention at the moment. Talia's too.

Painted in bold strokes in every color of the rainbow on that faded white surface were a pair of massive angel wings.

"Vivienne's mother painted those wings," Talia said. "You probably know that."

I nodded. She'd painted them the summer before she'd died of breast cancer. "There's a picture at the house of Kadence standing between them."

It was Vivi's favorite picture.

Arlo's warning about not painting this wall had been pointless. Vivi never would have erased those wings. Instead, her plan was to just walk away. To keep on pretending that the new owner would keep the wings forever.

I doubted Vivienne would ever come back here after she moved to Quincy. It would be too hard to see the physical memory of her mom missing.

"She hasn't said it, but I think a part of Vivienne wishes we could stay here," I said. "In Vegas."

"Is that what you want?" Talia asked.

"No." Montana had made a lasting impression this winter. So had the Eden family. Quincy was my future.

Vivienne wouldn't argue, because it was too important to me.

"I'm so fucking mad at her." My molars ground together. "She'll go to the extreme for the people she loves. Doesn't realize she goes too far."

Just like when she'd let Arlo push us into a marriage. It hadn't been for her. Sure as fuck hadn't been for me. She'd done it for Kadence.

Vivienne would move to Montana for me. For Kadence.

And she'd sacrifice our relationship because she was in love with Dex.

"I wonder if Arlo would have blackmailed you if Vivienne's mother had been here to stop him," Talia said.

"I don't know, love."

"Me neither." Talia reached for the door's handle and climbed out of the SUV.

I took a deep breath and followed, meeting her in front of the hood and taking her hand. Then together, we walked into the gym.

Angel's was nothing more than a square box of a building. In a way, it was a lot like the building I'd purchased in Quincy, though it was three times the size. Instead of an apartment, there were two offices.

Arlo had kept one, though he'd rarely sat behind his desk. He'd used it for closed-door discussions with fighters, me included. The business he didn't want anyone to overhear, like when he asked me for money.

Vivienne's office was the biggest of the two with two large glass windows that overlooked the gym space. Those windows were dark today.

Three boxing rings were spaced evenly through the room. Two younger guys were in the center ring, one practicing his punches while another held pads. Along the far wall were rows of free weights and three stationary bikes.

"Not much has changed," Talia said.

"No, not really." I tugged her hand, taking her toward an open section of mats.

"It smells the same. Like sweat and rubber and bleach and metal and cologne."

Arlo's cologne. The man was gone but that scent permeated these walls.

She let my hand go and spun in a slow circle. Then a smile tugged at her mouth as she pointed to the floor. "It was right here. This was where I was sitting when I saw you for the first time."

"I clocked you the second you walked through the door." I stretched for her elbow, hauling her close. Holding her was how I'd survived these past nine days. If she was within reach, then she was in my arms.

"It's quiet today." Talia glanced around. The space was clean and empty.

"It's early." Peak hours were usually in the afternoons and evenings. That's when people filtered in for lessons and sparring. The social aspect at Angel's was just as addictive as the fighting itself.

There was no set class schedule at Angel's. Men and women came in when they wanted to work. And usually, there'd be another person here, ready to work them over.

Mostly it was boxing with some martial arts for those of us who'd been interested. Drills were the foundation on which everything was built. There were instructors, like myself, who'd make sure to teach proper technique. But what made a fighter great was time honing those techniques. And time in the ring was priceless.

If you wanted to get better, you fought people who were better than you. People who pushed you. And for many years, the man who'd pushed the hardest had been me.

Was there any push left? Or had I used up my strength?

A man emerged from the locker room. "Foster?"

"Hey." I jerked up my chin. What was his name? There were too many young guys coming in and out these days. I'd stopped trying to keep track, to keep up appearances, after Arlo's death.

Hell, I'd even stopped training here. Jasper had a buddy who owned a gym. That's where I'd be meeting them this afternoon.

Arlo's was history now. I'd left Vivienne to run this place. And to move on with Dex.

"Wondered if we'd see you around here." The guy held out his hand, a bright smile stretching across his tanned face. "Looking forward to the fight Saturday. You ready?"

"Hope so." I forced a smile.

What if I just didn't show up? What if there was no fight?

What if I could leave and never look back?

"You here to work out?" He pointed to a ring.

"Nah. Just here to stop in. Check it out."

"And we'd better get going." Talia gave him a kind smile. "You don't want to be late to meet Jasper."

"Vale?" the man asked. "He's still training with you?"

"Yeah."

The guy opened his mouth but I extended a hand to shake his again before he could drag this out. "Good to see you," I said as he followed us to the exit.

"Yeah, yeah. You too, man. I'll be there Saturday."

"Appreciate it." With a wave, I held the door open for Talia to step outside, then we retreated to the SUV.

"Last time," she said.

I nodded. "Last time."

No matter what happened, I knew in my bones I wouldn't return to Angel's again. Maybe that was why she'd insisted on us stopping.

A farewell.

To end this the way it had started.

Talia and me.

"You need to eat something," she said.

"I'm not hungry." Nothing sounded good at the moment. Nothing but a meal made in Talia's kitchen. Or a dinner at Knuckles.

"I want a cheeseburger," she said.

"No, you don't." I chuckled. "You want me to get you a cheeseburger, probably two, and when you don't eat them, I will."

She giggled. "Maybe."

And I laughed for the first time in days. "If I vomit on Jasper while we're training, I'm blaming it on you."

"I'm willing to take one for the team."

Team. "We are a team. You and me."

"What do you want to do about the fight?" It was the first time she'd asked me that question. Instead of pressing, she'd given me time.

"I don't know," I admitted. "I didn't talk to you the last time this happened. Tell me what to do."

"I can't." She gave me a sad smile.

"Then I'm not buying you a cheeseburger."

Talia's laugh filled the cab and some of that anger, the frustration, eased. Regardless of what happened Saturday, I'd leave here with this woman.

"Do you want me to drop you at the hotel while I go meet Jasper? Or want to watch?" I asked.

"Watch."

"Good answer."

We stopped at a restaurant for cheeseburgers. After she ate one and I ate the other, we drove to the gym. Jasper was waiting with a group of guys I'd seen in my time training here.

It was different than at Arlo's. His ghost wasn't floating behind my back, ready to drive the knife deeper. I could relax here. Stop looking over my shoulder.

Jasper had been the one to suggest a change of scenery after Arlo's death, proving once again he had a direct line to my emotions.

"How are you?" he asked as I joined him in the ring to stretch for a few minutes.

"Good."

"Liar."

"You know I hate the press bullshit. Sets me on edge." Especially with a loudmouth asshole like Scott Savage.

It was the truth, but only a part of the story. I trusted Jasper with my life but I hadn't told him about the Vivienne and Dex clusterfuck. He'd be livid, and I needed him to keep focused. One of us had to concentrate on the fight.

I'd tell him about it later, after I made sense of it myself. After I figured out what to do.

"When's your first press event?" he asked.

"Tomorrow." For the rest of the week, I'd be adding various appearances to my schedule, all leading up to the fight this weekend. Thursday I had meetings with my agent and manager to talk about a new contract. Friday was weigh-in.

But today, I needed to train. So I smacked the floor and jumped to my feet, then walked to the edge of the ring, leaning on the ropes as I bent to talk to Talia, who'd pulled up a chair just beyond the ring. "Need anything?"

"All good." She shook her head. "Do your thing. Save a little energy for me later."

I grinned. "Maybe more than a little."

Two hours later, I was dripping with sweat, my muscles were warm and loose, and some of the haze in my mind had cleared.

Jasper had brought in some other guys from the gym, maybe sensing that what I'd needed was to burn. I'd done sparring round after sparring round. Most hadn't been much competition, but my last match had been with Jasper himself and he'd pushed hard.

"Saved yourself for last, huh?" I teased, chugging from a bottle of water. "Made sure I was winded before you stepped up."

Jasper chuckled, dragging a hand through his sweaty, dark hair. "That was the plan, but with the speed you're moving today, it wasn't necessary. How many body shots did you land? Two? Three? Savage is going to eat you alive."

He was taunting me. It was working.

"You're such an ass." I planted my hands on my hips, my chest shaking with laughter. "I landed more than three."

"Seven," Talia said from her bench. On her lap was a pen and notepad she'd pulled out of her purse. She lifted the paper, holding it up for me to see.

A sheet filled with tally marks.

A row for each of the sparring rounds.

"See?" I smirked at Jasper.

"How many did I get, Talia?" he asked her.

"Um...nine."

"Shit," I muttered as Jasper and every one of the guys watching roared with laughter.

"That is priceless." Jasper clapped me on the shoulder. "We're keeping her around."

I locked eyes with Talia, those sparkling blues dancing as she smiled. "Yes, we are."

Whatever doubts, worries, fears I'd had about this fight vanished.

In the beginning, I'd told her that I'd win this fight for her. That she was my motivation. Our past was scattered with enough broken promises. I wasn't adding another. So I waved her closer, meeting her at the ropes and dropping to a crouch.

"I'm not losing this fight," I said low enough for only her to hear.

She pressed a hand to her heart. "No, you're not."

It was like she'd known all along that would be my decision but had given me time to realize it myself.

The money for Dex and the situation with Vivienne, there was a way out of this. Neither of them might like it, but they didn't get to bitch. Not after what they'd done. Dex and his pride could go fuck himself.

"We'll figure the rest of this out," I said.

"After you win."

"For you."

"You already won, baby." Talia reached for my side, her fingertips brushing the Garnet Flats tattoo on my ribs.

A single touch and the future flashed in my mind.

Garnet Flats. A house built on her family's ranch. A home filled with love and laughter.

We'd be having a conversation at the hotel tonight about those pills she took each morning. If she was ready, they'd go in the trash. We'd fill our dream house with kids. Make Kadence a big sister. And I'd worship this woman for the rest of my years.

"Don't win this fight for me," she whispered. "Win this one for *you*."

Win this fight for the one I never should have lost. "Then I'll be done. Then I'll retire."

"But not yet."

I grinned. "Not yet."

CHAPTER 26

TALIA

The arena was booming. Lights flashed from every direction. The music rumbled like thunder. Or maybe that was just my heart.

"I'm going to puke." I didn't even bother whispering to myself. Everyone around me was standing, laughing and shouting to be heard as they talked. The crowd reveled in the spectacle.

Meanwhile I seemed to be the only person in a complex that held twelve thousand who was actually sitting in her seat.

My hands trembled. Sweat beaded at my temples, not from the heat but from nerves. I dragged in a breath, smelling concrete and beer and the guy behind me wearing too much aftershave.

The chairs beside mine, one on each side, were empty.

Foster had invited his parents tonight but they'd opted not to come. His mother had said his fights were too violent. His dad had said they'd get a better view at home on TV. I was grateful they'd declined because I was not going to be good company tonight. Besides, we'd see them next week before we flew home.

So I sat alone, knees bouncing, praying these front-row

seats would remain empty. Unlikely, but the idea of making small talk with strangers spiked my anxiety, so I didn't think about the chairs.

At my right, a bald man in a black suit coat raised his hand in a wave before returning to his conversation. Foster's manager. I'd met him on Thursday at a meeting. Foster's agent was probably milling around close by too.

I didn't even bother to smile as people walked by. I was too nervous to smile. Was Foster okay? Was he stretching or warming up? Was he drinking enough water?

His weigh-in had been yesterday morning and he'd been rehydrating since.

To call the past four days intense would be an understatement. Foster had shifted into a different mode since we'd come to Vegas. He'd trained harder. Pushed harder. Focused harder. He'd had press conferences and meetings.

I'd stayed by his side through it all. Every time I'd offered to give him space, he'd taken my hand, wordlessly keeping me close.

So I'd stayed, watching in awe as the man I loved prepared for his last professional fight. The culmination of his career. If he was upset, Foster hadn't let it show.

This fight tonight had been his focus. The only breaks in his concentration had been to call Kadence. And late at night, in the dark hours, with the Las Vegas lights streaming in through our hotel's window, when he'd lost himself in my body and let go.

It was the end.

And a beginning.

My knees bounced faster. Would he regret this? Would he miss this energy? It pulsed through the building, bouncing from wall to wall until it collected in the center of it all.

The Octagon.

Even empty, the eight-sided ring was intimidating. Those seated in the highest levels of the stands would watch the action from the enormous screens hanging overhead. Millions of people would be tuning in from the comfort of their own homes, including my family.

And I would be here, sitting in the front row, hoping I didn't vomit on television.

I hadn't been this nervous before taking the MCAT. I hadn't been this nervous on my first day at Quincy Memorial. I hadn't been this nervous delivering that baby all those years ago.

My stomach churned and I closed my eyes, willing the dizziness to ease.

When I opened them, Chase, the young man who'd escorted me to my seat earlier, was marching my way. He was Foster's manager's assistant or something. Did Foster need something?

I'd spent most of the afternoon and evening in the locker room. I'd hovered against the wall, doing my best to stay out of the way as person after person came in to talk to him. Then as time had gone on, as the arena had opened and people had flooded into the stands, Foster had given me a long kiss goodbye.

In Chase's hand was a notepad and a pen. His smile was wide, a kid who was loving every minute of this. I envied his unbridled excitement. Too much dread churned in my mind to enjoy the show.

If Foster lost, it would be crushing. I didn't want that sort of disappointment for him. Not after all that he'd been through to get here. Not after all he'd decided.

Chase glanced over his shoulder, and I followed his gaze.

"What?" I gasped and shot to my feet.

Lyla rushed over, her arms open for a hug.

Behind her, Eloise's mouth was hanging open as she took it all in.

"What are you doing here?" I asked, holding my sister tight.

Eloise joined the group hug. "Foster didn't want you sitting alone."

So he'd flown my sisters to Vegas to sit at my side.

Oh, how I loved that man.

"I'm glad you're here," I said, holding them tighter.

"Are you okay?" Lyla asked.

I shook my head. "Nervous."

"Can I get you ladies anything?" Chase asked as we broke from our hug. "Drinks? Food?"

"Drinks," Lyla said.

"And food," Eloise added.

"Of course." He nodded, then extended the paper and pen. "From Mr. Madden."

I glanced at the sheet. The top was blank but there was a slight darkening beneath the page, so I thumbed to the next. And found Foster's note.

I love you, Tally. Do me a favor. Keep track of how many times I punch Scott Savage.

I laughed, my eyes flooding as I pressed the notepad to my heart.

"What?" Lyla asked.

"Nothing." Just Foster knowing that there was no way I'd be able to sit idle tonight.

"I'll be back with drinks and snacks," Chase said. "Text me if you want anything else."

I nodded, waiting until he walked away, then took my chair with Eloise sitting on my right and Lyla on my left.

"He's going to win," Lyla said, taking my hand.

Eloise grabbed the other, squeezing tight. "And then we're going to party."

I held on to my sisters as the minutes passed and the anticipation built higher and higher. More people took their chairs. The referee came into the Octagon, making a loop around the edge. Then an announcer joined him, carrying a microphone and shadowed by three cameramen.

"This is intense," Lyla said. "Are you breathing?"

No. I gulped down some air.

The lights in the arena dimmed. Spotlights made a loop around the room before zeroing in on the Octagon as the announcer lifted the microphone to his mouth. "Ladies and gentlemen, we are live from Las Vegas! It's time!"

The crowd roared. The cheers spurred on the announcer, who only got louder, and the atmosphere went from electric to crazed.

There were five fights on the card tonight. Foster and Scott Savage would be the main event, taking place last.

Sitting through the first four was agonizing. The people around us cheered and yelled, rooting for fighters during the first four fights. Lyla and Eloise snacked and drank cocktails while I had to force myself to breathe.

In and out.

The wait was torture. I clutched Foster's note as Chase kept bringing food and drinks, none of which I touched, until finally, the fourth fight was over and the Octagon was prepped for the main event.

"Here we go," I said, closing my eyes. *Don't let him get hurt.*

Maybe another woman would have prayed for a win. But all I truly cared about was that Foster walked out of that ring.

The lights swung toward a tunnel. Scott Savage came walking out with at least ten people in his entourage. He puffed out his chest, yelling and pounding a fist against his sternum as he stepped into the ring.

"I can't wait for this guy to lose," Lyla said, leaning close so I could hear her.

"Look." Eloise pointed to the right as Foster emerged from a different tunnel.

A stone-faced Jasper walked at his side. Behind them were the other guys I'd met in the locker room as well as Foster's manager and agent.

Whatever the announcer said faded to a blur as I kept my eyes glued to Foster. And his focus was entirely on the ring—until Jasper nudged his elbow and jerked his chin my direction.

Foster's eyes locked with mine.

Love you, I mouthed.

The corner of his mouth turned up.

"Oh my God, you're so going to be on TV." Lyla laughed. "I hope Knox is recording this."

I couldn't think about TV right now. I just kept my attention on Foster, not caring what they said about me. Not caring if they knew who I was.

Foster shot Savage a scowl as he stepped into the cage, walking to his own corner and stripping down to only a pair of fitted black trunks that showcased the strength in his thighs and the perfect globes of his ass. Every muscle in his body was defined. His abs bunched as he bent, stretching his hamstrings. His corded arms rose high as he rolled out his shoulders.

The announcer droned on, running through a list of sponsors, naming the judges and introducing the referee.

After Foster stretched, he bounced on his toes, keeping his

body warm. His face was blank as a cameraman closed in tight. His eyes were narrowed. His wrists were taped in red and his knuckles covered in gloves.

Please don't get hurt.

"Introducing the undisputed UFC middleweight champion of the world." The announcer dragged out every word as he spoke, almost like a song. "The Iron Fist. Foster Madden."

Lyla and Eloise clapped, cheering with thousands of people as they jumped to their feet.

I stood, my heart racing as Foster held up an arm, greeting the crowd. He circled his half of the ring, then returned to the corner where Jasper was up on a stand, bending over the edge of the Octagon.

"And our challenger," the announcer said.

I didn't hear any of what came next because every person around me began to *boo*. Even Lyla and Eloise cupped their hands over their mouths, jeering Scott Savage, who adjusted the waistband of his white shorts.

Savage preened through his introduction, waving his hands to rile up the crowd and taunt Foster.

A woman dressed in booty shorts and a sports bra circled the ring with a giant number one. Two doors to the Octagon, opposite each other, were open, and as the announcer flipped to the last page of notes in his hand, people began filing out of the ring.

The crowd quieted as people took their seats.

We were beneath the television screens and unable to see what they were showing. Not that I'd look. My attention was locked forward as the referee waved both Foster and Savage into the center of the ring.

Foster held out his hand for a shake.

Savage turned and walked away.

"Asshole," I muttered, shooting Savage a glare before taking out my notepad. Keeping track of how many times Foster punched him was going to be my pleasure.

My heartbeat was frantic as the referee nodded. Then a ding echoed through the space and the first round started, both men facing off and maneuvering around the ring.

Five seconds of assessing each other, then Savage went on the offensive first. He attacked Foster with two punches that looked sloppy and wild. Foster blocked one and dodged the other. Then Savage attempted a front leg round kick that Foster caught with an elbow.

It had to have hurt because Savage hopped funny for the rest of the round, and when he came to his corner, even from a distance I could see the goose egg forming on the top of his foot.

Foster looked relaxed and calm as he spoke to Jasper. Entirely in control as they started the second round. Except I had yet to make a tally mark on my notepad.

"Come on, baby," I whispered.

Savage took a swing with his right arm that went wide.

Foster ducked, missing it, and when he rose up, his left jab smashed right into Savage's eye before his right fist connected with Savage's kidney.

Blood pooled from a cut in Savage's eyebrow as he stumbled backward just as the round finished.

Two. I drew two neat marks on the page. When I looked up, Foster stood in the center of the ring, his chest rising and falling. And instead of heading to Jasper, who was waiting, Foster stared at me.

I held up the notepad and two fingers.

He held up one.

What did that mean? One more round? One more hit?

He winked, then strode over to Jasper, who squirted some water past Foster's mouthguard. When he returned to the center, standing at the ready, Savage joined him again. The cut on his forehead was greased and taped.

"Win this, Foster," I said, inching to the edge of my chair.

The referee gave them the signal and they jumped straight into the third round, circling and weaving, trying to get in a shot.

Savage threw a cross, putting his entire weight into it, and all Foster had to do was lean back. Savage's glove barely skimmed Foster's nose.

And then he attacked. A left jab to the nose followed by a right uppercut to the chin. Foster's left swung again, this time connecting with Savage's jaw. And then the right, which slammed into Savage's temple.

Four punches and Savage hit the floor.

The referee rushed forward, likely to stop Foster from leaping onto Savage and punching some more.

But Foster just stood above his opponent, staring down as Savage attempted to push up on an elbow only to fall down again.

Knockout. "Yes!" I was on my feet before I'd even realized I was standing. My arms were in the air, the notepad clutched in a fist.

Lyla and Eloise were screaming, both jumping up and down beside me.

Tears poured down my face as Foster rushed to Jasper, getting a clap on the back.

My lungs expanded, able to draw in a full breath for the

first time in hours. My heart climbed out of my throat. And I clapped and cheered and joined in the frenzy as they announced Foster's win.

A champion. That man was a champion. And he was mine.

The celebration continued until the lights in the arena turned on bright and people in the upper sections began to trickle out of the center. Lyla, Eloise and I stayed in our seats, waiting until Foster was able to push through the door and hop down from the Octagon.

We rushed to each other. His arms wrapped around me as I held him tight. He buried his face in my hair. And above the noise, I barely heard his whisper.

"We won."

CHAPTER 27

FOSTER

"Is Kadence asleep already?" Talia asked as she came downstairs, joining me in the kitchen, where I was finishing up the dishes from dinner. She was wearing one of my T-shirts, the hem hitting midthigh. Her hair was wet from the shower, and her face was clean, her cheeks flushed.

In all my life, I'd never seen a more beautiful woman. Never would.

"What?" She walked closer. "What's that look?"

"Nothing." I pulled her into my chest. "Yeah, she's asleep."

"Damn. I feel bad for getting home late."

"She understands you were working."

Talia rested her cheek against my chest, her arms winding around my waist. "Don't let go."

"Never." I kissed the top of her hair.

I began swaying back and forth, not quite a slow dance, but enough that she moved with me.

Today had been Talia's first day back at work since we'd come home from Vegas yesterday. In the days since the fight, we'd been inseparable, and when she'd gotten up to leave for work this morning, I'd tried not to let my disappointment show.

"I missed you today."

She shifted, putting her chin on my sternum to meet my gaze. "I missed you too. But I'm glad we're home."

"Same here."

Vegas was history. Our last days spent there had been a nice way to say goodbye.

Sunday after the fight, I'd had meetings and appointments, mostly for press. Talia and I had decided not to announce my retirement. We'd ride the wave of the win for a while, then quietly step away.

The two of us had spent Monday in our hotel room celebrating, ordering room service and spending the day in bed. Then Tuesday, we'd driven into the desert for a sunrise hike. That evening we'd gone out to dinner with my parents, then yesterday morning, we'd packed up and flown to Montana. Kadence was as happy to have us home as we were to be here.

"My agent emailed me today, asking about a new contract," I told Talia.

"What did you say?"

"Nothing. I'm going to ignore him until next week." Be the champion for a few more days. Enjoy this time at home.

Then take the next step.

"What happened at the hospital?" I'd expected her home around six but she'd texted and said something had come up, so she needed to stay late.

"It wasn't bad, just busy," she said. "A guy came into the ER right before I was supposed to leave. He'd burned his hand while he was trying to cook an anniversary dinner for his wife."

"That's an anniversary they won't forget."

"No, they won't. His wife was really understanding about it and he just kept apologizing over and over again. It was sweet."

"How was it with Rachel?"

"She wasn't there." Talia had confessed yesterday on the flight that she was anxious about going back to the hospital after the accident. She hadn't seen Rachel since their encounter in the waiting room. "She actually took a leave of absence."

"Really?" I stopped moving. "Maybe that's for the best."

"I feel awful for her. I can't imagine what it would be like to lose your son. No matter the problems he might have had, he was still her child."

I shuddered, not wanting to think about that horror.

"The rumor with the nursing staff is that she won't come back."

For Talia's sake, I hoped that was true. "Give it time."

"I had a long talk with Dr. Anderson today."

"About?"

"Everything." She pressed her cheek to my heart, my cue to resume swaying. "He called me in to talk. I guess while we were gone, another one of the nurses told him about Rachel. She'd overheard what Rachel told me in the waiting room and she thought the reason I wasn't at work was because I'd quit, not because I was on vacation."

"And how did it go?"

"Good." She hugged me closer. "He told me that the budget cuts had nothing to do with my position. That the reason Rachel's sister was let go was because she was bad at her job."

That's what I'd suspected. "Feel better?"

"A lot." She looked up and smiled. A smile so full of light it illuminated the room. "He told me I was a good doctor."

"Because you are." I tucked a lock of hair behind her ear.

"Sometimes it's nice to be told," she said. "We picked a date for my license exam. It's going to get a little crazy with added study time but—"

"We'll figure it out. Whatever you need."

"He calls me Talia. Everyone calls me Talia." She paused. "I was worried that it was because they didn't think I was a good enough doctor. I'm sure no matter what, I'll always have doubts, but I'll give it my best."

"Yeah, you will." I leaned my cheek against the top of her head, swaying a little faster and spinning us in a slow circle.

"What happened in your day?"

I closed my eyes. "I got a call from Dex."

Talia stiffened, pushing out of my hold. The smile was gone and that worried crease was between her eyebrows. "What? When? Why didn't you tell me?"

"I am telling you." I chuckled and hauled her into my arms again, holding tight as she squirmed.

"Lead with that," she said, poking me in the ribs.

"Noted. Though I think today was the last time I'll be speaking to Dex."

"What did he say?"

" 'Fuck you.' "

Her jaw dropped. "Seriously?"

"Yup." I shook my head. "Over three million dollars and all I get is a *fuck you*."

Before the fight, I'd made a hard call to Tony Sabbatini. He'd been a loose acquaintance of Arlo's—filth tended to run with filth—and though I'd never met the man, I'd heard the rumors of his mafia ties.

Tony owned a handful of casinos around Vegas, all of them shady. Dex had truly fucked himself by getting involved with the Sabbatini family, but all I'd cared about was Vivienne's safety. So before I'd ever stepped into the Octagon with Savage,

I'd made a deal.

Three million plus what Dex would lose betting on my fight. I'd bought Dex's debt outright. In exchange, Vivienne was to be forgotten.

Maybe Tony would still go after Dex. I didn't give a fuck. If Dex's ego was bruised because I'd bailed him out, he could rot in hell. I'd done it for Kadence.

I'd paid to ensure my daughter didn't lose her mother.

"Why would Dex even call if not to say thank you?" Talia asked.

"To say *fuck you*."

She frowned. "Sorry."

I shrugged. "He's out of our lives."

"And Vivienne's?"

"She told Kadence tonight that she was almost done packing. Kaddie asked if Dex was coming too and Vivi told her that they broke up."

"Then it's over." Talia blew out a long breath. "Did you talk to Vivienne?"

"No. Just listened while she FaceTimed with Kadence."

Conversation with Vivienne was just as tense now as it had been before the fight. Other than trading logistics for Kadence, communication was short. She'd hurt me. And though she'd apologized profusely, we shouldn't have landed here.

Vivienne had stayed in Quincy while Talia and I had been in Vegas. When we'd gotten home, we'd traded the airplane and she'd flown back to the city to begin packing.

As of this morning, our house was on the market. So was Angel's.

Those had been conditions of mine. If I was going to pay Dex's debt, Vivienne was going to get her ass out of Vegas.

After the fight, when Talia and I had made it back to the hotel suite, I'd called Vivienne. She'd answered in tears, thinking Dex's life was over, until I'd told her that I'd paid his debt. When I told her that I expected her to move and soon, she'd agreed immediately.

Progress. We'd even scored some Quincy real estate.

Eloise had overheard a tip at the hotel. An older couple in town was moving to Missoula to be closer to their grandchildren and would be listing their house for sale. Bless that local phone book. Talia had looked up their number and given them a call. An hour later, my realtor had been drafting the buy-sell agreement.

I was paying cash plus fifteen thousand dollars to expedite their move. It would be tight, but if the timing worked perfectly, the home would be empty when Vivienne's own moving truck arrived.

The house was five blocks away. Kadence would be trading houses but at least those houses would be close.

"What do you think will happen with Dex?" Talia asked.

"I don't know. There's a chance they'll go after him. But the fact that he called me today…" The fact that he was still alive. "I just don't know."

"Do you think we'll be okay?"

There was fear in her voice, so I held her tighter. "We'll be fine."

Thanks to Arlo. That conniving bastard had been helpful after all.

Arlo had kept a book. It was no bigger than a notepad and he'd tucked it away in the safe at Angel's. I doubted Vivienne knew about it. I wouldn't be sharing it with Talia either. The less either of them knew about his connections, the better.

In that little black book, he'd kept names and numbers.

Information about the underground fighting circuit. Details about the big players and bookies in Vegas.

After years and years, that book had become Arlo's insurance policy.

He'd told me about the book once, and only once. On a night I was sure he didn't remember. A night when he'd been gifted a bottle of scotch, and instead of taking it home, he'd opened it at the gym. The guys had cleared out, leaving only the two of us behind.

And he'd had that book open on his desk.

Every bet he'd made, every contact he'd known, was listed in his small, neat script. He'd filled over three pages with information about Tony Sabbatini's crew.

Arlo had told me that if anything ever happened to him, anything suspicious, that the book was to be sent to the federal authorities.

The information could have been outdated. I didn't care. I'd told Tony that Arlo had a list of names. He'd asked me to name a few, so I'd rattled off those I could remember. After Arlo's death, I'd taken that book and kept it hidden. It had made the journey to Montana too.

Apparently the names I'd recited had been enough. Tony's lawyer had forwarded me a dummy investment contract for a business I was sure only existed on paper. And along with my multimillion-dollar wire transfer, this morning, I'd dropped Arlo's book in the mail to Tony himself as a good faith gesture that I wanted nothing to do with his world.

With any luck, that was the end of it.

Maybe it was foolish to believe it was over. But I was hedging my own bets now. I was banking on the fact that I was out of Las Vegas, and soon, I'd be just another forgotten, retired UFC fighter.

"That was a lot of money," Talia said.

"It's just money." There were more important things. "Besides, what do I need it for? I'm going to marry a doctor."

She arched her eyebrows. "Marry?"

"If she ever decides to wear her ring."

"Wait." Talia's eyes widened. "Are you asking me to marry you?"

"Something like that." I grinned, letting her go to dig in my pocket for the velvet pouch. "This has been in my pocket for months. I can put it back. Do a fancy proposal with flowers and candles and fireworks. Or I can put it on your finger and we can dance around the kitchen. I'll probably step on your feet a few times. Then I'll tell you how much I love you and carry you upstairs to our bed."

"You've kept it in your pocket all this time?" she whispered.

"Until you felt like wearing it."

"Tonight." She lifted her hand, her fingers shaking. "No fancy proposal."

"Thank fuck." I struggled to get the bag open. The ring was warm from being in my pocket all day. I fumbled it once before I finally slid it onto her finger.

Where it had always been meant to be.

"Oh my God." The diamond sparkled in the muted light as she held it up, that blinding smile on her face again. Then she rose up on her toes, her lips brushing mine. "I love you, baby."

"I love you, Tally." I fused my mouth to hers, my tongue sweeping past her lower lip. My hand skimmed under the hem of my shirt, gliding across the smooth skin of her hip. Then I hoisted her into my arms, skipped the dance entirely and carried her upstairs as promised.

Victory.

EPILOGUE

TALIA

One month later...

"**D**addy!" Kadence raced through Eden Coffee. Her new boots pounded on the floor as her braid swung between her shoulders.

Foster slid out of his chair just in time to catch her and she launched herself at him. "How was it?"

"So much fun." She giggled when he tickled her side. "Can we go again, Talia?"

"Of course." I'd taken her horseback riding at the ranch this morning. She'd instantly fallen in love with Neptune.

"Tomorrow?"

"Um, sure?" I laughed. "As long as it's not raining." Or snowing.

The April forecast was a gamble. It could be sunny and warm one day with a blizzard and six inches of snow the next. But if the weather was good, I'd happily take Kadence to the ranch and let her ride around the arena.

"Want a snack?" Foster asked, setting her down.

"Okay."

"Hit up Lyla." He nudged her for the counter, where Lyla was waiting with a smile. Then he walked over, bending to give me a kiss. "Good?"

"Really good. It was fun."

It had been Foster's idea for me to take Kadence alone to the ranch today. Since they'd moved into my house, we'd spent plenty of hours together, but it was rare for Kadence and me to have one-on-one time. So he'd decided to hang back and meet Jasper here for coffee while we had a few hours alone.

"You want something to eat?" he asked.

I scrunched up my nose and shook my head. "I'm not hungry."

"You didn't eat breakfast."

"I ate at the ranch," I lied. Tonight, after Kadence went to Vivienne's house, I'd tell him why I wasn't feeling well. But not with people here. "Hey, Jasper."

"Hey, Doc." Jasper raised a hand.

"Foster told me you're going to stick around for a while."

"Yeah, a little bit."

"He can't live without me," Foster teased.

Jasper shook his head, his chest shaking with a quiet laugh.

I was grateful that Foster's friend had decided to stay. Foster wouldn't have made that big of an ask, but when Jasper had volunteered to move, there'd been no objection.

Jasper had approached the owners of the cabin he'd been renting. Instead of extending his agreement, they'd offered to sell him the property. With him here, it meant Foster wasn't alone so much during the day.

I was working a ton and studying for my upcoming exams. And though Foster was adjusting well to retired life, when Kadence was at school, I was grateful that he had Jasper to keep him company.

For however long Jasper decided to stay.

"I'm going to say hi to Lyla and get some water," I told Foster, patting his abs before passing him for the counter.

Lyla slid a to-go cup to Kadence, whose eyes widened at the heap of whipped cream on top.

Kaddie lifted it to her lips, taking a sip. A dollop of white clung to her nose. "Yum. You should *definitely* get hot chocolate."

"Good suggestion." I laughed as she carefully carried her cup toward Foster's table, then I leaned my hip against the counter, my sister doing the same on her side. "Hi."

"Hi," she said. "Heard you took her for a ride."

"Yeah. It was cute." I smiled as Kadence went to the table and Foster wiped her nose. "What's going on here today?"

"Not much." Lyla sighed. "I'm about to head out. I was actually thinking of asking Jasper to dinner."

"What?" I stood taller, leaning in to lower my voice. "Really?"

"I don't know." She gave me an exaggerated smile. "He's hot. And sort of grumpy and brooding."

"Just your type."

"Exactly. But would it be weird?"

"Why would it be weird?"

"He's Foster's best friend."

"So?"

"So..." She sucked in a deep breath. "What if we go to dinner and then we start dating and it goes great for a while but then it starts to fall apart until we finally decide to call it quits but I'm still in love with him but he's not in love with me and it's not like you can hate him because he's your fiancé's best friend so it's awkward."

"Whoa." I held up my hands. "You've thought way too far ahead."

"I really like him. Like a lot. You and Foster disappeared to your hotel room after the fight, but that night...we all went out and had a blast."

"Did something happen?" This was news to me. Granted, I'd been pretty consumed with Foster, so I hadn't asked. And Lyla and Eloise had left the next day because both had needed to fly home for work.

Lyla opened her mouth to answer but then the bell above the door jingled and we both turned as Vivienne walked inside.

"Hold that thought." I held up a finger and returned to the table where Vivi bent to kiss Kadence's hair.

"How was your day?" Vivienne asked Kadence.

"So good, Mommy. We're going to go riding again tomorrow."

"That's great." Vivienne smiled at her, then looked to me. "Thanks for taking her."

"My pleasure."

Vivienne glanced at Foster but he didn't give her much. "Hey, Foster."

"Hi."

She waited for eye contact or a smile or anything, but that was it. That's how it had been between them for the past month. "So, I, um...I guess we'll just see you guys in the morning."

"Yep." He nodded. "Bring her over whenever."

Kadence was staying at Vivienne's house tonight. There was no routine or structure to their custody arrangement. For the most part, Kadence spent one day with her mother and one day with us. It was working for now, so Foster and Vivienne hadn't pushed to make changes.

If there needed to be a set schedule, we'd discuss it when

that time came.

My heart pinched as Vivienne looked at Foster. Guilt was etched on her face. It was how she'd looked at me since coming to Quincy. It was odd, being her supporter now.

She'd started calling me more to discuss Kadence's schedule, even though Foster wasn't working. But I understood. She didn't get the anger from me. And Foster, well…he wasn't ready to let it go.

Not yet.

All I cared about was that Vivienne was here because it made Kadence happy. Dex was history, and when I'd asked if she'd heard from him, she'd told me no with tears in her eyes. But Vivienne knew it was for the best. She'd walked away without regret.

Just a broken heart.

Since Foster had retired, the only people who contacted us from Las Vegas were his parents. They were planning to visit this summer.

"Okay, baby girl." Vivienne held out her hand. "Should we go?"

"Let me get a lid." I walked to the counter where Lyla had one ready.

A timer dinged and she nodded toward the back. "I need to get that. Will you holler if someone else comes in?"

"Sure." I took the lid to Vivienne so she could put it on Kadence's cup, then after Foster kissed his daughter on the cheek, we watched as they left.

"Are you going to be pissed at her forever?" Jasper asked as the door closed behind them.

"No." Foster dragged a hand through his hair. "Time to let it go, isn't it?"

I took the empty seat beside his, then held out my hand.

He took mine, his finger touching my engagement ring as he hummed. *Time to let it go.*

"Since you're both here. I, um, need to talk to you about something." Jasper glanced past Foster, to where Lyla had been standing. Then he sat straighter, taking a pause like he was thinking carefully about his words. "I, uh, well…I fucked up."

"What happened?" Foster asked.

Please be nothing bad. It had been a month of bliss. I wasn't ready for more drama.

"I sort of…I, um…fuck." Jasper rubbed his jaw. Then he closed his eyes and blurted, "I married your sister."

"What?" My jaw dropped. "You married Lyla?"

"Uh, not exactly."

Another jingle sounded from the door but I didn't turn. I was too busy staring at the empty counter. How in the hell had they gotten married? When? Where? Why hadn't Lyla told me? We'd been talking about him minutes ago. That would have been the perfect time to tell me she'd *married* Jasper Vale.

"Oh, uh, hi." Eloise stood at my side. When I whipped around to look up, her cheeks were flushed.

"Hi." I shook myself out of my stupor. "Jasper just told us that—"

"Oh my God, you told them?" Eloise shrieked. "How could you tell them? We agreed to keep this a secret until it was annulled!"

"Wait." Foster leaned forward, pointing between the two of them. "You two got married?"

"Now everyone is going to find out. Gah! Damn it. I'm never drinking again." Eloise spun around and jogged for the door.

"Eloise, wait." Jasper shot out of his chair, running to catch her.

Which left Foster and me staring at each other, dumbfounded.

"Did that just happen?" he asked.

All I could manage was a nod.

Shit. My parents were going to freak.

"Did Jasper leave?" Lyla asked as she came back to the counter with a towel in her hands. "Damn. I guess I'll have to ask him out another day."

I cringed. "Lyla, I think you'd better sit down."

. . .

"Well, that was interesting." I tossed my keys to the counter as we walked in the house. Then I checked my phone for the tenth time since leaving the coffee shop. Eloise still hadn't texted me back.

I set my phone aside and unzipped my coat, but before I could take it off, Foster was there, planting a kiss on my neck as he eased it off my shoulders.

"Got a call from the architect today," he said.

"On a Saturday?"

He shrugged, taking off his own coat. "Guess he was working on the plans."

"And?"

"Should have them done Monday. Wanted to see if we could meet and go over them together."

"I could do it over my lunch break."

"I'll find out if that will work."

A thrill of excitement chased away the unease in my stomach.

We'd wasted no time after coming home from Vegas to start

planning our future. My parents had insisted on throwing us an engagement party at The Eloise so more of our extended family could meet Foster. The next morning, we'd gone out to the ranch and asked to buy a chunk of land off it.

Of course my parents had said no—they'd gifted us five hundred acres instead.

We'd hired a local architect to start designing our dream home, and our wedding plans were in full swing for the summer. Knox's wife, Memphis, was planning it for us.

That was life with the Iron Fist, Foster Madden. Full tilt.

"It's great he's working so quickly," I said. "Maybe if we're lucky and he gets the design finished, we can get the builder to start earlier than expected. It would be so nice to move in before the baby is born."

"Yeah, that—" Foster blinked. "What did you just say?"

I smiled and walked to the coat rack to fish out the plastic sack I'd stashed in a pocket this morning. More importantly, the stick inside. "It happened faster than expected."

Good thing we both liked fast.

After the fight in Vegas, I'd stopped taking my birth control pills. Foster had asked if I was ready, and I'd assumed it would take a while. But here we were, one month later, and it was happening.

He took the stick, looking at the plus sign in the tiny window, then at me. Back to the plus, back to me. He shifted his gaze so many times I was sure he'd give himself whiplash. "You're pregnant."

"I'm pregnant."

He closed his eyes, fisting that bag close. Then he wrapped his arms around me, hauling me into his chest as he buried his face in my hair. "You won't stop, will you?"

"Won't stop what?"

He leaned back, framing my face with his hands. "Won't stop until every dream of mine has come true."

I smiled, leaning in to whisper against his lips. "Never."

EXCLUSIVE
BONUS
CONTENT

FOSTER

"Shit." I hissed as the needle pierced my skin.

"Don't move." Talia frowned, then shoved that needle in again, weaving the suture thread in and out of my flesh as she stitched up the cut in my eyebrow.

"Fuck, that hurts."

"You should have let me give you the lidocaine."

"No. If you're not getting the drugs today, then neither am I."

"That's the dumbest thing I've—" She winced, her face contorting as another contraction hit. One of her hands dropped to her belly. "Oh, son of a bitch."

"Breathe, love." I put my hands on her sides, holding my own breath as she endured the contraction.

"Ouch." She moaned as it passed, standing straight.

"Dr. Madden." The nurse hovering against the wall crossed her arms. "Please. Let me call Dr. Murphy in to stitch up your husband."

"No, I'm okay, Abbi." Talia waved her off and did another stitch. "Two more and we're done."

The nurse scowled but stayed quiet. Abbi was new to

Quincy Memorial. She'd started about six months ago as the new charge nurse to replace Rachel, who'd left town not long after her son's car accident.

Talia loved Abbi. There weren't many days when she didn't come home from work and gush about the nurse.

I loved Abbi simply for calling Talia Dr. Madden. Talia didn't need the title, but I loved it for her all the same. She'd earned it, through medical school and residency. And by passing her exams and getting her license. She was an attending physician now, poised for a long and wonderful career.

Dr. Anderson had even set his retirement date. He knew, like we all did, that when he quit working, Quincy would be in good hands. Talia's hands.

"Okay, done." Talia quickly tied off the last stitch and cut the excess thread. Then she smeared some ointment over the cut. "Where is that bandage?"

"I'll do it." Abbi held it in her hand, coming over to shoo Talia away. "You need to be in the other room. Now."

"Fine." Talia stripped off her gloves, tossing them in the trash. Then she put a hand beneath her belly, like she was holding the baby inside for just a few more minutes.

"Right behind you," I said.

Talia slipped out the door, and I was about to hop off my bed when Abbi leveled me with a glare.

"Sit," she ordered.

I didn't need a bandage. I'd been hit a lot harder and I'd had a lot deeper cuts than this, but I wasn't going to argue. The woman was stout, and if she wanted to blockade my exit, she'd be a formidable opponent.

So I tapped my fingers on the bed, waiting while she put the bandage over my stitches. Then I slipped past her and raced out of the room, heading three doors down to where Talia had changed into a hospital gown and was being hooked up to a bunch of monitors as she lay in bed.

"What do you need?" I asked, rushing to her side.

She glanced at my shirt. "I'm not excited about having this baby while my husband has blood all over his shirt."

The white cotton was what I'd been wearing at the gym when Kadence had hit me.

I glanced around the room, wishing like hell I had thought to pack my own stuff in her baby bag. But I had nothing. So I reached behind my head and tore off my shirt. "Better?"

"Much better." Abbi waltzed into the room and did a catcall.

The nurse hooking up Talia's monitors turned a violent shade of red.

"Can someone please get Foster a scrub top?" Talia rolled her eyes as another contraction hit, causing her to clench her teeth.

I took her hand, rubbing her knuckles. "You got this."

She nodded, her fingers squeezing mine until it passed.

"See this?" Abbi pointed to a monitor's screen. "That will show the contractions."

"Okay."

Another woman slipped into the room carrying a blue shirt. "Here you go, Dr. Madden."

"Thanks." Talia smiled at her and waited until I had it pulled over my head.

"Now what?" I asked, running my fingers through Talia's hair.

"Now, we wait." She sighed. "How's your head?"

"Fine." I waved it off.

"I still can't believe she hit you. Middleweight champion,

taken out by a second-grade girl."

I chuckled. "I'll never live this down."

After school today, I'd picked up Kadence and we'd gone out to the gym. Her summer activity had been riding on the ranch with Talia. But as Talia's pregnancy had progressed and fall had shifted to winter, we'd decided horses were a no-go. So in place of riding, Kadence had asked me to teach her kickboxing.

We'd been practicing in the afternoons. It probably wouldn't last much longer with the upcoming basketball season approaching. But it had been something fun for us to do together.

Our house on Garnet Flats was finished and we'd just moved in. I loved the space, the quiet countryside, but it was farther from Vivienne's house. It had put some distance between me and my daughter.

So, kickboxing.

I'd been distracted this afternoon. Talia had called earlier and said she'd been having contractions but they were far apart, so there was no need to rush to the hospital.

Of course my wife was working up until the moment she delivered our baby.

We'd been on the mats and I'd had my phone close by. I'd gone to check it for the tenth time, bending low, just as Kadence had said, "Watch this, Daddy."

Boom. Her fist had connected with my nose.

Not a big deal. Except it had caught me off guard and I'd tripped over my own goddamn feet, then stumbled to the side before colliding with a row of free weights.

Now *that* had fucking hurt. Not that I'd say it while my wife was in labor.

"People used to call you coordinated." Talia smirked.

"Good thing you're retired."

"Yes, it is."

There was no missing what we had ahead of us. The hard work, the years trapped under Arlo's thumb, had been worth it if this was my reward.

"Is Kadence okay?" Talia asked. When we'd rushed in earlier, Kaddie had been in tears. But Vivi had met us here to take her five minutes after we'd walked through the ER doors.

"She's good. Vivi will calm her down. They'll probably come back tonight depending on how this goes."

"To meet her brother." Talia ran a hand over her belly.

"She's so excited."

"Everyone is. Think he'll be born before midnight?"

Hell if I know. "Yes."

Talia hoped that he wouldn't be born until tomorrow because that was her dad's birthday. She wanted our son and her father to share the same special day. Harrison was hoping for it too.

I bent to kiss her forehead. "I love you."

"I love—"

The line on the monitor spiked.

"Breathe, love." I held her hand through that contraction and the next and the next. Until I could hold our son, Jude Matthew Madden.

Who joined our family at the stroke of midnight.

TALIA

"I love you." Foster gripped my hips, his fingers digging into my skin as he kept me pinned against the wall. The flowing white skirt of my gown was bunched around my waist. My silver heels were locked around his ass. My veil was...somewhere. Probably on the floor beside his suit jacket.

And my husband was fucking me. Hard.

"Yes," I panted as he eased out and thrust forward, my inner walls clenching around him. "More."

"Talia Madden."

A smile tugged at my mouth. "Say it again."

"Talia Madden," he murmured before sucking an earlobe into his mouth.

"I love you."

Our breaths mingled as he brought us together, faster and faster. There was a party going on in the building. A crowd of people were dancing and laughing to celebrate our marriage.

While Foster and I had snuck out of the reception and locked ourselves in a supply closet.

Our honeymoon suite was just upstairs at The Eloise Inn. When we'd snuck out of the ballroom, we'd planned to vanish upstairs, but neither of us had been able to wait.

As Foster had tugged me into the closet, I'd already been pulling up the skirt of my dress.

"Fuck, you feel good, love."

"Foster," I whimpered as my legs began to tremble, my toes curling in my shoes. My hands dug into his shoulders as I held on tighter, wrinkling the crisp white cotton of his shirt.

He sealed his mouth over mine just as my orgasm ripped through my body. He swallowed my cries, keeping them muffled as I shattered around his length, pulsing over and over until he tore his lips away.

He buried his face in my neck and came on a groan, pouring inside me until we were both spent.

The world was spinning. Stars danced at the corners of my eyes when I dared crack them open. And found my handsome husband's face waiting.

"I love you, Tally." He dropped his forehead to mine, our ragged breaths mingling.

"I love you too."

"We'd better get back." What I really wanted was to strip out of this dress, remove Foster's tux with my teeth and spend the rest of the night in bed. But there was still cake and dancing.

He kissed me again, slow and sweet, then eased out and tucked himself away. The moment I was on my feet, his come began leaking down my thighs.

"Where are my panties?" I searched the floor for the pale pink lace.

He bent and snagged them from on top of my veil, then helped me step into them, one leg at a time.

"Do you think anyone—" Before I could finish my sentence, a knock sounded on the door.

My eyes whipped to the door's knob and the lock that looked like it was pushed in but might have popped loose.

"Talia."

Oh God. That was my mother's voice.

"Shit," I whispered, dropping my gaze to Foster's. "Do you think she heard us?"

He shook his head.

"Yes, I heard you. Just be glad I came looking when I nearly sent your father."

I slapped a hand over my mouth as my face flamed.

Foster righted my skirt, then stood, fighting a smile.

"It's not funny," I hissed and smacked him in the gut.

"It's kind of funny," he said.

"It is kind of funny," Mom agreed.

"Mother." I grimaced. "You're not helping."

"Sorry." She laughed as a white envelope came flying through the crack at the bottom of the door.

The massive crack. It had to be two inches tall. No wonder she'd heard every word.

"Mateo wants wedding cake. You know how he is with wedding cake. Both he and Kadence are circling the cake table like sharks. So since it sounds like you're finished, er, celebrating, I'll just let everyone know we'll do cake next."

"Thanks, Anne," Foster said, chuckling as the click of her heels faded beyond the door.

"I really, really could have gone my whole life without my mother overhearing me have an orgasm."

Foster chuckled, stepping closer to splay a hand across my belly.

I wasn't showing quite yet, but my dress was definitely tighter around the middle than it had been when I'd initially gone shopping.

The pregnancy hormones were to blame for this insatiable craving for sex. Or maybe that was just my gorgeous husband.

"This is embarrassing," I said.

"Nah. It's just your mom. She's got six kids. I'm thinking she knows a thing or two about fuck—"

"Foster Madden, do not finish that sentence." I smacked him in the gut, then pushed a fingertip into each ear.

He threw his head back and laughed, the sight utterly breathtaking. Exactly how long did we have until someone else came searching? Did we really have to cut the cake? Couldn't people just eat it?

"Better stop looking at me like that, love." Foster bent and brushed a kiss across my cheek, his beard a rough scrape on my skin. "Or we'll miss the rest of the party."

A shiver rolled down my spine, but before I could reach for the zipper on his slacks, he was gone, swiping his jacket off the floor and brushing it off. Then he picked up the letter Mom had slid under the door, handing it over.

"What's this?" I pulled the seal apart, sliding out a neatly folded piece of ecru stationary filled with Mom's script.

Dear Talia,

It's your wedding day. I started this little tradition with Griffin and Knox when they got married.

Congratulations, my beautiful girl. I had this idea years ago to write each of you kids a letter on your wedding day. My letter to Griffin was a total bust. My note to Knox wasn't much better. But I've known for a long time what I wanted to say to you on your special day.

Did I ever tell you the story of how your dad and I got together? We knew each other in high school. That's usually what we tell people who ask how we met. But, like most high school romances, that didn't exactly end well. Then we both went our separate ways, heading to college. It wasn't until my senior year that I saw him again. Some friends invited me to a ski trip at a cabin and, when I showed up, there he was. There'd been a misunderstanding about the bedroom situation, and well, you can use your imagination.

We got a second chance. I like to think we were simply waiting until the time was right. Until we were the people we needed to be for each other. Until it was our time.

That's you and Foster. I'm so glad you've gotten your second chance too.

I love you. I'm proud of you. And I'm happy for you. For you both.

xoxo

Mom

A tear dripped down my cheek, landing on the paper. Except before I could wipe it away, another fell, nearly landing on the ink. Stupid pregnancy hormones. They'd turned me into a blubbering mess. "Damn it."

Foster slipped the page out of my hands. He wiped my eyes dry with a thumb. Then he blotted the water off the paper, making sure my mother's beautiful letter was safe. "Good?"

"Just emotional." I nodded, dabbing at my eyes again. "Will you keep that—"

I didn't have to finish my question. He tucked the note into the envelope, placing both in his jacket pocket.

Then he kissed the corner of my mouth and took my hand. "All good, Talia Madden?"

I'd waited a long, long time for that name.

I'd waited until it was our time.

I laced our fingers together. "Say it again."

Foster smiled. "Talia Madden."

ACKNOWLEDGMENTS

Thank you for reading *Garnet Flats*! Huge thanks to my editing and proofreading team: Elizabeth Nover, Julie Deaton and Judy Zweifel. Thank you to Sarah Hansen for the beautiful covers for this series. Thank you to all the members of Perry & Nash for being such an amazing group of readers. And thanks to the incredible bloggers, bookstagrammers and booktokkers who help spread the word about my stories. I am so grateful for you all! And lastly, thank you to my amazing family and very best friends. I love you!

Don't miss the rest of the Edens!

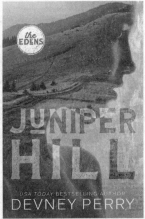

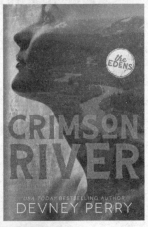

Don't miss the exciting new books
Entangled has to offer.

Follow us!

f @EntangledPublishing

⊙ @Entangled_Publishing

♪ @EntangledPub

an imprint of Entangled Publishing LLC